The Bastard's Tale
Dame Frevisse is drawn into the world of political intrigue . . .

"Anyone who values high historical drama will feel amply rewarded by Edgar-nominee Frazer's latest Dame Frevisse mystery . . . Of note is the poignant and amusing relationship between Joliffe and Dame Frevisse. History fans will relish every minute they spend with the characters in this powerfully created medieval world. Prose that at times verges on the poetic."　　　　　　　　　　　　—*Publishers Weekly*

"Frazer executes her exercise—inserting Frevisse into a dramatic episode in 15th-century history—with audacity and ingenuity."　　　　　　　　　　　　　　　—*Kirkus Reviews*

The Clerk's Tale
*Dame Frevisse must find justice for the murder
of an unjust man . . .*

"As usual, Frazer vividly recreates the medieval world through meticulous historical detail [and] remarkable scholarship. . . .History aficionados will delight and fans will rejoice that the devout yet human Dame Frevisse is back . . . a dramatic and surprising conclusion."　　　　—*Publishers Weekly*

The Novice's Tale
*Among the nuns at St. Frideswides's were piety, peace,
and a little vial of poison . . .*

"Frazer uses her extensive knowledge of the period to create an unusual plot . . . appealing characters and crisp writing."
—*Los Angeles Times*

Continued . . .

The Prioress' Tale
When the prioress lets her family stay at St. Frideswide's,
the consequences are deadly . . .

"Will delight history buffs and mystery fans alike."
—*Murder Ink*

The Maiden's Tale
In London for a visit, Frevisse finds that her wealthy
cousin may have a deadly secret . . .

"Great fun for all lovers of history with their mystery."
—*Minneapolis Star Tribune*

The Reeve's Tale
Acting as village steward, Frevisse must tend to the sick
—and track down a killer . . .

"A brilliantly realized vision of a typical medieval English village . . . Suspenseful from start to surprising conclusion . . . another gem."
—*Publishers Weekly* (starred review)

The Squire's Tale
Dame Frevisse learns that even love can spawn
anger, greed, and murder . . .

"Written with the graceful rhythms that have garnered her two Edgar nominations . . . [Frazer] transports the reader to a medieval England made vivid and a world of emotions as familiar then as now."
—*Publishers Weekly* (starred review)

"Meticulous detail that speaks of trustworthy scholarship and a sympathetic imagination."
—*The New York Times*

"As exquisitely woven as a medieval tapestry . . . dazzling."
—*The Cleveland Plain Dealer*

Berkley Prime Crime Books by Margaret Frazer

THE NOVICE'S TALE
THE SERVANT'S TALE
THE OUTLAW'S TALE
THE BISHOP'S TALE
THE BOY'S TALE
THE MURDERER'S TALE
THE PRIORESS' TALE
THE MAIDEN'S TALE
THE REEVE'S TALE
THE SQUIRE'S TALE
THE CLERK'S TALE
THE BASTARD'S TALE
THE HUNTER'S TALE
A PLAY OF ISAAC

A Play of Isaac

Margaret Frazer

BERKLEY PRIME CRIME, NEW YORK

This is a work of fiction. Names, characters, places, and incidents either are the product of the author's imagination or are used fictitiously, and any resemblance to actual persons, living or dead, business establishments, events, or locales is entirely coincidental.

A PLAY OF ISAAC

A Berkley Prime Crime Book / published by arrangement with the author

PRINTING HISTORY
Berkley Prime Crime mass-market edition / August 2004

Copyright © 2004 by Gail Frazer.
Illustrations by Brigid Collins/Arena Works.
Design by Leslie Worrell.
Book design by Kristin del Rosario.

For information address: The Berkley Publishing Group, a division of Penguin Group (USA) Inc., 375 Hudson Street, New York, New York 10014.

Visit our website at www.penguin.com

ISBN: 0-425-19751-4

Berkley Prime Crime Books are published by The Berkley Publishing Group, a division of Penguin Group (USA) Inc., 375 Hudson Street, New York, New York 10014. The name BERKLEY PRIME CRIME and the BERKLEY PRIME CRIME design are trademarks belonging to Penguin Group (USA) Inc.

PRINTED IN THE UNITED STATES OF AMERICA

10 9 8 7 6 5 4 3 2

For Don Wooten and the Genesius Guild,
without whom, none.

Chapter 1

The summer day that had promised so fair at its beginning with a primrose sky banded by cream-colored clouds above the sunrise had kept its promise through to a warm, clear afternoon this June day in the year of Our Lord's grace 1434. The good citizens—and others—of Oxford had come out from their dinners after Trinity Sunday Mass ready for sport of some kind, and for those who wanted something less bloody than the bear-baiting on Gloucester Green or less brutal than the half-barrel-boating fight on the Isis beyond Greyfriars, the company of players had been more than ready to oblige them with *The Steward and the Devil* in the innyard of the Arrow and Hind.

All in all, the play had gone out of the ordinary well, the innyard both crowded full of folk and full of laughter at it, and at its end Master Norton—the innkeeper and sharp as his kind proverbially were—had had his imposing bulk and two of his servants waiting at both the yard's gateway and the tavern door with baskets out-held to collect the audience's gratitude in coin on their way out.

Thomas Basset, playmaster and equally sharp, as *his* kind had to be, had thrown his Old Woman's wimple, veil, and gown into a heap on the nearest basket in the changing room and been at the gateway on the last of the audience's heels, to help Master Norton with the counting out of what they'd taken in, lest temptation and sticking fingers make problems where there need not be. Left behind, the rest of the players—all three of them—were undressing more slowly, seen to by Rose who had no part in their acting but tended to nearly everything else that needed doing to keep their company together. Just now she was sighing at Piers—her son and the small demon who had come leaping and chortling onto the stage at the play's end to join the Devil in harrowing the Steward's soul off to Hell—as she helped him off with his tail and horns, telling him, "You've ripped your tunic out under both arms again and I don't see how I'm going to mend it this time."

Joliffe, unbuttoning his doublet with care to lose none of the buttons, said, "I told you we should stop feeding him. If he isn't fed, he won't grow, and we'd save not only the cost of the food but the cost of having to re-clothe him all the time."

"It's you we shouldn't bother feeding," Ellis said from the depths of the fine linen shirt he was pulling off over his head. As the Steward, he had been garbed in their best-seeming shirt (at least the parts that showed were holeless) and doublet (the mended rend that had brought its first owner to sell it cheap did not much show so long as its wearer never fully turned his back to the lookers-on) and gaudy-dyed long-pointed leather shoes (never worn an instant longer than necessary once off stage, to keep them unworn out). Emerging from the shirt, bare to his waist and hosen, his dark hair as near to on end as its curls would allow, Ellis grinned at Joliffe and added, "Think of how little we'd have to listen to you if you didn't have the strength to talk."

"Just feed me a crust before we have to perform, to see me through, and leave me to starve the rest of the time?" Joliffe suggested.

"The thought has possibilities."

Joliffe laughed. Given the chance, he and Ellis could jibe at each other by the hour, but they had all had a hard push to reach Oxford by last night after the cart decided to crack a wheel outside of Witney. Then they had spent the morning putting up the scaffold and stagecloth in the inn-yard and crying their performance through Oxford before doing the play itself so for just now jibing at Ellis was too much effort and Joliffe let it go, laying his folded doublet aside for Rose to put away, because she'd snap at him if he tried to do it himself. As the Devil, he'd worn the company's high-necked, hip-short scarlet doublet, hardly long enough to keep the coiled tail hidden until the play's end, and a high black hat that concealed his devil's horns wire-held to his head and unseen until he whipped off the hat when he claimed the Steward's soul for his own at the play's end. The shirt worn under it all was his own, and stripped down to that and his own hosen and shoes, he was done undressing and sat down on the closed lid of one of the sturdy-woven wicker baskets while he coiled the de-vil's tail back into its bag.

He was tying the bag closed and yawning, wondering what his chance of a nap was—there was still the scaffold and stagecloth to take down—when someone shadowed the doorway to the innyard. He and Ellis, Rose and Piers stopped what they were doing and looked toward it on the instant, ready to be alarmed, because if Basset were back this soon it meant the day's take had been too small to need much counting and that would be very much to the bad— they hoped for today's coins to see them through to Thursday's Corpus Christi play so they could save up whatever they made between now and then to see them out of Oxford and on their way to wherever next they played. That would let them keep their Corpus Christi payment from St. Michael's church as cushion against whatever ill-paid stretches were sure to come later. Since last winter's stretch of bad luck that had stranded them for a time in remote St. Frideswide's nunnery where only a nun's help—Dame Frevisse still figured in Rose's prayers—had saved them from worse trouble, they had been living on a thinner edge of flat-out poverty than usual. A good take today would make the coming months more sure than the past half-year had been.

But it wasn't Basset in the doorway. It was the next most worrying thing, a man saying excitedly, "I've found you!" And adding over his shoulder to someone else, "They're here!"

Because too often someone looking for them meant trouble of one kind or another, Joliffe laid aside the bag and stood up, while Ellis moved to join him, and Rose pushed Piers to behind the heavy wicker baskets that held most of what they owned while shifting herself to where she could lay hands to both men's belts with their daggers, to hand them over if need be. But by then Joliffe had taken clear look at the stocky, undergrown, widely smiling man in the doorway and somewhat eased out of his readiness for trouble. He had rarely seen one of that fellow's kind grown to man-size because they mostly died young, but there was no mistaking their soft-fleshed, slant-eyed faces. Eden-children they were sometimes called, and children they stayed in most ways, no matter how long they lived, and there was rarely any harm in them. Whyever this fellow was glad to have found them, it was unlikely to be for trouble. The question was where were his keepers, since it took only a glance to see he was no stray, not someone's cast-off left to wander at will with the hope he'd not come home. From his rolled-brimmed cap to his square-cropped hair to his fine-made doublet and hosen to his low-cut, fashionable shoes, he was well dressed and well-kept and must belong to someone.

As Joliffe wondered whose he was, two men appeared behind him from the yard, one of them saying, more amused than angry, "Lewis, what do you think you're doing, going off like that?"

The Eden-child turned to him and declared triumphantly, "I found them, Richard. Simon, I found them!"

Both men were as well dressed as the Eden-child and both were young, one of them probably barely twenty, the other somewhat the oldest of all three of them and carrying himself with the easy confidence of wealth and settled living as he said, a little laughing, "We see you did. But have you thought to ask if they wanted to be found?"

Lewis took a moment to think that through, then, stricken, looked back to the players to ask, faint with sudden uncertainty, "I did it wrong?"

Ellis instantly made a flourished bow to him and answered as formally as if to an Oxford burgess, "No wrong at all. You've done us honor, good sir, both in the seeking and the finding."

Lewis's round face blossomed into delight again. "I did it right? I can stay? Richard, Simon, I can stay!"

"That's not quite what he said," the younger of the two men began. "He. . . ."

"But I can, can't I?" Lewis asked of Ellis, eager as a puppy.

Probably mindful of Basset's saying, "Never turn away smiling men who look to have money," Ellis said over Lewis's shoulder to the older man, "He's welcome to a visit, if that suits you, my masters?"

"If it's not a trouble to you," the man said with equal courtesy.

"Our pleasure."

Lewis pointed at Joliffe. "You were the Devil!"

"He usually is," Ellis muttered without moving his lips and too low for anyone but Joliffe to hear.

Ignoring him, Joliffe swept Lewis a low bow in his turn. "Indeed, good sir, you have it right. I played the Devil."

Lewis laughed, pleased with himself, and pointed at Ellis. "You were the Steward!" A quick frown of concern furrowed his soft brow. "The devils didn't hurt you really, did they?"

"You can see he isn't hurt," the younger man said a little impatiently. "What they do is only pretense. It isn't real. I've told you."

"I know," Lewis said, impatient back at him but a little uncertain all the same.

A woman hovered into sight behind the men, well-dressed, too, as well as wimpled and veiled several layers deep in beautifully pressed, whitely starched light lawn. With an uncertain look at the players but claiming her place in things, she laid a hand on the older man's arm, claiming him, too, as she said, "Lewy loves plays, doesn't he, Richard?"

Joliffe immediately judged she was his wife and that they all were a tidy little family group—two brothers, probably, and the wife of the elder, with somehow an idiot in tow. Another brother?

Lewis was saying happily, "Plays and plays and plays.

It's almost Corpus Christi and there'll be plays and plays and more plays."

Piers, never one to keep out of anything for long unless he were forcibly stopped, made a small leap onto the sturdy-lidded basket nearest Lewis, struck a pose, and said, "We know! We're to play the third play. The one at St. Michael's Northgate. *Isaac and Abraham. . . .*"

"*Abraham and Isaac,*" Ellis corrected.

". . . and I'm Isaac," Piers went on, uncorrected. He and Ellis often differed on their views of the world and, presently, particularly on the name of the play they had been hired to do for Oxford town's Corpus Christi plays. To Piers's mind, if he was playing Isaac then Isaac had to be the more important. "I even cry when my father is going to kill me," he said proudly.

"He kills you?" Lewis breathed, looking awed at Ellis.

Ellis was too often mistaken for Pier's father for Piers to care; he went on, heedless of it, "My father in the play. Abraham. No, he doesn't kill me. The angel stops him, remember. That'll be Joliffe."

"But aren't you afraid he might kill you?" Lewis insisted, wide-eyed.

"No," Piers said with bold scorn and friendliness. "The sword we use wouldn't cut hot butter. I'll show you." Quickly, the way he did almost everything, he slipped off the far side of the basket and had it open and Lewis was come to join him before anyone could gainsay them.

The woman with her hand still on her husband's arm said in embarrassed despair, "Oh, Lewy!" while her husband said to Ellis, "I'm sorry. He's like that about things. Simon, can't you . . . ?"

The younger man was already going toward Lewis and Piers as if taking responsibility for Lewis were a long accustomed thing for him, while Rose came forward, saying with a smile, "It's no matter, sir. He's welcome to see. But, Piers, if you mess things about, you'll spend the afternoon straightening them."

"I won't," Piers said in the voice of one forever much put upon by others.

Lewis echoed, "We won't," sounding so much like him that over their heads Rose and Simon unexpectedly widely smiled at each other with much the same depth of affection.

But beside her husband the woman was saying, "We really should have brought Matthew. He's the only one who manages Lewy well, he really is. Richard, shouldn't we be going home?"

Simon looked to Richard who slightly nodded agreement to his wife's insistence. Unhurriedly but firmly, Simon set to extricating Lewis and Piers from each other's company and the depths of the basket with a casual hand on Lewis's shoulder and, "We must needs go now, Lewis. You heard Geva and Richard. We have to go home. The players have things to do. We have to go."

Lewis surfaced from behind the propped up lid. "Do we, Simon? I don't want to."

"We do," Simon said gently, firmly.

Great grief shimmered dark into Lewis's odd-formed eyes, but even as he protested, "I don't want to go," he was moving to follow Simon, probably too used to doing what he was told to do to make real trouble over it. Then suddenly delight as utter as his grief had been bloomed across his face. He stopped where he was between the baskets and said, "They can come, too! They can come and do plays for me!"

Geva cried with instant and complete dismay, "Oh, Lewy, *no*!", while her husband said more moderately, "I don't think so, Lewis."

Only Simon kept countenance, saying calmly, "Lewis, the players can't come with us. They have things to do."

"They can do things with me. Where I am," Lewis insisted.

"We don't have any place for them to stay," Simon insisted back patiently.

"Or time for them," Richard said, not quite so patiently. "Not with everyone who's coming and everything that has to be done this week. Nobody is going to have time or place for players on our hands."

"I have time. I have place," Lewis insisted. "There's lots of places."

What Simon would have said to that, Richard cut off with, "There aren't places. Everywhere is going to be full in a few days. Now come on. We're expected home. We've been here long enough."

"I want them!" Lewis said. He crossed his arms over his chest and dropped solid-rumped to the floor, defying anyone to change his mind or make him move.

Simon made a small gesture at Richard and Geva to stay quiet and sat down on his heels to come eye-to-eye with Lewis. Lewis looked scowlingly at him, but Simon said slowly, calmly, "Lewis, we have to go home now and the players can't come with us. It's no good worrying at them and no good worrying at us. They have other things to do. They can't," firmly, "come with us."

Intent on the dealing with Lewis, Joliffe had not noticed Basset come back from his dealings with Master Norton, but from the doorway he said now in the mellow, warm, commanding voice he used when he played God, a prophet, an apostle, or a saint in a kindly humour, "Not necessarily so, my good lord. Not necessarily so at all."

He must have been listening long enough to know something of what was toward, and with everyone now looking at him, he finished his entrance like the practiced player that he was, bowed first to Richard's wife, then to Richard, and finally to Lewis and Simon. In his younger days a strong-built man, Basset was, with years and gray hair, gone somewhat to bulk but carried his years well when he chose, and now, at his top of dignity, turned all his heed to Richard with yet another bow, deeper than the first, and said, "If there's some way we could oblige the young lord, we'll be more than merely glad to do so, sir."

Half-wit he might be but Lewis knew an ally when he heard one and scrambled to his feet so fast he nearly overset Simon who rose somewhat more slowly and with a shading of . . . relief, Joliffe thought. At the same time he wondered at what Basset was aiming. Lewis, not bothered with any wondering, said, simply happy, "They can come! They can come!"

"That's not what he said, Lewis," said Richard, whose rapidly shifting expressions betrayed he was looking for his best way out of the tangle in which he suddenly found himself. He took the shortest one by saying to Basset, "What do you mean?"

If it had been to a cue written in a play, Basset's answer could not have come more pat. "Why, simply, that we're not tied to anything or anywhere these few days from now to Corpus Christi. If it would make the young lord happy . . ."

"Master Fairfield," Richard said. "His name is Master Fairfield. Not 'lord'."

"Lord, Lord," Lewis burbled happily.

". . . Master Fairfield," Basset smoothly amended. He had taught Joliffe early on that you never went wrong giving someone a title higher than was actually their own. They would correct you, but they would remember the pleasure you had given them. "If having us to hand would please him for that while, we could make do with anywhere given us to stay. A corner of a stable. A loft somewhere?"

"Loft, lost, loft," Lewis said, close to singing now.

"It isn't . . ." Richard began.

But Simon moved away from Lewis to Richard, taking him by the arm and turning him aside to say, low-voiced, "Listen a moment. You know as well as I do what it's worth to tell Lewis he can't have a thing he's set to. If he thinks we're giving in, he'll come home with us, and when it comes out he's not having what he wants, he'll throw his fit there instead of here with everyone to see him." Simon suddenly smiled. "Besides, there's always the chance your father will say they can stay and then there'll be no need for tempers lost at all."

Except perhaps by Geva who said, "We can't troop through the streets with a band of players at our heels. I won't!"

She sounded as ready to make trouble over having her own way as Lewis was, but Basset, putting something of her own dismay into his voice, instantly agreed, "Assuredly not, my good lady. But if I came and . . ." He threw a quick look past Ellis in his shirt and hosen and bare feet to Joliffe, marginally more dressed with shoes already on and his workaday brown doublet in his hand. ". . . and Master Southwell with me, we can talk to whomever the decision lies with or . . ." He dropped his voice and leaned a little forward, conspirator-wise. ". . . at least have Master Fairfield home without trouble. You see what I mean."

She saw, and her struggle between choosing to go through the streets with a wailing Lewis or with two men who, after all, *looked* presentable enough, despite what they were, was both visible to Joliffe and brief before she said, taking hold of her husband's arm again, "Yes. That would do. Yes, let's do that. Simon, would you make him come now?"

Simon turned back to Lewis, quiet now that things seemed to be going his way. Joliffe flung on his doublet, and Basset turned to Rose who briskly smoothed his hair, centered his belt buckle, handed him his hat, and when he had put it on, nodded he was fit to be seen. She was his daughter and Piers his grandson but she saw to them both with an almost identical and frequently aggravated affection. Now, for good measure, she also ran a quick eye over Joliffe to be sure of him, which he acknowledged with a twitch of a grin at the corners of his mouth, knowing that to Rose he and Piers were much of an age and often of like trouble.

With the dignity he kept despite how much the world at large sought to take it from him, Basset faced Richard again. "We're ready when you are, Master Fairfield."

"Penteney," Richard corrected. "I'm Master Richard Penteney. Master Fairfield and his brother Master Simon are my father's wards."

Which went some way to straightening how matters stood—but not to explaining the mingled glint of wariness and question that crossed Basset's face, there and quickly gone and probably undiscernable to anyone who didn't know his face as well as Joliffe did. Besides that, Joliffe knew, too, how well Basset could keep hidden behind his face what he wanted to keep hidden. What had disconcerted him that much in the little that Master Richard Penteney had said?

There was time only to wonder at it in passing. Lewis, persuaded by Simon that at least some of the players were coming with them and the rest would follow, was eager to go; but after taking Simon's hand he turned back to say at Joliffe again, "You were the Devil."

Joliffe admitted that with a slight bow. "I was, indeed."

"I liked you."

"You were supposed to," Joliffe said, answering Lewis's grin with his own.

"Lewy, come on," Mistress Geva ordered from ahead, already away into the innyard on her husband's arm. "Be a good boy."

"Good boy, good boy," Lewis repeated under his breath, as if the words tasted bad, but Joliffe patted his shoulder and said, "Go ahead. We'll be with you," and Lewis went away with Simon, leaving Joliffe and Basset to follow in their wake as they left the innyard.

Joliffe took the chance to shift near enough to Basset to say, private under the general talk of passers-by around them, "What are you about? You really think they'll have us stay? Or are you just being obliging, helping them take their idiot home?"

"Obliging, to be sure, my lad, and at the worst likely to have a few pence for our trouble. Then again, this is a very well-kept idiot. If they indulge him this far, they're likely to indulge him farther, maybe even to keeping us these few days to keep him happy."

"And if they do," Joliffe said, catching up to Basset's thought, "we won't have to pay for lodging and maybe not for food the while." And so save what they'd made today and be that much ahead, along with whatever else they might make in the streets in the three days between now and Corpus Christi.

Basset laid a comfortable hand over the pouch hung from his belt. "A little trouble and a large profit is how it looks to me."

"How was the take today?" One of the two constant questions that rode with any company of players. First there was: Would they find an audience? Then: If they did, would they collect enough coins at the end of their playing to pay for the next meal and to see them to the next town?

"Today's take?" Basset said with satisfaction so thick it could have been laid on with a trowel. "It was good enough that even Master Norton didn't growl too deeply over his share of it."

So even if this possibility with the idiot didn't go through, they would still be comfortably off for a while to come, and a while was all, even at best, they could ever count on. It went with being a player, especially one with no noble patron to fall back to for protection from such troubles as the world—or, to be more precise, as mankind—might choose to visit on them. Comfortable "for a while" was boon indeed, and added to a warm, bright summer's day, a well-performed play behind him, and almost a week's sure work ahead of him, Joliffe enjoyed the easy walk along Northgate Street with its narrow shops rowed in front of tall, narrow-fronted houses crowded wall to wall, and out through North Gate into broader St. Giles beyond the town walls.

The houses were larger here, for richer folk who wanted out of the town's crowding, but the people in the street were the same, a mixed crowd of townspeople and students out to enjoy the good Sunday weather. Ahead, the Penteneys and Simon and Lewis turned leftward through a stone gateway arch leading through a building that ran blank-walled along the street but above was timber-built, with windows looking out. Joliffe and Basset followed through the gateway's passage into a cobbled yard that was wider and longer than the inn's. The far end was closed off by a plain gateway and a large barn, while along one side were what looked to be stables and a cattle byre, and across the yard from them a house that lived up to the rich look of all the rest. Stone-built below, its two upper stories rose in timber and plaster work, with glass in every window and in the midst of it all the steep-pitched roof of a great hall, with a square stone porch for entrance from the yard.

Joliffe whistled almost silently with admiration and said for only Basset to hear, "If this goes our way, we've fallen in clover this time."

Basset didn't answer, probably because the Penteneys and Lewis had gone inside but Simon Fairfield had turned back at the porch, waiting, saying when Basset and Joliffe came up to him, "Master Richard has gone to tell his father what's toward and see if he'll see you."

Basset bowed his acceptance of that and they were left with a pause that usually Basset would have filled with easy talk to make the waiting time pass less awkwardly. Instead, having taken off his hat when Simon turned to speak to them, he stood turning it slowly and steadily in his hands, looking downward as if in thought. Simon Fairfield, for his part, was equally, awkwardly silent, frowning aside into space with the look of someone trying to find something to say. Joliffe, too used to being kept waiting by his "betters" to be uneasy about it but unsettled by Basset's silence and a little sorry for Simon, said, "Your brother seems a good-hearted fellow."

Simon smiled with both affection and rue. "He is. He's small of wit but very good of heart."

"He was born so?"

"Born so, yes."

And was the elder, since he was Master Fairfield and also—at a safe guess—was heir to something sufficient to make it worth Master Penteney's while to have him in ward and keep him well. The oddness lay in the fact that usually an heir like Lewis would have been long since put aside in favor of a brother as well in mind and body as Simon apparently was. Joliffe was curious about that but manners meant he should not ask more and another pause began, this time ended by Simon asking, obviously grabbing at something to say, "You've been in Oxford long?"

"Only since yesterday. This time," Joliffe answered when Basset did not.

"You've been here before?"

"Most years we're here around Christmastide, usually through Twelfth Night. Sometimes we come again in spring or summer, depending."

"On what?"

"On how the world is going."

"Ah," Simon said vaguely.

"You see, there's good years for players to be on the road and bad years," Joliffe explained. "The bad years, like these last few have been with the poor harvests, when there's not much money and not much food to spare, folk may welcome us but they don't have much to give and, alas, we need to eat, like anyone else. So we have to circle wider, farther, to more villages and towns, to make as much as we'd otherwise hope to make in fewer places."

And a footsore, wearisome business it was. They had a cart and a horse: Tisbe served to pull the cart, the cart served to carry the necessities of their work and lives, neither served to carry any of them. Where they went, they walked, and while their usual route took them a long enough way, along the Chilterns and around through Berkshire and into Gloucestershire and up so far as Warwickshire, these last two years they'd had to go as far eastward as Hertford and as far north as Nottingham in their quest to keep flesh on their bones.

"Ah," Master Simon said again, this time with open interest. "Have you ever been as far as London?"

Basset finally roused to an actual answer, saying with something of his seemingly forthright way, "Alas, no, sir.

Our company, fine as it is, is too small to venture there just yet."

Master Simon looked ready to ask or say more, but a servant came to the door and while giving both Basset and Joliffe a sidewise look said, "Master Penteney says he'll see them, please you, Master Simon. He's in his study-chamber. Would you have me take them there?"

"I'll see them to him," Simon answered, and added to Basset with a smile, "I brought you to this. I should see you through it."

The porch opened into the screens passage that protected the great hall from draughts. The servant went ahead of them and aside, through a doorway to the left, probably toward the kitchen. Simon led Joliffe and Basset the other way, through a rightward doorway into the great hall. At this hour of a fine-weathered Sunday afternoon, with even servants let off all but the most necessary work and folk able to be outside and elsewhere, the hall was quiet, its long, wide space, open to the raftered roof, empty so that the pad of their soft-soled leather shoes over the stone-flagged floor was nigh to loud as Simon led them up it to one of the doors flanking the dais at its upper end. Joliffe had time to note that the arras showing beautifully dressed men and women riding across a flowery meadow and covering all the broad end wall save for the two doorways, was painted rather than woven but that the painting was of the very best, before Simon knocked lightly at the open door and went through, into the room beyond it. Basset and Joliffe followed him.

The chamber was far smaller than the great hall, well-proportioned, with a low ceiling and much sunlight through a long window looking out on a stretch of close-cut grass and a garden bright with flowers, bounded on the far side by what looked to be someone else's blank housewall. With a single sharp flicker of his eyes as he entered, Joliffe took in the tall, closed aumbry standing along one wall, the flat-topped chests to either side of it, the long-legged writing desk angled to the window so the light would come over the left shoulder of whoever worked there, and the smaller clerk's table to one side of it, everything plainly made but of golden oak, while under foot, rather than the bare stone or rush matting there might have been, there was a carpet woven in strong and intricately patterned colors.

Everything told there was more than a little wealth in this place, whoever Master Penteney was—and almost surely he was the man standing beside the desk, a man who very definitely went with the room. He was of late middle-years, with his hair beginning to draw back from his fore-head and his belt beginning to quarrel with his belly; but the belt's buckle was silver and his knee-length houpp-lande was of a burgundy-dyed wool that came no more cheaply than the soft lambs' budge that edged it at wrists and hem. Like the room, there was nothing of excess about him but everything there was was of the best.

What did not match was how, as he saw Basset, the easy welcome on his face began a sharp shift that Joliffe—see-ing him over Basset's shoulder—thought would be open startlement in another instant; but in the same moment that Master Penteney's eyes began to widen and his mouth to open, Basset twitched his head in the slightest of denials, and Master Penteney's expression shifted smoothly back to simply welcoming as completely as if nothing else had ever been there.

But something had been. What?

And why?

Chapter 2

Whatever had passed between Basset and Master Penteney, Joliffe thought no one but himself had seen it. Simon had been in the middle of turning from one of them to the other and Master Richard was across the room saying something at Lewis who was nodding and jigging a little on his toes, heeding nothing but that he was going to have his players. Now Basset was simply making the expected bow to Master Penteney, and Joliffe matched him, both their bows deep but, this time, unflourished, one of Basset's dictates being that a player should always make a flourished bow to both country folk and the nobility—to the first because they were impressed by it, to the latter because it amused them—but that for merchants, craftsmen, and almost any other townspeople a plain bow was best. "Because," Basset had said, "they're on the watch, always, to keep from being robbed by their betters or cheated by their fellows, by lesser folk, and by assuredly such useless troublemakers as they're sure we are. Be too fantastical to them and all they'll do is distrust you the worse."

So here Basset's bow was carefully graded with respect to a wealthy man, and Joliffe's bow was slightly deeper, to show that as Basset's man he was even more humble—another of Basset's dictates being that a man was always deemed more important if he had followers. Since players needed any slight bit of importance they could glean, Joliffe was his humble follower whenever necessary.

Master Penteney acknowledged their bows with a slight bending of his head and said, "I'm told you're to perform one of the Corpus Christi plays."

"At St. Michael's Northgate, please you, sir," Basset answered.

"The *Abraham and Isaac*, I believe?"

"But the sword won't even cut butter!" Lewis interrupted happily. "The boy . . ."

He broke off, looking to Basset with a troubled, asking look.

"Piers," Basset said.

Lewis's face shone with happiness. "Piers!" he repeated, swaying happily from foot to foot.

Master Richard dropped a hand onto his shoulder, quieting him as Master Penteney went on, "You surely have plans for between now and then. Rehearsals and suchlike and somewhere to stay?"

"For where we stay, last night we were at the Arrow and Hind. Tonight . . ." Basset made a light shrug to show the matter was open, though in fact Master Norton had grudgingly granted they could stay where they were if they could pay and so long as he didn't need the space for someone who would pay more. "As for rehearsing, we know the play well. Our practicing will be slight and otherwise our time is our own. Or yours, if we may be of service," he added with a slight, respectful bow.

Master Penteney was probably no more deceived by

Basset's smooth words than Joliffe was. Just as Basset would not have survived his years as a player without sharp wits and skill at bargaining, neither would Master Penteney be where he was without the same. Apparently he likewise appreciated good bargaining when he met it, because he said, level-voiced but with a warm glint of laughter in his face, "Well, Master Fairfield has taken an interest in you . . ."

"Plays," Lewis said happily. "They can do plays for me."

". . . and I see no reason to deny him the diversion, if it's convenient to you. Besides, we're to have guests this week. Somewhat many and of importance at an evening feast on Wednesday, a few friends and neighbors to Thursday supper. Would you be interested to perform for us those times?"

"In return for staying here?" Basset asked politely.

"If that would seem a fair exchange to you. Board and lodging these five days in return for obliging Lewis and performing for our guests?" Master Penteney asked back as politely.

The offer was more than fair. It was all that Basset had hoped for and probably more than he'd thought to get and it had come more as a gift than by bargaining. But Master Richard said with the quiet certainty of someone pointing out a reasonable thing, "Father, there's going to be no room to spare. Once Lord and Lady Lovell and their people come . . ."

"I hardly think Master Basset and his company expect to stay in our guest rooms," Master Penteney said.

Basset immediately, smoothly, agreed. "Assuredly not, sir. A corner of any clean place suits us very well."

And when pushed to it, so did unclean places if there was no other way to have a roof and walls between them and the weather, but neither he nor Joliffe was about to say so.

"There then," Master Penteney said to his son. "The winter stores are mostly emptied and the hay hardly yet begun to come in. Why not the great barn? They can stay there at no one's inconvenience, surely."

"Who's going to see to Lewis going back and forth to them?" Master Richard asked.

"Matthew, as always. Nor is there any reason they can't come to the hall. They'll want to work in it before they perform in it anyway."

Master Penteney was knowledgeable as well as generous, Joliffe thought. All too often people had to be persuaded players did not step out of thin air into a place to do a play.

He was knowledgeable of more than that, too: he had said Basset's name without—to the best of Joliffe's remembering—anyone having said it either here or at the inn.

"It's going to mean five more people to feed," Master Richard said. "Shouldn't you ask Mother . . ."

"Five more mouths won't break us. Say we do it in honor and for the sake of our Lord's Body."

Everyone, Lewis a little behind the others, crossed themselves at the mention of Corpus Christi. Then Master Penteney paused as if waiting for something. When nothing came, he cocked a questioning look at his son. "No other objections?"

Master Richard solemnly shook his head.

"I can't say you made much of a case against them being here," his father complained.

"I didn't see there was much of one to be made," Master Richard returned. "If there's somewhere for them to stay and you're willing to feed them and they'll earn their keep, what else was there to protest?"

"That they're vagabonds and therefore probably rascals

and so shouldn't be allowed inside our gates, let be spend whole nights here, able to work who knows what ill doings?" Master Penteney suggested.

Master Richard smiled. "It seemed a rude thing to say to their faces, especially considering we know nothing actually ill against them. Haven't you said it's better to let others do wrong to us than to do wrong first?"

"Hm. A point well taken." Master Penteney returned his heed to Basset. "You see, when raising a son to follow you, it's ever a peril that he may learn to follow so well he never learns to lead. Therefore, I've encouraged him to argue with me."

"Sometimes and by your leave," Master Richard said.

"And sometimes without my leave," his father returned.

"But we're more private about those," Master Richard said, smiling.

Master Penteney returned his smile. "Granted." He turned back to Basset. "By the time you've brought the rest of your folk, we'll have a place ready for you and I dare say Master Fairfield will be waiting."

Lewis clapped happily. "I have my players!"

"You have your players," Simon agreed and held out a hand. "Now we have to find out Mistress Penteney and tell her about them."

"I want to go with them!" Lewis protested.

"No," Master Penteney said firmly. "Go with Simon now."

"They have to fetch the other players," Simon said, going to take Lewis by an unwilling hand. "They have to go for Piers."

"Piers!" Lewis said, delighted.

"And we're going to tell Mistress Penteney about them," Simon repeated. "So come on now."

Lewis went peaceably enough then. When the door had shut behind them, Master Penteney said to Basset, "Thank you for your kindness to Master Fairfield. It's appreciated."

Basset bowed. "As is your kindness to us."

"We're both well satisfied then. Richard will see you out, please you."

It was a gracious dismissal and Basset took it graciously, he and Joliffe both making deep bows before following Master Richard from the room and through the great hall. He left them in the porch and they went on by themselves, across the yard and through the gateway, Joliffe waiting until they were to the street, to say, "It looks like we've landed on our feet this time and no mistake."

"It does indeed," Basset agreed. "I'll light a candle to St. Genesius for it." The patron saint of players, beheaded in ancient Rome after suddenly converting to Christianity in the middle of a play—part of the miracle being that his fellow players had not martyred him for spoiling the performance, before ever the Roman lords laid hands on him.

As they went back toward the inn, Joliffe kept curbed his curiosity at what he had seen pass between Basset and Master Penteney. Curbing curiosity was a necessary courtesy most players kept among themselves. A company of players lived too much together to go asking questions about things someone else might not want to tell. Whatever their lives had been before they joined a company, they mostly knew no more about each other than what each one chose to say by chance or purpose, and mostly it was better that way. Assuredly there were things in Joliffe's life he was content that neither Basset nor anyone else should ever ask about or know. Leaving Basset to his own secrets was the least he could give in return.

Besides, if he asked something that he shouldn't, Basset would likely flay him front and back and down both sides with a few very well chosen words. Best not to give him the chance.

At the inn they found that Rose and Ellis, because it was always best to keep the company's belongings safely basketed except when needed, had the company's wicker hampers packed. With that already done and the good news given, it was the work of merely moments for Joliffe to hitch Tisbe to their cart while Rose, Ellis, and Piers loaded the baskets in and Basset went to make his farewells to Master Norton, who tried to gouge another sixpence out of him but did not get it.

At the Penteneys they found Lewis waiting in the gateway for them, behind him a man almost as short as he was but older and more strongly built and with nothing lacking in his wits, to judge by the sharp look-over he gave the players while Lewis greeted Piers with, "I'll show you where! Come on!" and started away at a shambling run.

Piers looked to Basset, who nodded he could go. He did, and the older man, left behind, gave a hard look at him light-footing after Lewis but, seeming satisfied of something, said to Basset, "This way, then."

At Joliffe's urging, Tisbe started the cart forward again, following Ellis and Rose who were following Basset who was saying as they went, "Thank you, Master . . . ?"

"Matthew," the man said. He sounded as if he were still of several minds how much he approved of them being here. "No 'master' to it."

"You see to Master Fairfield," Basset ventured.

"I'm his keeper is the way most folk put it, like he was an animal. Which he isn't. He's just simple."

"And good-hearted and clear-spirited," Basset said, "which is more than can be said for a great many men who *ought* to have keepers and don't."

The man give Basset a shrewd sideways look. "You're

in the right of it there. Master Fairfield doesn't need 'keeping.' He just needs watching out for, like you would with a
child. I'm the one who does it most of the time and that
means, from what Master Penteney has said, that we'll be
seeing something of each other these few days."

"Indeed," Basset agreed. "So by your leave, I'll depend
on you to keep us straight with him. Tell us if we start to
lead him some way he shouldn't go."

"Aye," Matthew said. "There's none know him better
than me. You listen to what I say and it'll go well enough."

"Would he be able to be in one of our plays, do you
think. A small part but . . . ?"

Joliffe grinned to himself. Basset would have the man as
much on their side as Lewis was before they finished crossing the yard.

As the cart rattled off the cobbles of the fore-end of the
yard onto hard-packed bare ground that went the rest of the
way to the rear gate, Piers and Lewis disappeared through
the double-wide doorway of the barn at the yard's far end.
Joliffe, with the practiced glance of someone who often
needed to know quickly as much as he could about where
he was, took in the barn's size, over-large for some place in
town, even if on the town's edge. The well-built stables and
long cattle byre facing the house were more than might be
expected, too, as well as, on the house side of the yard, the
several low, strongly built sheds with hasped and locked
heavy doors in a line from the house's end to the barn
where Piers and Lewis had disappeared. To make it all
more strange, the whole yard was oddly empty, with no
men in sight nor any animals besides a few chickens
scratching in the dust. There was not even a muck heap beside the stable.

Ahead of him, Ellis must have noted that, too, because
he asked something and Matthew said over his shoulder to

him, "Aye, nothing much going on just now. It's because
Master Penteney is a victualler, see. Supplies their beef
and mutton and pork and all to a goodly number of the colleges and halls and St. Frideswide's monastery right here
in Oxford, as well as I don't know what all he sells to London merchants. Whatever the butchers need for the holiday
they already have, so he's cleared the place out for there to
be room for Lord and Lady Lovell's people and horses as
they'll be bringing with them. Then, God willing, we'll be
coming on to more haying. That'll take up a big part of the
great barn where you're to stay, but there's room in plenty
for you folks for now. Along harvest-time he'll be buying
grain, and right through into winter we're full up and busy
with cattle and sheep and all, as well as whatever he buys
in from overseas in the way of spices and the better wines
and suchlike. That's what's in there." Matthew nodded at
the locked sheds. "He deals back and forth for Lord Lovell
and some others, too, that doesn't want to merchant for
themselves. He does all right, does Master Penteney. It's
quiet here only for the while."

All that explained how Master Penteney could afford to
please Lewis to—frankly—excess. What it didn't explain
to Joliffe was why Master Penteney bothered with pleasing
him. He held Lewis and Simon's wardships, yes, and that
meant he was responsible for their care and up-raising until they came of age, meanwhile running their inheritance
and taking the profits of it. How well or ill a ward was kept
depended on their guardian and on how much of a profit he
meant to have out of the wardship. A ward could be nearly
starved and go in rags the while they were in an unkind
person's keeping, though it was rare for that to happen and
there were laws to prevent it; but there was nothing that
forced Master Penteney to indulge Lewis with as much
care and freedom as he plainly did—not when, as an Eden-

child, Lewis could simply have been locked in a room and fed, even removed as heir and Simon put in his place. Joliffe came back to wondering why hadn't he been.

They were nearly to the great barn. Reared up to the sky and spread wide to either side of its broad double doorway, it was larger than some village churches Joliffe knew, maybe larger than the hall in the house behind him. Piers bounded out from the shadowy inside and called "Come on! Wait 'til you see!"

The others went ahead. Although horse and cart would go easily through the doorway, Joliffe stopped and spoke to Tisbe, then left her standing outside before he followed the others into the high-raftered space, thick with shadows after the bright day outside, in time to hear Matthew say, "All the rain this spring brought the grass along. With the good weather these past few weeks, Master Penteney had some meadows mowed, making early hay on the chance the weather turns again, the way it has these past two summers and we get to make no more hay. There's not much, though, and still plenty of room for you." He raised his voice. "Master Fairfield, you stay off that mow! You got your good clothes on!"

Well away toward the far end of the barn and the golden mound of hay there, Lewis and Piers pulled up short and looked at each other, before Lewis hunched his shoulders toward his ears in a massive shrug and together they turned back.

"Have my work cut out for me with two of 'em to watch," Matthew muttered, but it sounded like token grumbling and he added, "Won't hurt him to have some new company for a change, someone to play with, like, and your boy's not making fun of him. That's good."

But then, anyone who would let Piers talk and show off all he wanted was going to find him good company, Joliffe thought. The rest of them might even be spared Piers's chattering at them for the while, if Lewis was willing to listen enough.

"You're welcome to bring your cart right on inside. Settle down wherever you like," Matthew went on. "Help yourself to hay for bedding if you like. Master Penteney says you're not to be grudged it if you want it. He says, too, your horse can be put to pasture with his if you like. Save mucking out here, don't you see, and feeding it since you're not going to need it these few days."

"That's kind indeed," Basset said.

"Where?" Joliffe asked, knowing he'd be the one to take her.

"You go out the rear gate here into the lane and head north," Matthew answered. He went on to tell Joliffe how to know the place when he saw it while Rose called to Piers and Lewis, headed now for the cart, "You two leave those baskets alone for now. When we're settled in, you and Master Fairfield can go through them, Piers, but not yet."

"Ask for Walter Glover," Matthew said "He's Master Penteney's pasture-master there. He'll see you right. He's a stiff man, is Master Glover. Keeps things the way they should be and has trouble keeping men to work there for him because of it. He knows his business there, though, so he'll never be let go. This time of year there's only need for one or two other men there anyway. If you're in luck, it'll be one of them you meet up with, rather than him."

"They're off away," Rose said, watching out the door as Piers and Lewis, with Lewis in the lead now, disappeared down a narrow gap between two of the sheds.

"That's Mistress Penteney's garden they're headed for. No harm there," Matthew said, making to follow after them, adding over his shoulder as he went, "If you don't see us before, you'll catch up to us in the hall at supper, no fear."

He disappeared the way they had gone and the rest of them set to the settling in. It went easily enough. With the cart brought into the barn but no need for the tent here or a fire for warmth or cooking, even though the barn's bare dirt floor would have made that easy enough, their unloading was only some small wooden boxes of belongings, some canvas-covered cushions for sitting, and their bedding. For all their beds, Joliffe and Ellis brought a few armloads of hay so fresh it still smelled of sun and summer. While Rose spread their blankets over the long, thick heaps they had made—humming to herself while she did, sure sign that she was happy—Basset sat down on a cushion, looking tired but satisfied, his brow for once unfurrowed with worry, and Joliffe went to unharness Tisbe from the cart. Looking around, Ellis said, "I'd say this time we've fallen into it properly for a change."

Chapter 3

Joliffe did not mind walking Tisbe to the pasture. Besides the mare being good company, he never minded a chance to go off on his own and well the rest of the players knew it. Basset, Rose, and Piers were family to each other, being father, daughter, and grandson, and Ellis was as near family to them as he could be short of marriage and actual fatherhood. That maybe made the difference for Joliffe, but Joliffe suspected not. He did not remember a time in his life when he hadn't sometimes simply liked to have himself to himself, and living as the players did—practically in each other's shoes days and nights together—wore on him sometimes more than it ever seemed to wear on the others. No one would be surprised if he made no haste over going to the pasture or coming back, and he and Tisbe strolled together the whole way, past other people's backgates and rearyards into the more open country of Oxford's city burgage meadows, the lane lazy between summer-sprung hedges, with people Sunday-wandering in no more haste to anywhere than he and Tisbe were.

Pacing along roads was mostly an everyday thing for Tisbe and him but this walk was, in its way nothing for the two of them because she was without the cart for once and for once he had no need to worry over where supper and the night's stay would be.

Master Penteney's place with its green-painted gateposts along the lane was as easy to know as Matthew had said it would be. The yard beyond them was enclosed along one side by a long shed, a cattle byre, and at the far end a pigpen where, by the squealing, piglets were waiting to be someone's pork-roast dinners. On the yard's other side was a small timber-and-plaster house against a barn as large as where the players were staying. Everything, from house to pigpen, looked to be as well kept, clean, and prosperous as the Penteney place in town, and the man who came from the house as Joliffe passed through the gateway with Tisbe was well-kept, too. Dressed in a doublet and loose surcoat better than a plain servant would have worn, he stood on the doorstep and demanded, "What do you want here?"

It was a fair enough question but could have been asked more courteously. Still leading Tisbe onward, Joliffe—having long since found that a firm stand on his dignity often threw people out of their stride toward despising him—answered courteously back but with a look down his nose and the slightest hint in his voice that told he had heard the insolence but was willing to overlook it this time, "Master Penteney has given leave for our horse to graze in his pasture these few days our company is in his service. Master Glover, are you?"

"Aye." The man started across the yard toward him. "Company of what?"

"Players."

Glover regarded him with mingled disbelief and disapproval. "Master Penteney has taken on a clot of players?"

"For Master Fairfield's pleasure," Joliffe said, giving no ground.

"Ah. Master Fairfield." That seemed to answer everything for Glover. Some of the unwelcome went from his voice. "Well, we've grass enough." He reached the middle of the yard when Joliffe did, enough into his way that Joliffe stopped. Master Glover walked around Tisbe with a judging eye. "She looks healthy enough."

"We'd have small use for a sick horse, would we?" Joliffe said easily, not looking to make a quarrel with him.

Glover half-laughed. "You wouldn't, no." He slapped Tisbe lightly on the shoulder, said, "We might even manage some oats for you while you're here, old girl." He pointed toward one of the gates at the far end of the yard. "That's where we keep the horses presently. Turn her in. She'll do fine."

He went back toward the house and Joliffe led Tisbe on to the gate at which Glover had pointed. There were three gates, all opening into well-hedged pastures, with a marshy stream running along the bottom of them to make for easy watering of any livestock kept there to wait for market. Just now some young sheep were in one, a few cows in another, while half a score of horses were grazing the thick-grown grass in the middle one. With all of that and the barn and byre and pigs and storage shed and being so near to town, this was a place suited and fine for a victualler supplying colleges, halls, and a monastery in Oxford. Besides there, Joliffe could guess that Master Penteney's business probably went across a wide swathe of country from the Welsh border to London, with links overseas to France and Flanders at the least. It was not that Master Penteney owned or needed much land of his own, since he wouldn't trouble to grow much of his grain and hay or breed his own livestock. As a victualler, he would contract with others who did that, would buy from them and sell in better markets than they could hope to reach, making fine profits for himself from it all.

Joliffe led Tisbe into the horse pasture and closed the gate behind him while he made his farewell, rubbing the deep hollow under her jaw while he told her, "Don't eat yourself out of shape here, my girl. You'll have to go back between the cart shafts one of these days, you know."

Tisbe did not deign to answer. With head stretched out and eyes half-closed, she would have let him go on rubbing under her chin forever; when he stopped, she rolled a re-proachful eye at him, still holding her head out in hope of more. Laughing at her, he slid her halter off, gave her a scratch behind the ears, and said, "That's enough, you spoiled madam. Go enjoy yourself."

Tisbe blew down her nose at him, swung her head to bump him in the chest for her own farewell, and ambled away, not toward the half dozen other horses in the pasture but in search of a patch of grass all her own. Usually she had only whatever grass was in the compass of her lead rope when they staked her out of a night beside a road or else a little plain hay if they were in a town, with—as Mas-ter Glover had certainly guessed—rarely a mouthful of oats from one month's end to the next. Compared to the sturdy, smooth-flanked horses here, she was an unimpres-sive sight, under-tall and bony, but she had come cheap five years ago when their last horse, Hero, having lain down sometime in a night, had quietly failed to rise in the morn-ing, fading from sleep to death with the players standing mourning around him.

They had had to pull the cart to the next town themselves and spend half a day looking for a horse they could afford, and even then Tisbe had taken most of the coins in Basset's purse. They had lived on vegetable pottage and bread for a week afterwards, unable to buy any meat, but in the long go of things Tisbe had proved to be worth more than they had paid. She was not much to look at but she was what they needed—a plain horse that no one would ever envy or likely have urge to steal, but hardy enough to hold up to the work they asked of her. Besides that, she was sweet-humoured, and Joliffe was glad she'd have this while of rest along with the rest of them.

Leaving the pasturage, he turned back for Oxford with no particular thought of what he meant to do but in no hurry to rejoin the others. Since the few silver farthings in his pouch totaled somewhat less than threepence and he misliked spending himself flat out of coin unless there was black need of it, he did not have much choice of what he would do, but walking, sitting, and looking cost nothing, and he turned off the lane at the first stile he came to, going over it to a fieldpath headed vaguely eastward through the countryside. He made no haste: sat for a while on another stile between one field and the next to watch the world do nothing in particular around him, ambled on eventually, and when the path brought him to a stream's bank, sat there among a scrub of alders for another while, pitching idle stones into the water. The path finally brought him, as he had supposed it would, to a narrow bridge over the River Cherwell and into another lane that he followed southward, back toward town, still in no haste. Among summer's beauties was how long the days lasted. The sun had over an hour to go to setting when he reached the Iffley Road and joined the flow of townspeople and students turned back from their Sunday strolls or visiting, done with their day's idleness and heading to the surety of supper and somewhere familiar for the night. Having no thoughts of home to draw him and fairly certain he had time before supper, he stopped on the bridge outside the town's East Gate, to lean on the railing and watch the water flow away under him in satin darkness and rippled light. It was something, in other days, he had done often here, and he was paying no heed to the talk of passing people behind him—students as always louder than everyone else—until a man asked, "Joliffe?"

Too surprised to be wary, Joliffe straightened and turned around from the railing.

Drawn aside from the people-flow, the man was standing uncertainly a few feet away. Soberly dressed in a scholar's dark, long gown, with a simple, brimless scholar's cap over his smooth, short-cut hair, he was much about Joliffe's own age and clearly of two minds as to whether he should have spoken or not. For a moment Joliffe was equally puzzled, until something in the slight, questioning turn of the man's head jarred memory loose and Joliffe asked uncertainly back at him, "John Thamys?" Growing certainty surprised him into pleasure and he repeated, certain now, "John Thamys!"

"Yes!" Certain, too, Thamys shifted the leather case he was carrying—Joliffe would have bet his less-than-threepence that it held books—into the crook of his left arm and thrust out his right hand to clasp the hand Joliffe put out to him. "I thought it was you but couldn't believe it," Thamys said. "It was the way you were leaning there on the railing, looking as if you were seeing anything except what was in front of you. It made me think of you. I haven't thought of you . . ."

"In years," Joliffe said, smiling.

"Six months," Thamys said. "At Christmastide. I thought of you then, when someone put double cinnamon in Master Bryton's spiced wine and Master Bryton choked and coughed wine clear across the high table."

"*That* brought you to think of me? I never did that."

"That's why you came to mind. I wondered how you'd come to miss that trick. You tried enough other things."

"I never had the money to buy that much extra cinnamon. Nor," Joliffe added thoughtfully, "cared to waste good wine that way."

"That explains it," Thamys said as if deeply satisfied on some point of difficult scholarship. He shifted the leather case again. "Which way are you bound?"

"Townward."

"Go a ways with me, then? This thing is heavy and I'd rather be quit of it sooner than later."

"Gladly," Joliffe said, surprised to find himself more willing to company than he would have thought likely a few moments ago. On his side, he couldn't have said when he had last thought of Thamys, but they had been friends in their time and it was good to see him again and see him so obviously thriving, too. His scholar's gown was of good cloth and cut and he did not look under-fed, as scholars did whose love of learning outmatched their income and forced the choice of books over food.

Jostled together as they came off the bridge into the crowding of people toward the East Gate, Joliffe asked, "You're still at New College?"

"Not these three years past. I'm at St. Edmund's Hall, assistant master to Master Bryton now."

"Are you? How did that come about?"

Thamys shifted his burden back to both arms, carrying it against his chest, but around its awkwardness he managed a shrug. "I was ready to move on from being only a scholar. I wanted to do as well as to learn. Master Bryton offered me this chance and I took it. Do you remember Master Bryton?"

"Maybe." Joliffe had never clung to his Oxford memories. A great deal of lesser matter had faded, including Master Bryton. "Not to put a face to."

"A good man, a solid scholar. Not brilliant, but then most of us aren't."

"Speak for yourself."

"You weren't brilliant. Merely brazen."

Joliffe laughed. Into broad High Street now, they were walking less crowdedly, drifting toward the right through the homeward flow of folk. Toward Queen's Lane, Joliffe guessed; if he remembered rightly where St. Edmund's Hall was.

There were places like St. Edmund's Hall all over Oxford, lacking the rich endowments and patronage that supported the great colleges and dependent on luck and their masters' skills to keep them going, but they offered residence and learning to students who otherwise could not have afforded them. Such places rented spaces here and there as chance and their ever-imperiled finances allowed, gaining or losing students by the master's reputation, flourishing or fading for, sometimes, no discernable reason at all. At best, running such halls was a chancy business, but St. Edmund's was still here after more than a few years, and that Thamys had involved himself with it suggested it stood a good chance of going on a few years more. There had never been anything slack about Thamys' wits.

"You've finished your studies then?" Joliffe asked.

"Nearly. If things go as planned, I'll be ordained priest sometime in next Lent."

"Well done," Joliffe said, fully meaning it. Priesthood had been something John Thamys had wanted ever since they had met at New College as scrub-faced boys.

"And you," Thamys said. "What have you been at since I last saw you?"

"As you see." Joliffe held out his arms as if his well-worn, plain clothing told all. "Wandering."

Turning into Queen's Lane's narrow way, they were suddenly clear of the crowd, and Thamys came to a halt to look him openly down and up before saying, "But not idly wandering, I'd guess. You were never idle."

"As I recall, one of the great complaints against me in my days here was that I never worked enough."

"The great complaint was that you rarely worked at what you were supposed to work at. But idle? No, you were never that. In truth," Thamys said judiciously, "there were times when you would have been better idle than doing what you did. Such as the ten cats in the privyhouse."

"Eleven cats."

"A close count was difficult at the time," Thamys said, solemn as if they were settling a theological point.

"I'd hoped to make it twelve."

"I'm sure you did," Thamys agreed. "But when you consider the effect upon Master Hampton when he opened the privy door, I think we may agree that ten cats—eleven, I beg your pardon—was sufficient to your purpose, was it not?"

"Yes," Joliffe granted as solemnly, "I'd have to say it was."

They regarded each other straight-facedly a moment and then, together, convulsed with laughter at mutual memory of Master Hampton standing in the way of a surge of angry cats intent on being somewhere else.

A flurry of scholars, robes flapping with their hurry, surged by, much like the cats in their somewhat heedless haste to be elsewhere. Joliffe and Thamys faded aside, against the housewall there, and then drifted in their wake along the narrow street, Thamys asking again, "But what have you been at? More than merely wandering, surely."

"I'm a player."

"Are you?" Thamys looked at him with widened eyes and laughter. "That suits, at any rate. You're here for the Corpus Christi plays then?"

"We're to play St. Michael Northgate's *Abraham and Isaac*."

"A small company then."

"Yes."

"But successful or you'd not be here. Is this your first time back to Oxford in all this time?"

"Contrariwise. We come once most years and sometimes twice."

"And you never came to see me in all this while?"

"You never came to see me," Joliffe pointed out.

"True. But that's because I don't go to see players and didn't know you were here, while you knew quite well that I was."

Joliffe paused, then said in all seriousness, "I wasn't certain how welcomed I'd be."

"Joliffe! Considering all else I'd seen you at, you think I'd balk at you being a player?"

"There was . . ." Joliffe searched out the best word. ". . . scant approval of my leaving, as I remember."

They were nearly to the gateway into St. Edmund's yard. Thamys stopped short of where they might be heard by the porter sitting easily on a barrel beside the gate, keeping eye on who came and went. "I don't know how you'd remember whether there was approval or not of your leaving," Thamys said, "let be whether it was scant or otherwise. One morning you were here and then, come supper time, there was only your note saying you were gone and weren't coming back. Nor did you. I think that was the only time I was ever truly angry at you. Except," he added thoughtfully, "for when you put the dried toad inside my borrowed copy of the *Polychronicon*."

"There was naught wrong with that toad," Joliffe protested. "It couldn't have been flatter than it was."

"Flat or otherwise, the *Polychronicon* is no place for a dried toad."

"Better a dried toad than a wet one," Joliffe pointed out. "Consider, too, that it cost me a right sum from the apothecary, when I could have had a live one free for the catching."

"True, but that doesn't mean I'm going to thank you for the dried one."

"Better it was a dried one anyway," Joliffe mused, "considering you threw it at me."

"I would have thrown the *Polychronicon* at you, too, if it hadn't been only borrowed."

Joliffe shook his head in mock sorrow. "It's a sad thing when mortal man is so adverse to one of God's creatures."

"Nor do I much like toads either," Thamys said blandly.

They laughed together again. Joliffe had forgotten how easily he and Thamys had been friends—better friends than he had remembered, for them to take it up so readily from where they had left off.

Thamys nodded toward the gateway and its watching porter. "I'm not going to ask you in."

Joliffe would have been surprised if he had and said, unoffended, "Better not to be seen with someone as riff-raff as me?"

"Precisely so," Thamys agreed. "Though if anyone asked, I suppose I could always explain I wished to show you to my students as example of what happens to someone who deserts the scholar's life for lesser ways." Thamys shifted from the blandness that nearly always meant he was jesting, said crisply instead, "No, you idiot. I have to deliver

this to Master Bryton and then ready lessons for tomorrow
that I should have done yesterday. Where are you staying?"

"We've been taken on by a Master Penteney for the
week."

"Master Penteney the victualler?" Thamys asked.

"You know him?"

"Somewhat. A good man and something of a friend to
St. Edmund's. He gives us good consideration on what we
buy from him. I'm to dine with some others at his house
Wednesday evening."

"Then you'll be seeing me. We're to perform for his
guests that night."

"Good then," Thamys said with what looked real pleasure. "I'll look forward to it."

"Until then," Joliffe said, beginning to draw away in
parting, then thought to add, "Oh, by the way, if for some
unlikely reason you hear me called by the name Southwell,
don't mind. It seems to be who I presently am."

Thamys frowned. "Are you in trouble of some sort?
Will I give away too much if I know you?"

"No. It's nothing more than that when I met Master
Basset, I wouldn't tell him all my name at first. For the
sport of it, he gave me one of his own choosing and ever
since then gives me a different one now and again, as the
fancy takes him."

"I may like your Master Basset," Thamys said, smiled
farewell, and turned away into St. Edmund's gateway with
its paved courtyard with the usual long buildings of student
rooms and lecture halls on either side, leaving Joliffe to go
his own way.

Joliffe did, wondering as he went why Thamys had not
asked why he had left Oxford as he had. Was it because he
thought the business was Joliffe's own and not his . . . or
because he knew the reason?

Chapter 4

Joliffe reached the Penteneys' in time to go into the house to supper with the other players. There in the great hall they were shown to a place near the low end of one of the two long tables that faced each other down the length of the hall for those of the household who were not serving the meal, while Master Penteney sat at the center of the table on the dais at the hall's other end, able to overlook the lower tables. A round-faced, smiling woman who must be Mistress Penteney was seated beside him, with Simon next to her, then Lewis, then a somewhat younger fair-featured girl. To Master Penteney's other side were Mistress Geva and Master Richard.

Joliffe sorted them to his satisfaction: Master and Mistress Penteney; and their son (their one son?) Master Richard and his wife; and Lewis and Simon Fairfield, Master Penteney's wards. That left only the fair-featured girl unplaced. Was she a Fairfield or a Penteney or someone else altogether? Perhaps another profitable ward to Master Penteney?

Servants began to bring in food then and Joliffe lost interest in the high table. He could not see what was carried up the hall to the Penteneys, but what came his way among the lower servants was rabbit in a spiced sauce, a salad of greens, leeks, and garlic, and a date-laden cheesecake, all of it cooked well, nothing scanted or burned or underdone, and all of it in generous portions. Joliffe said something to the household man on his right about how the eating looked to be good here, and the man readily agreed, "Aye. There's no stinting in this house. They're a good master and mistress, are the Penteneys."

"They've just the one son?" Joliffe asked.

"Master Richard, aye. There's nothing to be said against him either. He has his father's head and enough of his mother's heart to do him good."

"I've met him and his wife. Mistress Geva, is she?"

"That's her. Mistress Geva. She does well enough, too. Given us a grandson, she has. Master Giles. It goes hard with her, though, I've heard some of the women say, her not to have place of her own but being under Mistress Penteney's sway. Still, she's young. Her time will come."

Joliffe had learned early on from Basset that the better a player knew a household, the better was his chance of doing well in it, and since this fellow seemed ready to talk, he tried. "I've talked with Master Fairfield and Master Simon, too."

The man, having just spooned a piece of rabbit and sauce into his mouth, nodded while he chewed, swallowed, and said, "Same as family, they are. Grew up here after their father died and Master Penteney got their wardships and all. Master Simon likes books out of the ordinary but is good enough. It's pity he's not the heir, but there it is. When you get used to Master Fairfield, he's none so bad either. Wouldn't want that Matthew's job, though."

Making busy with cutting a piece of rabbit to stir into the sauce, Joliffe murmured, "I'm surprised, though, Master Fairfield hasn't been set aside in favor of his brother."

"There's many as is surprised by that." The man was cutting his own share of rabbit into smaller bits and so had chance to talk but that was all he said.

Joliffe, though, had been thinking things through in his walk and ventured, "Is it because if Master Simon was heir, when he came of age he'd take over his properties and all? With Lewis as heir, it's likely, isn't it, Master Penteney will keep control of everything?"

The man favored him with a sharp, approving look and agreed, "Aye. This way, look you, he'll not lose by having kept such good care of him all this time, see."

He knifed a bit of rabbit into his mouth and Joliffe took the chance to say, "Sounds good sense to me. Now, who's the girl sitting next to Lewis?"

"Kathryn Penteney, aye," the man answered around his mouthful "Master's daughter. Going to be betrothed . . ."

The woman on the man's other side jostled his arm, wanting him to pass over the tall mug of ale they were sharing, and Piers on Joliffe's other side began to pester for Joliffe's share of cheesecake.

Their lengthy debate over why Joliffe was not going to give it to him saw them through to the meal's end and then, during the general upheaval of servants starting to clear away the meal's dishes and table linens so other servants could take the tables down and out of the way, Basset gave the word and the players slipped together out of the hall, back to the yard and away to the barn. If they lingered in the hall there was likelihood someone among the house-hold folk would think that since they were players they should play something. Then there would be hard feelings on the household side if they did not, and hard feelings on

their own if they did. That made it easiest just to leave, but
as soon as they were back at the barn, Ellis said, "Who's
for going out for a drink?"

"Plans first. Ale later," Basset said. "It's time we talk
about this week."

"Money first, ale later, plans tomorrow?" Ellis suggested hopefully; but when Basset shook his head against
that, he sat down on a cushion beside where there would
have been a fire if they'd had one and said on a martyred
sigh, "Where's the horse, Piers?"

Piers was already fetching the thing from the small
chest beside the cart where his own things were kept. The
horse had started as a piece of beechwood picked up at the
edge of a clearing where they'd camped last week. Piers
had claimed its rough shape was something like a horse—
"If you've had enough to drink or a cant-eye," Joliffe had
said unhelpfully—but it looked much more like one now
that Ellis had been whittling at it a few evenings. It would
be a warhorse, Piers had decided. "Then next you can make
a knight to ride it and then we'll do like we did before."

Which did not mean Piers would play with it. Joliffe
could not recall when last he had seen Piers play with a toy,
not counting the rag doll he dangled in the St. Ursula play
when he was supposed to be a sweet little girl saved by St.
Ursula from an evil stepmother's plan to kill her. Joliffe's
own thought was that if the little girl was anything like
Piers really was, it was the stepmother who would likely
have needed rescuing, but no one would let him rewrite the
play in her favor.

As for the wooden horse, if things went the way they
had other times with other bits of wood, Ellis would make
what Piers told him to make and it would be quite good because Ellis was good with his hands that way. Then Piers
would paint whatever was made with some of the paint

kept for touching up the painted cloths that mostly dressed their playing places, and then he would sell it to some-one—a mother, a peddler, a shopkeeper, whoever seemed likely to pay the most. Then he'd keep all the money for himself and Ellis would let him because Ellis was besotted with Rose and happy to make her son happy. For all the good it did him. Despite Piers's father had gone his own way before Joliffe ever joined the company, with never word heard from him since, Rose held that until she knew differently she had to believe she was still married and therefore there could be nothing between her and Ellis ex-cept friendship or else adultery.

Bitter though that was to him, Ellis accepted it because, as he'd said once to Joliffe when they were swaying home from a tavern together and there was no one else to hear it, "She's right, so what else can I do?"

"Leave her?" Joliffe had suggested, though Basset would have flayed him if he'd heard. By that time, after the disaster, they had been barely enough to be a company as it was. "Go find someone else?"

"Can't." Ellis had shaken his head, staggered sideways, righted himself, and said, throwing an arm around Joliffe's shoulders, a thing he would never have done if sober, "It's that I love her, you see. I love her."

He'd gone on tearful about his love the rest of the way back to camp, until Joliffe, not so drunk, had dug an elbow into his ribs and told him to shut up.

"But I love her," Ellis had insisted.

"So I gather. But you'll wake Piers if you keep on about it and then, love or not, she'll skin you."

"And well I deserve it, tormenting her with my love. Tormenting her . . ."

Joliffe had given him to understand that if he didn't shut up, he'd be the one who was tormented and not with love but a pail of cold water over his head and a solid kick where it'd do the most good. Ellis had settled to mournful but safe muttering.

Not that he was always without comfort. Sometimes, out of her own need or Ellis's—or both—Rose gave way and for a night, sometimes two, it was as it should have been between them, until her conscience took hold and she drew away again. She would make confession then as soon as a priest or friar could be found and do penance for her sin, made the heavier because Ellis, grim and short-tempered for days afterwards, refused both confession and penance, darkly insistent there was no sin in them being together and that penitent was the last thing he was.

While the cycle was at its worst between them, not only Joliffe but Basset and even Piers carefully kept from jarring Ellis until the darkness passed, its end usually announced by Ellis demanding why everyone was so brooding, had he missed some trouble they all knew about but he didn't?

At present they were a few weeks past the last time and everything was peaceable for now. While Basset sat himself down on his cushion and readied himself for talk, Ellis set to carving on the horse, with Piers leaning against his shoulder to watch and Rose quietly listening from where she sat on her hay-piled bed. Joliffe sat beside the cart, leaning back against a wheel, ready to prop his head against the spokes and drowse if talk went on too long.

Basset started off briskly enough anyway, saying, "Foremost of everything this week, we have to be sure as possible of the *Abraham and Isaac*. First thing come the morning, before breakfast even, we'll run through our lines."

"For Christ's sake . . ." Ellis started in protest.

"Precisely," Basset said. "For Christ's sake we want this

to be as good as can be. Then we owe the Penteneys a play
and we want to make it a good one in return for all that
Master Penteney is doing for us. So we have to decide what
we'll do and rehearse it, too."

Ellis groaned and Joliffe could have echoed him but
didn't, just put his head back against the wheel and looked
up at the broad barn rafters disappearing into shadows
while he waited for more.

"Then there's Lewis to keep pleased."

Ellis did not even bother to groan, just shook his head
and kept on carving.

"Piers," said Basset, "if we put on *The Steward and the
Devil* for the Penteneys—not for Wednesday night when
there'll be the feast and fine company, but tomorrow
maybe, for just the household—do you think Lewis could
be a devil with you in it?"

Ellis gave a disbelieving croak and stopped carving to
look at Basset, apparently expecting to see other signs he'd
lost his mind. Even Rose frowned slightly. Joliffe just
waited, somewhat interested.

"No lines," Basset went on. "Just capering with you on
the stage. Could he do that, do you think?"

"Aye, he could do that," Piers said, poking Ellis to set
him carving again. "Lewis isn't stupid. He's just . . ." he
made a face, looking for the word, ". . . simple."

Ellis, who had started to carve again, stopped and
cocked his head around, eye to eye with Piers. "You understand the difference there?"

"Aye," Piers said with the patience of someone much
put upon by lesser folk. "It's like there's not as many wits
in his head as other people have, but what he has he makes
good use of. Not like some who have all their wits and
don't half use them. Like Joliffe."

"Best use your wits to curb your tongue or there'll be

burrs under your blanket by morning," Joliffe said without
heat. Burrs in the bed were a constant threat between Piers
and him. Once Piers had even done it. But only once, because in return Joliffe had put burrs in the toes of Piers's
hosen. Working them to the bottom of the hosen's feet had
been tedious, but Piers's yelp when his toes met them and
the grumbling he had done while working them out—with
bits left behind to bother him through a few days afterward—had made it worth the while. Since then burrs had
remained a threat, not a practice, and Piers made a face at
him while Rose asked, keeping to Lewis, "Will his folk let
him? Be in a play, I mean."

"We'll have to ask," Basset answered. "I doubt there's
harm in asking and I'm willing to warrant they will. His
man Matthew seemed to have no trouble with the thought,
anyway."

Ellis sighed and went back to his carving. "Ask away. It
can't hurt."

Rose and Joliffe both nodded agreement.

They talked a while more, and the choice for Wednesday's play came down to *The Pride of Life*, one of their
best. It was more work than they truly wanted to do, with
Corpus Christi the next day and the need to have the *Abraham and Isaac* as perfect as might be for it, but neither did
they want to cheat Master Penteney.

"Besides," said Basset, "it won't hurt to do our best in
front of Lord and Lady Lovell either, let alone whoever
else may be there. But it's been a while since we've done it,
so best we run its lines tomorrow morning even before
Abraham and Isaac."

That brought groans from Ellis and Joliffe both: *The
Pride of Life* was longer by far than *Abraham and Isaac*.
But groan was all they did because Basset was right; it had

been some few months since they had done it and the sooner they found out what they had forgotten, the better.

Dusk was thickening into dark now. Summer nights were short, there was small point in wasting candles to light them when sleep would be a better way to spend the time, and at Basset's word, they made ready to go to bed, Joliffe finding out just how tired he was now he had stopped moving. It seemed to be the same way with the others; even Ellis was forgetful of his ale-thirst and rolled into his bed willingly enough, with very little restless rustling from anyone before sleep soundly took them.

Joliffe awoke in darkness with no way to tell what the hour might be, but when he rolled his head sideways and looked at the gap around the barn's door, the line of paling gray in the darkness told him the night was nearly done. No one else was stirring, though, and seeing no need to be the first, he settled more deeply into the straw with quite an unreasonable sense of holiday, despite that holiday was likely the last thing the next few days were going to be. Not with an extra performance of *The Steward and the Devil* if it happened Lewis would be allowed to do it, and *The Pride of Life* to sharpen up, and *Abraham and Isaac* to finish perfecting, along with need to be sure all was well with everything they would wear and use for those plays and making right anything that was not.

But not to be loading and unloading the cart every day, and walking miles between one hope of work and the next with never certainty the work would be there when the time came —instead sleeping in the same place five nights in a row and certain of every meal—that looked like holiday to him.

The feeling stayed with him even after he rose with
everyone else to go through the morning business of putting on the hosen and doublet he'd taken off for sleep last
night, seeing to his body's needs, washing his face and
hands in the waiting water bucket, and combing his hair
because Rose was firm on them looking no more unseemly
than could be helped.

So as not to spoil the pleasure she took in ordering them
around, he carefully kept from her that he at least—he
would not answer for Ellis and Piers—would have done it
anyway.

Only when Basset sat them down and said, "Now. *The
Pride of Life*. From the beginning," did the sense of holiday not so much fade as die a brutal death, as all too
quickly it became plain that neither Ellis nor Joliffe had a
firm hold on their lines anymore. Worse, Basset *did* have
firm hold, and Rose, prompting from the script, shook her
head over how often she had to give Ellis and Joliffe, turn
and turnabout, a word or words to keep them going, until
Basset stood up with a frustrated roar, swore at Ellis and
Joliffe both for wash-brained idiots, said he was going to
breakfast and that they'd better, too, though, "I'll be mazed
if either one of you has wits enough to keep straight the
difference between chewing your food and breathing," he
snarled.

If Ellis had any better answer to that than Joliffe did, he
wisely kept as silent as Joliffe, neither of them moving as
Basset stalked out the barn door, Piers beside him, their
backs matchingly eloquent with indignation. Even Rose
held silent while she put the script away in the box where
all their scripts were kept, only giving Ellis a sideways
look that Ellis answered with an uncomfortable, sheepish
shrug; but she relented before she left, saying as she moved

toward the door, "Come on then. You won't do any better for being starved."

"I think I'll stay," said Joliffe. "I'll go in after you've come back. Someone should stay to keep an eye on things here."

Ellis said, "Come on. Basset won't bite your head off in front of others. We all went in to supper last night."

"That was last night. By now all the Penteney servants and everyone up and down the street if not half of Oxford know we're here. I don't think we should leave our things simply to strangers' good will."

Ellis frowned at that, but Rose said, "You're probably right. Well thought of, Joliffe."

Basset would have thought of it if he had not been so irked this morning, Joliffe thought as he watched Rose and Ellis out the door. He waited until sure they were well gone, then leaped for the script box.

With reading, his lines began to crawl back out of whatever hole in his memory they had sunk into; he was feeling at least a little less a fool by the time Rose and Ellis returned. By then he was also more than ready to go to his own breakfast but asked as he pointedly held the script out to Ellis, "Where's Basset?"

Taking the script ungraciously but willingly, Ellis said, "Gone to speak to Mistress Penteney. He asked the chamberlain or someone if he could see Master Penteney. The fellow said we're a household matter now and it was Mistress Penteney who'd deal with him.

"Where's Piers?"

"Lewis claimed him as soon as he'd done eating," Rose said. "That man Matthew has them."

"Good luck to him," Joliffe said from the heart.

He made it to the hall in time to help himself to the last

of breakfast, spreading a fist-thick slab of new-baked bread
with soft butter, layering a few cold slices of beef onto it,
and catching up a wooden cup of ale just ahead of the servants clearing the benchless single table set up in the middle of the hall. Breakfast in even the largest households
was usually a simple matter, with bread and ale and yesterday's left food set out for folk to help themselves without
sitting down, the quicker to get them onward with the day.
Accordingly, there were no servants lingering for him to
draw into talk, and a long look around while he ate told
him that wherever Basset was, he was not here, nor Piers
either.

But Kathryn Penteney still was, standing not far away,
near the doorway to the screens passage, in earnest talk to
a man Joliffe guessed might be the household's chamberlain: he plainly belonged to the household but his tunic was
of better cut and cloth than a mere servant's and his manner toward her was both respectful and assured, suiting
someone who both served here and had authority. Joliffe
was too far away to hear what was being said between
them, but he took his time over eating his bread and meat,
watching them.

Well, watching the girl more than the man he admitted,
and liking what he saw. She would probably someday fill
out with womanhood to her mother's fullness of figure, but
presently she was merely slender in her girlhood, with her
fair hair in a long plait down her back, her hands moving
quickly while she talked, her laughter brief and bright at
something the man said.

He did not know Basset was behind him until Basset
slapped him between the shoulder blades deliberately hard
enough to stagger him a step and said, all his ill-humour
seemingly gone, "Come on then, boy. Finish up. We've a
new player to set to work."

Joliffe gulped the last swallow of his ale, set the cup
down, shoved the last bite of the bread and beef into his
mouth, and followed Basset from the hall, pausing only at
the basin and towel set by the door to wash his hands and
wipe them clean, giving a last, quick look backward at the
girl, still in talk with the man. She was no harder to look at
close up than farther off, though maybe younger than he
had guessed, but that was all he had time to note before
Basset caught him by an arm around the shoulders and
moved him out of the hall, saying as they went, "I don't
want to think what kick in the shins the goddess Fortuna
will give us next time she turns around, but for the present
I have to tell you we've landed hip-deep in a pot of cream."

"Your talk with Mistress Penteney went well, I take it?"

"Well and better than well. No trouble over anything.
She saw no reason Lewis couldn't be in a play, simply that
we weren't to tire him. Seems he's not so stoutly strong as
he looks. She said to ask if there was anything we needed
for that or anything else, and to speak with the chamberlain
if there was something particular to how the hall should be
set up for either Lewis's play or Wednesday's. We should
be so lucky in our hire all the time!"

Joliffe couldn't quarrel with that. All too often the best
they could hope for was not to have too much trouble put in
their way.

"All she asked was that Wednesday's play be somewhat
to the point of Corpus Christi, it being the feast's eve," Basset went on. "I told her what we had in mind—I didn't tell
her I had idiots as bad as her own in my company who have
to learn their lines all over . . ."

" 'For no doubt death has mastery, to make to weep and
sorrow. From holy writ and prophecy this knowledge I do
borrow,' " Joliffe declared, raising a dramatic hand.

Basset clapped him happily on the back again. "There! I

knew the part was still in your addled head somewhere. It was just a matter of grubbing around till you found it. Anyway, she said it would do well."

"There's the part where the Devil makes somewhat rude sport with the Bishop," Joliffe warned.

"I told her of that and said we could cut it out, but she said laughter could be as much to God's glory as prayer and she'd trust we keep all within bounds. There's a woman I'd marry if I could."

"Pity she's wed and can't accept the honor," Joliffe said, with cheek enough he knew to duck as Basset made to cuff his head.

"You keep a courteous tongue in your head, boy. And don't think I didn't notice you noticing the daughter either. Just mind that noticing her is all you do."

"Tell it to Ellis. He's the one has an eye for the women."

Basset snorted. "And you don't? Heed me. There's to be no loosening of the loins while we're here. You hear?"

They had reached the barn, were just outside its door. Joliffe paused to sweep Basset a deep and flourishing bow, declaiming as from his very soul, "Your command is ever the wish of my heart."

"Oh, lord. What's he thinking of getting up to now?" Ellis called from inside.

"Nothing, if he knows what's good for him," Basset growled, and then, on the instant all brighter humoured, added, "Ah, here come our fine young devils," as Piers and Lewis came out of a narrow gap between two of the buildings ranged between the barn and the house, Lewis's Matthew following behind them.

"We've seen Mistress Penteney! Piers called. "She told us!"

"But does Master Fairfield want to do it?" Basset called back, as if he did not know the answer.

"Of course he does," Piers said, scornful that his grandfather had to ask.

"Of course I do!" Lewis echoed.

Basset looked skyward for the divine help that never seemed to come when called for, sighed with mock despair, "What have I done?", clapped his hands and declared, "To work then!"

Chapter 5

But Basset did not intend to shape all their work to Lewis. Instead, he said they would begin with a run-through of the *Abraham and Isaac* to see how much (with a glare at Joliffe and Ellis) they'd all forgotten.

"That can wait," Piers protested. "We know the thing backwards!"

"I want to see if we know it forward, too," Basset said quellingly. "Besides, Rose needs to measure Lewis for his devil-wear. Go on."

He pointed them aside to where Rose was laying out a length of somewhat battered red cloth, bought last autumn cheap off a stall in Warwick marketplace from a batch spoiled in the dyeing. At the time Basset had said, "At that price, we'll sooner or later find it fit for something or other," and today he was proved—as usual—right: some of it could easily be made into a devil's tabard for Lewis. Diverted, Piers and Lewis went to Rose, leaving Basset, Ellis, and Joliffe to outline a square-cornered shape the size of their scaffold in the barn's dirt floor and set out the two stools that would serve, for now, as God's throne and the sacrificial altar.

Joliffe, with his fair, smooth face, was inevitably the Angel but on their way to Oxford there had been, yet again, debate between Basset and Ellis over which of them should be Abraham and which should be God this time. Both parts were better suited to Basset, with Abraham supposedly being somewhat over one hundred years old and God being . . . well, God. Either way they played it, they were both going to be bearded heavily enough to obscure their actual years and Ellis had tried, "If I'm God, all I have to do is sit. I won't have to remember to move old."

"Meaning I don't have to remember because I *am* old, you young whelp?" Basset had growled in mock anger.

"Meaning Abraham is the better part and you should have it," Ellis had growled back.

"What you mean," Joliffe had put in, "is that you want the fewest lines and the chance to sit watching us do all the work. Let me play God. Then I can do the sitting."

They had both snapped at him for that and he had gone off laughing to help Piers fetch water from a stream to the camp and come back to find that, as usual, Basset would play God, with Ellis to be—as usual—the patriarch Abraham.

Now Basset took his place upstage on the stool that was presently God's throne and Ellis knelt as if in prayer downstage, nearer the audience, while Joliffe as the Angel stood at God's right hand. They had begun running their lines with each other last week on their way to Oxford, and despite Basset's jibing at them, all of them had their words firmly in their heads. It was the business that went with the words they needed to make smooth again, not having done the play since sometime in Lent, and Basset was set on making this as perfect a performance as lay in human power. "We're few enough," he said, "but, by God, we're better than most and as good as the best." And if they weren't, he plainly meant they would be before he was through with them.

He set right off to it with, "Now, Joliffe, face me more than Ellis, remember, as if you've been listening to me, until he starts his prayer. When he starts to pray, turn your head over your shoulder to look at him so it seems we're both pausing to hear him. Ellis, raise your head more. Remember the damn beard is going to be over most of your face. Talk to heaven but be sure they can see your eyes. Now, when I start to speak, Ellis, you go on mouthing silently as if still praying and, Joliffe, you look back at me, and if you can put less grin and more adoration into it, it will help. Ellis, begin."

Ellis obeyed, his voice rich on the words, giving them weight and worth. "Father of Heaven, omnipotent, who neither beginning nor ending has, with all my heart to you I pray . . ."

He prayed at length, giving thanks in particular for his dear and long-desired son Isaac. Then God spoke to his Angel, and the Angel spoke to Abraham, and only then was Piers needed as Isaac. With the time Basset took over every bit of business among them, Rose was long since done with measuring Lewis, but she knew as well as anyone what trouble idle boys might make—or, more accurately, what idle Piers might lead Lewis into—and Joliffe, waiting while Basset showed Abraham exactly how he was to rise and pretend to be dusting off his knees and turn with great surprise when the Angel spoke to him, watched her setting Lewis and Piers down together with a few handfuls of hay between them, telling Piers, "You show him how to braid this to make his tail so it will be ready when I need it."

"Devils don't have hay tails," Lewis protested.

"You'll see," Rose said with a smile and made to ruffle his hair as she would have done Piers's but remembered in time he wasn't a child. For all that he was childish, he was man-grown and properly to be called "Master Fairfield" and was certainly no one whose hair she had any business ruffling. Joliffe saw her look a little uneasily toward the door where the man Matthew was leaning comfortably against a post, keeping out of the way while he watched. To her look he merely smiled and nodded to let her know all was well. Then Joliffe needed to pay heed to his own business with Ellis until Basset said, "Right. Now, Piers, you're on. You have your hoop?"

Piers, already on his feet and coming, no hoop in hand, as his grandfather could well see, froze, one foot in the air and a rather frantic look on his face. "I thought. . . ." He stopped, straightened, put his foot down, and glared at Basset. "You said no properties today. I don't need the hoop."

"Good. You do remember what you're told sometimes. Get over here."

Some days it was a close-run thing whether Basset would keep the upper hand with his grandson but more times than not he did. Thus far.

Lewis made to follow Piers, saying, "And me," but Rose said, "Not for this play, Master Fairfield. This one has no devils. He has to be a boy and all alone in this one." Lewis's round face began to draw toward a pout at that but Rose added, deliberately cheerful, "Besides, you're not ready to be a devil yet. We still have your tail to finish. Bring me what you've made and we'll do that, please."

She held out her hand and Lewis went to her, taking the two feet or so of braided hay he and Piers had done, while Basset said, "Come on from over there, Piers, the way you've done before, if you remember it," pointing, and they went on from where they were, sorrowful Abraham taking

Isaac away to the mountain to sacrifice him at God's command. Joliffe, withdrawn to the side of the throne of God, had only to watch while Abraham told Isaac his fate and Isaac made his plea for life and then submitted to God's will, at which point Joliffe's Angel stepped forward to save the boy and praise Abraham for his faith in God, bringing the play to a glad end.

The whole business with the ram miraculously appearing in a bush was put off for later, Basset being presently more interested in how well they had their lines and movements than any of the special business that went with them—the crowd-pleasers, as he called such business rather rudely when he was out of good humour with the world in general and audiences in particular. Besides, the ram was Rose's business and she was presently busy sewing a long strip of the red cloth tightly around the braided hay, with a point to one end to make it into a credible devil's tail. It would not hold up to much rough use but for the few times they would rehearse and the once Lewis would perform it would do well enough, and for now Basset settled for granting rather grudgingly that they all seemed to know their lines sufficiently well. "Better than I hoped, that's certain."

Low enough Basset could pretend not to hear him, Ellis muttered, "If we don't have them now, we never will. You've had us saying them every other mile the last two weeks."

"But how does it stay on me?" Lewis protested as Rose held up the finished tail.

Before Rose could answer, Piers skipped out of the stage-space to him, saying, "There'll be a band wrapped around your waist and between your legs . . ."

Lewis giggled and made to touch his crotch but Matthew by the door made a loud clearing of his throat and

Lewis's hand moved vaguely off into space as Piers went on, ". . . and the tail is stitched to that and it sticks out from under the tabard. Here. I'll show you mine, how it does."

"And then," said Basset, "we'll run your part of *The Steward and the Devil*, if you will, Master Fairfield."

"Yes!" Lewis said eagerly. "Yes!"

"Sit down while you can," Basset added aside to Ellis and Joliffe who promptly did, with Ellis asking a drink of water from Rose who brought cups for him and Joliffe both, then went to explain to Lewis why he and Piers would not either of them be wearing their devil tails just now, not for a first practice. When Lewis would have protested that, Piers made it all right by saying, "I never wear mine for first practices. There's too much else to think about." He looked to his grandfather. "But what about the horns? Couldn't we wear those?" Adding aside to Lewis, "They're more trouble than the tails. The tails won't fall off, once they're on, but the horns do if you're not careful."

"A point well taken," Basset said as if it were a great matter worth heavy consideration. "Yes. I'd say you should wear the horns."

Being smaller and rag-stuffed, the horns were not so liable to damage as a hay-stuffed tail, and Piers, with Lewis following him, dove for the basket where the horns were kept, not only Piers's small ones but several man-sized ones from when they had been a larger company, able to send more "devils" onto the stage. Lewis's somewhat stubby fingers made clumsy work of tying on the black cap that held them to his head. Piers helped him, then did his own while Lewis went over to Matthew to show himself off.

Basset took the chance to say at Joliffe and Ellis, "Since we did this only yesterday, I'm going to suppose, St. Genesius reward my faith, that you remember your lines . . ."

"Rest it, Basset," Ellis said impatiently, never good at being jested at, which was what made it such a pleasure to do.

"So we'll do just the last few speeches before the end." Basset held up a warning finger. "But we'll probably do it maybe five times, to satisfy Master Fairfield and take some of the edge off him. You see?"

Joliffe and Ellis both saw. You had to care more than a little for the craft of playing to be willing to go on and on at a part, working it over and over into the best you could make it be in whatever time you had. If someone looked on it all as little more than a light game, as a chance to show himself off, the work of it soon palled, and it surely would for Lewis. The trick was going to be to rehearse him well enough that he could do his part, without quenching his interest in it along the way. Or maybe quenching his interest just enough he would be satisfied with what he was being given to do and want no more. To Joliffe's mind—and to Basset's as well, he suspected—that would be the very best of all.

The Steward and the Devil was mostly taken from one of Geoffrey Chaucer's tales, with changes made to suit their company but the story much the same. The Steward, a lord's officer given to extorting money from hapless folk in his power, meets a friendly man who claims to be a Devil come from Hell. They make agreement to travel together a while, each taking their share from whatever people offer them. They overtake a man—Basset—carrying and damning to the devil a sack too big and heavy for him. When the Steward urges the Devil to take what he's been offered, the Devil declines, saying the man did not truly mean it. Likewise, when they come on a drunken man (again played by Basset with a change of hat and doublet) damning himself to the devil because his wine bottle is empty, the Devil says again he doesn't mean it, the offer doesn't count. But when the Steward seeks to grind a false fine out of an old widow (likewise played by Basset in loose gown and wimple and veil) and *she* wishes him to the devil, the Devil cries, "Now there is a wish made from the heart and fully meant!" Revealing his horns and tail, he summons the demon Piers to help him drive the Steward off to Hell, ending the play.

It was quick-paced and with laughs in plenty. The Penteneys would probably be well pleased simply because Lewis was in it, a second demon with Piers, no matter how ill Lewis might do his part.

The surprise, as they began to play it, was that it seemed Lewis would not do ill at all. He understood easily when Basset showed him where and how he was to follow Piers, and he readily copied, albeit clumsily, Piers's leap and caper around the playing space. Basset brought them to a stop then with a sharp clap of his hands and said, "That's the way of it. No trouble there. Now here's the part you have to careful with." He held out his hand for the two spears Ellis had brought from the cart. Ellis gave them over and Basset showed them to Piers and Lewis together. "They're only painted wood, even the heads, but they're sharp" he said sternly. "You wouldn't want to be poked with a sharp stick, would you, Master Fairfield? No. Nor does Elis. You can poke them *at* Ellis but you must never, never touch him with them. You understand?"

Lewis frowned, puzzled, and said slowly, "Piers did. I saw him."

"You *thought* you saw him, but he never really did," Basset said, slowly and clearly back, because it was very necessary Lewis understand this. "Come. Stand with me, and Piers and Ellis will show you."

Still frowning, Lewis obeyed. Ellis took his place as the

Steward, Piers took one of the spears, made his long leap onto the "stage" and capered and jumped and bounded around Ellis, thrusting at him with the spear without ever touching him while Ellis yelped and flinched and tried to dodge and flinched and yelped some more until driven off, Piers thrusting and poking the spear behind him all the way.

His frown gone to a grin, Lewis clapped wildly. "I see! I saw how they did it! Let me! Let me!"

"Slowly," Basset said, handing over the spear but holding up a warning finger. "Slowly at first. Faster later. You understand?"

Lewis nodded eagerly and went to join Piers, and shortly showed that he did understand. He even understood, without being told, that his own movements were less sure than Piers's and was the more careful because of it. They were doing it a third time, at a little better speed, when Ellis did catch a hard jab in the ribs and Lewis stepped hurriedly back with a shocked gasp but Ellis said quickly, with a grin, "My fault. I bumped into the spear, not the spear into me. But you," he added at Piers. "You slow down, you little demon. Lewis is doing better than you are."

Piers stuck out his tongue, Ellis took a slap at his head without any chance or intent of reaching him, Lewis laughed, and they started again.

Joliffe's part, when he had said his last line, was simply to get out of the way and stand with hands on hips, laughing devilishly, then follow his demons off the stage. For now he simply waited aside with Basset, so interested in watching Lewis and Piers that he hardly noticed when Simon sidled in past Matthew and around to Basset's other side, to stand silently watching with them until Basset said quietly, with a nod at Lewis, "Your brother is simple, Master Simon, but he's not a fool."

Simon looked at him with surprise, then past him to Joliffe who nodded agreement. Simon smiled. "There's not many can see that about him. Thank you."

Matthew eased over to join them, keeping a servant's place a little behind Simon but saying, "Begging pardon, but maybe best call this enough for Master Fairfield for now." He made a small nod toward Lewis. "He wears down sudden, you know, Master Simon. We don't want him going blue."

"True," Simon agreed unwillingly. "But it's good to see him at such fun."

With happy yells and much flailing of spears, the devils had just chased yelping Ellis off the stage yet again and Lewis was begging to do it one more time but Basset clapped his hands at them and Piers immediately swung around and came toward him. Lewis turned, too, his wide grin dimming as he looked from Simon to Matthew and back again. He would have stayed where he was except Ellis laid a friendly hand on his shoulder, saying, "You have to come when Master Basset calls. We all do."

Smiling, Simon held out a hand to his brother. "It's time to go, Lewis. Come on."

"Go away," Lewis said firmly, putting his hands behind his back. "I don't want to."

"It's time to go," Simon repeated, still easily, his hand still out. "It's time for dinner."

How odd did Simon find the necessity of seeing to Lewis as a child when Lewis was the older of them, Joliffe wondered? Or was he so used to it that he never thought about it as strange at all?

"You're hungry, aren't you?" Simon said.

"No," Lewis answered.

"Our guests are. They're going to eat. It would be discourtesy not to come with them."

"I'll put our spears away," Piers said cheerfully, offering to take Lewis's.

Lewis looked about to refuse but Joliffe, taking on his "Devil" manner and voice, said, "Here now, young master demon, there's time for sport and time for feast and as your lord I say 'tis time to feast, that afterwards we may have strength enough for seizing souls. Hand over here . . ." He put out demanding hands toward both Piers and Lewis. ". . . and away with you both till time for sport again."

Among Piers's few virtues was the ability to know a prompt when he heard it. With a flourish of his spear, he knelt and held it out to Joliffe. Lewis, grinning again, clumsily copied him, going heavily down on one knee and holding out his spear, too. With a solemn, approving nod, Joliffe took them both and ordered, "Away with you then, my devils, until we meet again to win this stinking soul to hell." He pointed arrogantly at Ellis who rolled his eyes and turned away as Piers and Lewis, laughing now, scrambled back to their feet, Piers saying, "Race you?"

But Matthew quickly put in, "No, best not. Master Simon wants to hear what you've been doing this while."

"How the play is going and all," Simon said. He held out his hand again and this time Lewis took it and they went out together, Lewis talking happily, Matthew following a few paces behind.

At Basset's word, the players lingered, to let Lewis, Simon, and Matthew reach the hall well ahead of them before going themselves, leaving Ellis to his turn of keeping watch in the barn. By the time they took their places at the farthest end of one of the hall tables, below all the household folk, Lewis and the others were at the high table with Matthew standing against the wall behind Lewis, who—to judge by his gestures and bouncing on the bench through the meal—was telling Kathryn all about the morning, pay-

ing more heed to that than to his eating and sputtering
much of his food in consequence. The girl seemed used to
that. She took it in good part anyway, nodding to what he
was saying and wiping his chin when need be, helped by
Simon sometimes drawing Lewis's attention his way, giving her chance at her own food. Joliffe, watching while trying to seem he was not, judged it was something well
practiced between her and Simon.

Seated between Piers and Basset, he had no chance to
speak with anyone else but decided that, first chance that
came his way, he would make talk with someone of the
household—a pretty maidservant for choice; no reason not
to mix one pleasure with another—to find out more about
this care and coddling of Lewis. Even if Master Penteney
hoped to go on running the Fairfield properties—and they
must be considerable—after Lewis came of age, that was
hardly reason for all this care of someone who anywhere
else would at best have been kept unseen and never talked
of. There had to be more than money in it somewhere and
Joliffe wondered what it was.

At the meal's end, when Master Penteney said the grace
and the household was beginning to draw back from the tables, making no great haste toward their afternoon's work,
Lewis ducked away from both Kathryn and Simon and
around the high table's end, avoiding even Matthew reaching out for him as he made eagerly toward the players at
the hall's far end. Basset, seeing all that, said, "Rose, Piers,
you go on. Get Ellis's food and go. Joliffe, keep with me."

"Why me?" Joliffe muttered at Basset's back, not expecting answer and getting none as he followed Basset up
the hall, their progress slow against the flow of folk the
other way. They met Lewis halfway, just as Matthew overtook him, with Simon and Kathryn not far behind. When

Matthew laid hold on one of Lewis's arm and Simon took the other, Lewis started to thrash against them both, yelling toward Basset, "There! See! He's come for me!"

"Uh-oh," Basset said, for only Joliffe to hear.

That was an echo of Joliffe's own feeling and he silently doubled it as Mistress Penteney swept down on them. She was a wide-bosomed woman of middle-years, suitably dressed for a housewife running her weekday household in a plain gold-brown gown held in at the waist by a buckled belt hung with a housewife's keys and a small cloth purse, her hair covered by a white headkerchief neatly pinned to the white wimple around her face and throat. What told she was a rich man's wife was the finely woven linen of gown and veil and wimple, and the thick gold and garnet ring on the hand she reached to lay on Lewis's shoulder. The hand was gentle, though, and so was her voice as she asked, "Oh my, what's toward? Does Master Basset need you this afternoon, too, Lewis?" at the same time giving a firm shake of her head at Basset.

Lewis, turning around too late to see the head-shake, complained at her. "I have to go! We're practicing!"

With a low swept bow to both Mistress Penteney and Lewis, Basset said, "Praying your pardon, Master Fairfield, but I was coming to tell you that this afternoon we mean to rehearse the play we're to do for the household on Wednesday . . ."

"I want to watch!"

". . . and I must needs ask your kindness in not watching us, lest it be spoiled for you on the day."

Lewis's face crumpled like a small child's told he was not going to have a longed-for treat after all. "No?" he asked faintly.

Basset said regretfully, "I fear so."

"Master Basset will want you later," Mistress Penteney said kindly. "Best you be rested when he does. Go on with Matthew now, like usual."

"Usual, usual, usual," Lewis said unhappily and trailed away with Matthew toward a doorway at the near end of the dais.

"Thank you for trying to help," Mistress Penteney said to Simon and her daughter. They made bow and curtsy to her, and Kathryn cast a smile toward Basset and Joliffe before she and Simon went off together a different way from Lewis. Mistress Penteney smiled at Basset and Joliffe, too, and said, "Master Fairfield must needs lie down every day after dinner, lest he tire himself too much. I should have told you that, but he knows it as well as anyone. Thank you for your ready help."

"It's ever my pleasure to serve you, my lady," Basset assured her.

"And this is . . . ?" she asked toward Joliffe.

"Master Joliffe Southwell," Basset said. "One of our company. You'll see him as the Devil tonight and tomorrow."

Joliffe swept her a slightly flourished bow. "And as the Angel of the Lord on Corpus Christi, may I assure you, my lady, lest you think ill of me."

Straight-faced but with a merry enough twinkle to her eyes, she said, "But you're only a man most of the time, I trust? Neither angel nor devil would be comfortable to have around the house for long."

"Only a man most of the time," Joliffe agreed, "and at your service."

"You've both served well thus far, surely," she said, "keeping Master Fairfield so happy. But one of you was missing from dinner just now. There's nothing amiss, I hope?"

Basset explained about the need to keep watch on their belongings.

Mistress Penteney made an impatient sound at herself. "Now there's a thing of which I should have thought. You were surely going to take him his dinner, though, weren't you?"

"One of our company is seeing to that, my lady," Basset said.

"I'll tell our chamberlain that you're to have a padlock and key so there's no need to trouble yourselves any more with keeping watch and missing meals."

Basset and Joliffe both bowed their thanks. She bent her head to them in return and said, "Now I'll leave you to your business and go on with mine. But, again, my thanks for your help with Lewis."

She went her way and Basset and Joliffe went theirs, Basset musing as they went, "A worthy woman. Still, what's amiss with our Lewis, I wonder, that he's not to tire himself too much and must needs lie down to rest at midday, as if he were more an infant than a man-grown youth. I do have to wonder."

"And about the care being taken of him?" Joliffe prompted.

"About that, too," Basset agreed, but neither of them took it any further, not then, keeping to themselves whatever were their own thoughts about it.

Chapter 6

Despite what he had told Lewis, it was the Abraham play that Basset kept them at through much of the afternoon.

"Three days," he said to Ellis's grumble at that. "That's what we have. Three days to make this good enough not to shame ourselves, and some of that time must go to keeping Lewis in good spirits *and* putting together *The Pride of Life*. Now, I've another thought on what you can do, Piers, when you understand he means to kill you. You're standing here, see . . ."

He finally gave over working them but only because a servant from the priest at St. Michael Northgate sought them out with word that Sire John wanted to see Basset about what was planned for Thursday.

"Right, then," said Basset. "I'll go along with you. Piers, help your mother. If Lewis shows up, he's yours to divert." He caught his hat that Rose tossed to him and added as he put it on, "Ellis, Joliffe, you can run your lines for *Pride* while I'm away."

Ellis and Joliffe both gave him respectful half-bows. Only when Basset and the servant were well gone did Ellis exclaim, "Christ and the cripple!" and fling himself down in disgust on one of the cushions.

"Ellis, not that oath," Rose admonished. "Not this week of all weeks, especially."

Ellis sprang to his feet and went to kiss her by way of apology. Joliffe settled on another of the cushions, waited until he judged they had had a long enough apology between them, and said "Shall we get on with it?"

Ellis groaned and came to join him. For the next hour they belabored their way through the play, far enough better than their first attempt this morning that Piers, listening while he helped his mother hem Lewis's devil tabard, said when they'd finished, "That wasn't bad. Maybe Basset won't kill you after all."

"Our hearts are gladdened that you approve," Joliffe said with a mocking bow from where he sat.

Ellis suggested Piers could put his approval and his head into the water bucket and keep them there.

"Should you run it again?" Rose suggested.

They were spared saying what they thought of running it again by Basset's return. There was a fine glow of pleasure on him that made Ellis say, before Joliffe could, "The good priest was kind with some rather good wine?"

"The wine was indeed good and he was indeed surprisingly kind," Basset said. "It seems our vicar has a fondness for plays and is vastly looking forward to ours come Corpus Christi."

Unimpressed by that, Rose asked, "You made agreement with him on payment?"

"There was talk that he needn't pay us so much, since we weren't having to pay lodging this week . . ." Rose drew in a sharp breath and Basset finished hurriedly, ". . . but we

talked it around to where we'd started from and all's settled. Guess who I met on the way back?"

"Trouble, if I know you," Rose said.

"Jack Melton."

Ellis slapped his hands down on his knees. "Melton! We
haven't crossed ways with him since that Midsummer
gathering, what, two years back? How's it going for him?"

"His company is doing *The Birth of Christ* at All Saints.
That's after us. We'll be able to see them, like."

"Hai, Piers." Ellis reached out to punch his arm playfully.
"Wasn't there a sweet-faced girl you liked with them?"

"No," Piers said with scorn. "There wasn't." And
punched him back, less playfully.

"We're to all meet at the Black Bull tonight after supper," Basset said. "Talk over times, trade word about other
companies . . ."

"Spend money we haven't earned yet," Rose said,
threading a needle with unnecessary viciousness.

Ellis jerked his head for Piers to shift out of his way and
moved over to sit beside her. Cautious because of the needle, he put an arm around her waist and, when she made no
jab at him, gave her a small squeeze and said, "We've
money, love. There's not a farthing been spent from yesterday's take and no necessities to spend it on all this week.
What harm to have a little sport with it?"

Rose laid her sewing and her hands in her lap. "It's not
a 'little' sport I'm worried over. What I worry over is the
'ale for everybody in the place' kind of sport." But she was
jesting at him about it. Or half jesting. Willing to be persuaded, anyway, and she said past him to her father, "I'll
tell you what. It's time we counted out shares from yesterday's. Do it, and when you and Ellis have put yours into my
keeping, I'll give you each a penny for tonight. One each
and no more."

"Ah, sweetling," Ellis started, clearly purposing to woo her out of more.

She cocked an eye at him. He silenced and Basset, knowing he'd not get a better deal without a quarrel, pulled a pouch out of his purse.

"We count," he said.

They did, on a place smoothed in the dirt, and better than her word, after writing their shares into the small scroll she kept for it, Rose gave two pence apiece to Basset and Ellis from their shares, a half-penny to Piers from his and a penny to herself from hers, pushed Joliffe's coins toward him and scooped the rest into the company pouch. Joliffe, as always, took out a few of his own pence and pushed the others over to her, to be kept with the rest.

"Now there's unfair," Ellis protested, as always. "Why give him chance to keep his and not me?"

"Because he's halfway to having the sense of a goose about money in hand and you're not," Rose returned, tucking the pouch into her belt-hung purse, under her apron, to be hidden later in the cart.

Lewis showed up not long after that, faithfully followed by Matthew. To keep him happy they ran the devils' part of his play twice through, before Matthew said it was time Lewis went to wash for supper.

"Tomorrow you'll wear your tail," Basset promised and Lewis went off happily.

While Rose was scrubbing around Piers's neck, with a firm grip on his shoulder and no pity, Joliffe offered, despite it was her turn, to stay with the cart through supper since the promised padlock had not yet shown itself.

"Why?" she asked.

"Because I know you'll talk whoever you need to into letting you bring my share back and I'll probably get more that way."

"On the other hand, I may just talk her into letting you starve," said Ellis.

"On the other hand I may just offer the both of you to the cook for stew tomorrow," Rose returned. "Yes, I'll fetch you food back if you want to stay here."

As usual, no one thought twice about him wanting only his own company; nor did anyone probably think at all about Rose turning back as they were going out of the barn, taking off her apron and calling out to Joliffe to come take it. He did, unsurprised as he took it from her to feel the weight of the coin pouch hidden in its folds. He gave no sign, merely leaned against the barn door, watching until they were all into the hall and the two men crossing from the stable were gone in after them and the yard was empty of anyone. Only then, leaving the apron on Rose's cushion, did he take the pouch—pleased with the weight of it in his hand—and step up into the cart, make his way around and over the hampers they'd not bothered to unload, and finally crouched among them just behind the driver's seat. The seat was made of seemingly a single thick slab of wood, but he felt along the slab's bottom until he found the slit there, big enough for him to put two fingernails in. Pushing carefully, he was able to slide aside the panel set so cunningly in grooves that anyone who did not know about it would need to have the seat out and upside down in full daylight to know it was there.

Rose had said when showing the hiding place to Joliffe, "He's good with wood, is that man I married. That I'll say for him. I had him make this so I'd have a secret place for things. I've not ever even told Basset. It's so no one can come at our money except me, and now you."

"Why me?" Joliffe had asked, more in protest than pleasure.

"What if I drop dead? Better someone knows where our money is than only me."

"Why not trust Basset?"

"Because if it comes to buying a play or some other thing he thinks might help our playing, he'll spend all we have without half thinking whether he's paying too much or whether we really need it or that there might be dire need of money to hand somewhere down the road. You know that."

Joliffe also knew better than to ask why not Ellis. The one thing he doubted Rose would ever do again was trust a man she deeply loved; her judgment had been too deeply betrayed by Piers's father. Instead he had said, "So don't trust Basset. But why trust me?"

Rose had smiled a grim little smile at him and said, "Because you're just idiot enough to be honorable."

He had not much liked hearing that, not liked having her know him so well, because, yes, he was just idiot enough not to betray a trust if he could help it. Aside from that, he loved the game they had between them—of her sometimes giving him their money to be hidden or, other times, having him be the one to secretly bring it out and slip it to her, so that neither Basset nor Ellis had yet figured out how she managed to keep their money hidden from them.

With most of the money safely put into the leather pouch waiting in the hiding hole, and the panel carefully closed, Joliffe crawled back out of the cart, put the other pouch back among the folds of Rose's apron, and settled down on a cushion with his back against one of the hampers, his legs stretched out in front him with ankles crossed, ready to have the evening go as simply as the day had. Given the tangles into which life could twist itself, a simple day like today, full of straight-forward work and no problems, was as near to wealthy as he ever expected to come, and he was watching sparrows flitting among the rafters and not thinking about anything much at all when, true to expectation, Rose came back with a goodly portion of supper for him. He did not rise, just smiled up at her and thanked her as she set the tray down beside him. A padlock and its key were lying beside the thick, broad slice of meat pie and the berry tart in a bowl of cream, and as Rose straightened to stand over him, hands on hips, she said, "We can lock up now, with no need to keep watch, so what about this going out to the tavern? Basset says you have one of your black humours on you and will want to stay here. Do you?"

"My humour is more the shining blue of a summer day's clear sky," Joliffe said.

"There is no blue humour," Rose pointed out. "You can have black, yellow, red or . . . What would phlegm be? Gray? White? You cannot have blue."

The four humours ruled the health and passions of human bodies: the black bile of the melancholic; the yellow bile of the choleric; the hot red blood of the sanguine; the cold, pale phlegm of the phlegmatic. If the humours were in good balance, all was well. If out of balance, they made for disease of body and mind. But Joliffe gestured her protest aside with, "It's an oversight on the part of physicians throughout history. There is a sky-blue humour and I am filled with it."

Rose heaved an impatient sigh at him. "Are you staying or going? Basset is having a few words with Master Penteney. The others are waiting at the gate."

"I'm by all means staying." Because he had not liked Jack Melton the other times they had met. As Basset well knew. Joliffe waved a hand at her. "Go and disport yourselves. I'll tend to my own business here."

"Tend to your lines in *Pride*," Rose said, to remind him all wasn't as well with the world as he might think, and left.

Too used to her ways to be bothered at all, Joliffe took

his time over the food. It was both plentiful and good which spoke well of Mistress Penteney's housekeeping. She did not do the cooking herself but surely she had chosen and oversaw whoever was the cook and she likewise determined what was cooked and how it was apportioned, and he thought he might fall in love with her on account of the meat pie alone, never mind the berry tart in its cream.

Food finished, a long drink of ale taken to wash it all down, and the bowl cleaned and set by to be returned to the hall, he took out *The Pride of Life*'s playbook and, not to suit Rose but because he had intended to, went twice over his lines. By the time the light was faded enough that reading was passing from difficult to impossible, he knew both his part and Ellis's well enough to count on making fair fun of Ellis tomorrow when they practiced.

The playbook put away, he strolled to the barn door again and stood looking out, stretching his back and considering what to do next. It was too early to sleep and he was weary of words, spoken or read, and even if he had felt like going to some tavern after all and locked the barn behind him, there was no spare key to the padlock, no way for the others to get back in if they returned before he did. That was no problem, though, since he did not feel like being in company of any kind. Nor did he look in any danger of having any here, that was sure. On a warm summer's evening of a holiday week, with the day's work done and sports of one kind and another to be had all over Oxford, no one seemed to have lingered around the yard for someone to find something for them to do. The place had an air of pleasant desertion. Except for . . .

Joliffe cocked his head, listening to laughter from beyond the line of sheds, muffled by them but seeming to come from behind the house.

Deciding he could leave the cart to itself for a while, he

pulled the barn door shut without padlocking it and crossed the few open yards between the barn and the sheds to the narrow gap out of which Piers and Lewis had come this morning. The sheds were made with close-joined plank walls instead of wattle-and-daub, and the roofs were of slate instead of simply thatch. All of that and the locks on every door testified to the worth of whatever goods and foodstuffs Master Penteney kept stored here. Since he was a victualler and therefore dealt in a variety of things, not all of them on the hoof, that was very reasonable and expected. What was not reasonable—and still in Joliffe's mind—was that moment of understanding between him and Basset when they first met. They were two men with nothing alike in their lives except they were something of the same age. Where or how had they come to know something about each other that made them want to keep secret they knew each other at all?

Tiredness and satisfaction yesterday and work today had kept Joliffe from wondering about that, but the wondering came back now as he went into the gap between the sheds. He knew nothing about Master Penteney beyond these two days but the man looked so set and settled into his life that it was hard to think he had ever been other than he was. And Basset, on his side, had the thorough seeming of someone born under a player's cart and never away from it since then. But Joliffe had that same seeming, he knew, and for himself at least, it was not the truth. So Basset's seeming could likewise be not the truth. And Master Penteney's seeming, too.

But since none of that was something about which he could question Basset—and certainly not Master Penteney—he shoved his wondering away as useless.

The gap proved to be a short, narrow alleyway, with at its farther end a closed gate between the sheds' back walls and too high to see over. The laughter that had drawn him came from beyond it, and Joliffe, not in the least bothered to be spying, put his eyes to the thin opening between the gate's latch-edge and the gatepost. On the gate's other side was the garden he had seen from Master Penteney's study yesterday. From what he could see now by shifting a little, he could guess it stretched along the back of the house and sheds to where a high wall cut it off from the lane behind the barn. He could glimpse a gravelled path and flower beds but what he mostly saw was a stretch of the close-cut green grass with three birch trees in the middle, their shade and the round bench set among them surely making a pleasant place to be through much of a summer's day. Even now, in the thick gold light of the westering sun, the low-swept branches gave a flickering shade, and Mistress Penteney and her daughter-in-law were sitting there, with sewing in their laps but watching their husbands and Simon, Lewis, Kathryn, and a very little boy playing catch-and-chase around the garden with a large canvas ball. The ball had to be lightly stuffed, to judge how even the little boy could lift it, big as his head though it was, and throw it, albeit he sat down on his bottom thereafter and had to scramble up, laughing, to run after Simon who had caught it and was trying to dodge being tagged by everyone else, only at the last moment before Master Penteney laid hands on him throwing the ball to Kathryn who squealed with delight and horror and raced to put her mother and Geva between her and everyone else until—as her brother and father came around for her from both sides—she threw the ball at Lewis who caught it surprisingly well but promptly threw it at Master Penteney too wide aside for him to catch it so that there was an immediate free-for-all of everyone after it at once, with Mistress Penteney and Geva laughing so hard that Mistress Penteney was wiping tears from her eyes and Geva had wrapped her arms around her hurting sides.

Joliffe, watching unwatched, smiled at their pleasure, at first surprised by, then ignoring the unexpected pang in him that was not jealousy but sharp awareness of how there had been a time when something like that much happiness with family had been a possibility for him. Just as John Thamys yesterday had been a reminder of yet another way he could have taken his life instead of the way he had. But everyone's life always came down to choices. He was living out his choices and still preferred them to the ones he might have made and nonetheless was still smiling at the Penteneys' pleasure as he drew back from the gate and returned to the barn.

He was stretched out on his pallet, a pillow comfortably under his head but no need for a blanket yet, the evening still warm though the sun was finally down, when Basset came into the barn, carrying a sleeping Piers. Joliffe, who had drifted to somewhere between thinking and dozing off, roused and rolled onto his side, propping up on one elbow to ask, "Just you and Piers?"

"Just us," Basset said softly, laying the boy down on his bed. Piers did not waken, merely sighed happily, rolled onto his side, and curled up into deeper sleep.

"Talked somebody into playing nine-penny merels with him, did he?" Joliffe said, not trusting Piers's happiness even in sleep.

"He did." Basset straightened with a sigh of his own and pressed his hands to the small of his back. "He's getting too big and I'm getting too old to be hauling him about like this much longer. He's going to have to use his own feet after this to get home."

"Did he take them for much?"

"Enough but not too much. Ever moderate when it counts, is the boy."

Moderate in the hope of taking them again a few more times if he had the chance, before they caught on that nobody ever won against Piers at nine-penny merals except when he let them. Come to that, nobody won against him at quite a few other games either. Joliffe was sure that if all else failed him, Piers could make his living as gambler, at least while he was still young and golden-haired and looked like a guileless cherub. After he outgrew that, he might find the going a little harder. Or then again, being Piers, he might not.

Joliffe thought of asking Basset how things had gone with the other players but that was something that could keep until morning. He'd rather sleep now and Basset had probably been the one to bring Piers home because he was ready to be a-bed himself.

First, though, instead of undressing to lie down, Basset rolled his shoulders as if to ease them and said, "I think I'll take a turn around the yard to work the twitches out, unfume my head a little. I'll be back."

Already settled to his pillow again, Joliffe made a sound to say he had heard and in very few moments he would have been asleep, but as Basset went out, partly closing the barn door behind him with a soft creak, his eyes flew open and he lay staring into the dark. And not because of the door.

If Basset had said nothing, had simply gone out, Joliffe would have had no second thought about it at all. But to unfume his head a little? All Basset ever wanted to do when he was fumed with drink was go to bed. Joliffe rolled off his own bed, stood up, and silent on bare feet, went to the door. It still stood half-open, with no need for him to creak it on its hinges. Easing his head around its edge, he saw Basset—or rather the black shape of him in the blue starlight—just as it merged with the shadows of the alley between the two sheds, the same way Joliffe had gone earlier. Joliffe slid out the barn door and sideways and, aware he could be seen in the naked starlight should Basset happen to look back, kept in the thicker darkness of the barn's eave-shadow until he was past where anyone in the alley itself could see him unless looking out from just inside it. Basset had been moving with enough purpose to suggest he should be more than a few paces along it by now, able to see only a little of the empty yard if he looked back, not Joliffe crossing to the shadow of the nearer shed.

Joliffe had not much thought about what he was doing or why and did not stop to think about it now. More than once, his curiosity had set him to do things he could just as easily not have done if he had only taken the trouble not to be curious. Unfortunately, that was usually too much trouble to take, and because just now he was curious why Basset had felt the need to lie about where he was going, he moved along the shed's shadow to the alleyway's mouth, stopped, held his breath to listen, and was just able to hear Basset still going away from him, then the soft opening of the gate, and the light crunch of steps taken on gravel.

Two steps on the graveled path . . . then nothing. Not the closing of the gate or more footsteps. Basset had either stopped just inside the gate or else crossed onto the grass. Was either still at the gate, or was going away across the garden, or had taken unexpectedly to flying.

Now, Joliffe knew, was when he should go back to his bed and the pretense he had never left it. He also knew he would not. Instead, he slipped around the shed's corner and into the alley's darkness, glad he knew there was only clear earth along it and nothing nasty to step barefoot in. What he need worry about instead was keeping silent, and he did. And when he neared the alley's other end, he pressed himself flat-backed against the right-hand wall and edged nearer to the gateway, keeping himself as much part of the darkness as possible. From there, with his head turned sideways and against the wall, he could see Basset standing on the path, looking away toward the house.

If the set of Basset's body and head were anything to judge by, he was waiting for something. Or more likely someone. Joliffe had barely time to wonder for what or whom when a faint crunch of footsteps told him it was someone, and Basset took a step forward to meet them, almost beyond where Joliffe could see him. Joliffe silently cursed at him to stay where he was and Basset did, though probably not for Joliffe's cursing but because the other person had reached him, just barely into Joliffe's sight. Master Penteney.

Even in the pallid starlight Joliffe had no trouble knowing him and seeing he was readied for bed, a bedgown of some dark stuff loosely belted around him and his hair rumpled as if maybe he had already been to his pillow before coming outside. He held out a hand that Basset took in a welcoming grip that Master Penteney readily returned, saying low-voiced as he did, "Your pardon for asking you to meet like this. It's not for shame."

"It's for good, solid sense," Basset returned, equally low. "Even after all this while, there's still folk might be reminded of too much if they saw us being friends together."

"There's too much truth for comfort in that. But by St. Christopher, it's good to see you again, Thomas." They had dropped hands but he reached out to slap Basset on the upper arm. "Damnably good."

"And you. I'd not have sought you out—haven't done all these years—but I'd agreed to come with your young

Lewis before your name came into it and it was too late then to back off without it looked odd."

"There've been times when I knew you were in Oxford and I didn't seek you out either." Some of the pleasure went out of Penteney's voice. "We've paid our price, haven't we?"

"We have that," Basset agreed. But a smile came back into his voice as he added with a movement of his head toward the house, "It's not turned out so ill for you, though, has it?"

"It hasn't, true enough. But you?"

Penteney's doubt was plain but Basset's answer was unhesitant. "As far as any man is likely to get what he wants in this world, I've the life I want, no fear. And even if I didn't," he added jestingly, "it's a better life than the one I might have had if we hadn't paid our price."

"Longer, at any rate," Penteney returned, matching the jest but with something more than jest behind it.

Something less than jest was in Basset's voice, too, as he asked, "And Roger? Do you ever hear aught of him? Or from him?"

There was silence then, making Joliffe wish for more than starlight by which to see Penteney's face before he answered, "I've never seen him since, but I hear from him once a year. Sometimes twice. He's well. He's . . . doing well."

"And best not spoken of," Basset said.

"Best not," Penteney agreed. "Basset, come inside. I've wine in my study. Let's risk the time to talk . . ."

"It's not worth the risk, Hal. Even this is more than we should."

"But you're well?" Penteney insisted. "You can assure me of that?"

"As well in my way as you are in yours. I swear it."

Not knowing how long they would talk and afraid it would not be much longer, given their unease at it, Joliffe slid silently away along the wall. Given one thing and another, he thought he would rather be in his bed and seemingly asleep when Basset next saw him than be caught here listening.

Chapter 7

In the morning Joliffe was, as usual, first to awake among the others. He lay in the darkness, listening to the early rustle and murmur of birds in the barn's rafters and thatch and the even breathings of his fellow players. For a mercy none of them—including him, he supposed, or he would have heard about it by now—was given to snoring. "Would take too much effort," Basset had grumbled when Joliffe once mentioned it. "Or maybe nobody wants to die, because I'll kill any fool who wakes me from a good sleep."

To judge by the deep rumble of his breathing, Basset was sleeping soundly enough now. And well he should be, after his lurking last night, Joliffe thought.

Joliffe had been well settled on his bed and feigning sleep by the time Basset returned to the barn; had fallen actually to sleep while Basset was readying to lie down and had awakened only enough when Rose and Ellis came back to know they were there before falling straight back to sleep, his tiredness greater than his curiosity about how their evening had gone.

He was fully awake now, though, and it wasn't their evening he was wondering about but what he had heard between Basset and Penteney. He had been already sure they had known each other before now and had half thought their secrecy was because Penteney did not want to admit acquaintance with a player and Basset had been willing to accept that. But last night Joliffe had unmistakably heard a friendship still warm between them after apparently years of never speaking to or seeing one another. Friendship . . . and some trouble heavy enough to keep friends apart. A trouble that despite they were years away from it, they felt they still had to pay the price of it because there were still people who could be "reminded" of it. Reminded of what? What had Basset and Penteney known or done—or, St. Genesius forbid, known *and* done—that it was dangerous even now for people to remember they had known each other?

And who was this Roger who was "best not spoken of"?

Joliffe rolled onto his back and damned his curiosity for dragging him into this. He couldn't even pretend to himself he would let it go and forget about it. His questions would twitch at him worse than an itch would. Likewise worse than an itch, he couldn't even go straight at them. There was no simply asking Basset. Even aside from the fact he shouldn't have been listening at all, there was the never-spoken pact among the players never to ask about each others' lives before they had met. Any of them could tell whatever he chose to tell, but no one ever asked questions. "It's the best way to keep throats from being slit, boy," Basset had said in their early days together. "What a man doesn't know, he can't use against you if there's a falling out or we end up going separate ways. All we need

know about one another is that we all do our work, share
and share alike, in plays and otherwise, no slacking, and
the rest doesn't matter."

That had suited Joliffe well enough at the time and still
did, but it meant there was no way he could be asking Basset outright what was toward between him and Master
Penteney.

Come to that, how had Basset and Penteney come to
know each other at all? Or at least to know each other
well enough to get into such trouble. On the face of it,
there wasn't much likelihood of it. Players were set too
far aside—below, some would say, but Joliffe made his
own choices on how to see things—from a settled, wealthy
merchant like Penteney for there to be any deep dealings
between them, let alone ground on which friendship
could grow.

Joliffe stretched his arms out to the sides and muttered
toward the roof, "This is what comes of being lazy." If he
had fought his curiosity instead of letting it haul him out of
his bed last night, he'd have no problems this morning beyond making sure of his lines for *Pride* and hoping Ellis
wasn't quarrelsomely sore-headed from too much ale. It
served him right and on a platter to be stuck with questions
he had small hope of ever having answered and maybe
he'd finally learn his lesson by it.

That settled, he closed his eyes, determined to slip to
sleep again. And promptly opened them to stare into the
thinning darkness. He hadn't even a prayer of fooling himself into believing he would let his questions go or convince himself to make light of whatever was between
Basset and Penteney. Whatever it was, they were still so
wary about knowing each other that last night Basset had
left the gate open behind him so he could make a swift re-
treat if need be, and if the thing was that dangerous to Bas-

set, it was dangerous to all of them, if only because without Basset there would be no company and not even the thin livelihood they presently had. If nothing else, without Basset they would be down to two men and a boy and there were too few plays they could do with only that many. As it was, they were almost too few. Only Basset's determination and Joliffe's skill at making over plays to fit them had kept them going this long. But more than that, it was Basset who had brought them together, Basset who kept them together. Without Basset it would all be over.

Not that they couldn't find work of one kind or another elsewhere. They could even join other companies of players if they were that daft; but staring into the rafters now taking shape out of the darkness, Joliffe had to admit—to the darkness and to himself but never to anyone else—he liked the company he was in. He was used to them and they to him and he was not minded to be forced to change. If Basset was in trouble, so were they all and Joliffe wanted to know what the trouble was, either to help Basset if he could, or else be forewarned of disaster coming.

Besides, all else set aside, he was curious. Damn it.

He was still lying there when Rose awoke and eased from under her blanket. The dawn was cool enough that she paused to be sure Piers was still covered, no bare back or leg thrust out from beneath his blanket, before she pulled her gown on over her shift and went silently, a shadow-shape in the barely lightened darkness, to the cart, took something from the small chest that held her few belongings, sat down on one of the hampers, and set to unbraiding her long hair that during the day she wore wound up and fastened out of sight under her headkerchief, never seen. Going on pretending sleep, Joliffe watched her as she shook her hair out loose to her waist and began to comb it in long, slow strokes unlike her usual briskness toward everything she did.

Watching her, it came to him that their stay at the Penteneys was holiday time for her even more than for the rest of them. For the while they were here, she was spared most of the things she usually had to do. No worry over the buying or bartering for their food; no cooking of it and cleaning up afterwards; no constant troubling over where and how their things were packed and unpacked from the cart—nothing put where it couldn't be readily found when they next stopped and needed it, nor anything left behind when they moved on—no bother with starting a fire and keeping it going when they spent the night by the road rather than at an inn or somewhere. Her other usual worries were still with her—of seeing to their clothing and such of their properties that might need finer mending than what the men could do—but the great worries of food and travel were put by for now and instead of her usual early morning bustle she was simply sitting, combing and combing her hair.

It was a soothing thing to watch a woman comb her hair that way, and Joliffe was somewhat back toward sleep again when Ellis and Basset began to stir. That meant time for him to stir, too, and he did, stretching as if just awakening before getting up and going outside about his business. When he came back, Basset was sitting up on his bed, rubbing his face and grumbling to himself—mornings were not his best time—and Ellis was prodding Piers awake, saying, "Time to fetch water, you slug."

Piers made to grab Ellis's bare ankle but Ellis was too quick for that and Piers—a grumbling small copy of his grandfather—shambled up and toward the water bucket. His mother caught him on the way and combed down his hair, saying, "Let's at least pretend we're seemly folk, shall we?" before letting him go.

Piers was gone, still grumbling, and the rest of them were straightening their blankets over their beds when Ellis said, "Know what we heard last night after you left, Basset?"

"Of course. I always sneak back into a tavern to listen to you after I've gone to bed."

Ellis ignored that. "Rose and I fell into talk with some Penteney servants that were there. Lewis is to marry the Penteney girl."

Basset turned around from his tidied bed. "Marry her?"

"Marry her," Ellis repeated.

"They're going to marry her—what's her name?—to Lewis?"

"Kathyrn," said Joliffe. He looked to Rose. "Truly?"

"Truly," she said.

"The Penteneys have been putting it off on the likelihood he'd die before he came of age," Ellis said, "but he hasn't, and he comes of age at midsummer. So while Penteney still has control of Lewis's marriage they're going to marry him to this Kathryn and be done with it. The talk is they mean to do the betrothal this week, while Lord Lovell is here to witness it."

"I'd have thought they'd rather have young Simon for her," Basset said. "Penteney holds right to his marriage, too, as I understand it."

"Simon isn't the heir." Ellis was dry about that.

Basset frowned. "Not that I have anything against Lewis, but I wonder why they haven't seen to having him set aside from inheriting. Given how he is, that would be possible."

"Costly, too, what with lawyers and fees to the king and Church and all," Ellis pointed out. "Besides, if it's set up for

Simon to inherit when he comes of age, he'll surely take everything into his own hands, the way Lewis never can."

"Ah," said Basset, immediately seeing the point.

Joliffe saw it, too. Had seen it earlier, in his talk with the serving man at supper their first night here. With Lewis married to Kathryn, Master Penteney would go on running the Fairfield properties and go on having the profit of them just as he had for all these years, rather than giving everything up to Simon, to *Simon's* profit.

Thinking aloud from there, Joliffe said, "And even if Lewis dies after he's wed, Master Penteney will likely go on running the properties for his daughter's sake."

"So the girl is to be sacrificed to the idiot on the great altar of her father's profits," said Rose coldly.

"Or the girl is to be set up for life as prosperous wife and prosperous widow," Basset returned. "There's few would quarrel with that. And they have waited as long as they could, in hope it wouldn't come to this. You have to give Penteney that. Lewis has already lived past the time most of his kind die. He's not likely to last all that much longer, come what may, but even if he doesn't get a child on her, to keep all the Fairfield properties in the family, the girl's dower-third of it in Penteney hands will be better than none. And she'll be free to marry again."

All that was not so much heartless as merely reasonable. As Basset said often enough about other matters, there was rarely point in shying clear of what was true and couldn't be helped; but Rose nonetheless gave him her disgusted look that said, *"Men,"* though aloud, she only warned, "Best not say anything of this around Master Ears." Meaning Piers.

To that they all nodded agreement and got on with the day.

After breakfast Basset talked with Mistress Penteney,

and at his asking the hall was given over to them at mid-morning, that they might run the play there with Lewis so he would be used to doing it there. Until then, they worked at *Pride*, Basset beginning to be satisfied with it by the time they had to go to the hall.

The practice there went well, too. Lewis was happy with his devil's tunic and twitching tail, and though he made a larger, more lumbering demon than Piers, it somehow made the business the funnier. And he remembered to be careful with his spear, never once jabbing Ellis.

They were not without lookers-on. Matthew was there, of course, sitting out of the way on a stool, and sometimes a servant's head would ease around the corner of the door-way to the screens passage for a brief look. Mistress Geva came once, carrying on her hip the little boy Joliffe had seen in the garden. She stood near Matthew until there was a pause and then went to Basset while Rose mended some stitches in Lewis's tail—she had come with her sewing basket in expectation of the need—and said, "Mistress Penteney sent me to remind you Lewy isn't to do too much and tire himself."

The little boy on her hip waved at Lewis, calling, "Lewy!"

Lewis waved and called back. "Giles! I can't come. She has my tail."

The boy laughed as Basset gave his mother a bow and assured her that care was being taken.

Mistress Geva, who seemed no more certain how play-ers should be dealt with than she had on Sunday, was ap-parently unsettled by Basset's courtesy to her, and said stiffly, "Well. Just see it is." She looked around as if for something else to say, did not find it, and with her chin a little jutted in the air, left the hall.

"Bitch," muttered Ellis.

"Or maybe just very unhappy." said Joliffe.

"About what? Living easy and not having much to do?"

"Living in someone else's household with nothing to do but what she's told?"

Ellis grimaced, seeing what he meant.

They let Lewis caper two more times before Basset traded looks with Matthew and said, "Well, that's enough for now, I think, Master Fairfield. You have it to perfection and we, alas, are growing tired."

"Once more?" Lewis begged.

Matthew, coming forward, said, "They must needs rest. If you tire them out too much, they'll be no good tonight or tomorrow at the feast."

"Rest, rest, rest," Lewis muttered, but he let Rose help him out of his tunic, and when Kathyrn came into the hall he called happily to her, "I've been a good devil!"

"I don't doubt it," she answered, smiling.

Joliffe's assessing look at her was different than it had been, now he knew she was meant for Lewis. She was somewhat young for marrying but not by much. Others, both girls and boys, were married off younger than she was for the sake of profit. But had anyone considered what might happen if she came to full womanhood still bound to a husband who was, to most intents and possibly purposes, forever a child? However it went between them in bed, their companionship would always depend on her care of him, with never an equal meeting of minds or hearts. Or if no one else had considered it, had she?

Presently anyway, she was saying to Basset with her pretty smile and far more ease than Mistress Geva, "Please you, my mother said I was to ask if the servants could ready the hall for dinner now."

Bowing with an excessive flourish that made Kathryn laugh the way he had meant it to, Basset said, "It is our

pleasure to oblige. I pray you tell your lady mother from
me that Master Fairfield is so excellent at his work that we
need do no more with him this afternoon."

Lewis started to protest but Kathyrn said to him firmly,
"You know she wouldn't let you anyway," and held out her
hand. "Come. She'll want to hear what you've been doing."

"Come, come, come," said Lewis disgustedly, but he
went with her, Matthew following them out of the hall.

After an ample dinner and their return to the barn, Basset, with an unwonted inclination toward repose, said that
he thought he would nap a while. "With maybe we rehearse
Pride afterwards," he added.

Joliffe waited until he had laid down and shut his eyes
before taking Ellis aside and saying, too low-voiced to disturb Basset, "I think I'll away to see how Tisbe is doing."

"Mind you're back before he wakes," Ellis warned.

"But if I'm not, we won't have to run *Pride* again, will
we?"

Ellis brightened. "Have as long a walk as you like. No
need to hurry back. None at all."

"I want to come," said Piers, nudging at Joliffe's elbow.

"If Joliffe says you may," Ellis said.

"And your mother," Joliffe added.

Rose gave her leave. Joliffe complained it wasn't fair
that because they needed Piers for the plays this week he'd
have to bring him back alive no matter how much a pain he
was. Piers, used to being complained of, already had his
hat on and was heading out the door as Joliffe added, "Of
course we could always hire Lewis, I suppose."

Piers turned back long enough to say, "Or I could come
back without *you*, and we could hire Lewis to take *your*
place. It wouldn't make much difference," then ducked
outside as Joliffe set off after him.

They made a dodge and tag game of it out the rear gate

and for a way along the lane before Joliffe bothered to catch him with an arm around his waist and a hand free to pull Pier's hat over his eyes.

"Hai!" Piers protested. "My feather!"

His hat's bright green feather from a popinjay's tail had been given to him by a lady at a manor where they had played last autumn. She had been charmed by his sweet face and fair curls, been more charmed by the grateful kiss he gave her on the cheek and had given him a coin to go with it. He had refused to share the coin and had Rose fasten the feather to his hat, been careful of it all winter, and now wriggled free of Joliffe and snatched off his hat to see if there was damage. Joliffe had been careful of it, and assured his feather was unharmed, Piers put the hat back on and started to ask questions as they walked.

Joliffe had never decided whether Piers's questions were a way to be sure someone was paying him heed or because he really wanted to know about whatever he was asking, but at least they were rarely dull. Today his questions were about Master Penteney and how he had come to be so rich. Joliffe explained as best he could what it was to be a victualler, and at the end, after silently thinking on it a while, Piers said, "Then he does no work with his hands himself. He gathers in what other men do and has the money from selling it to other people who'll have to do the work with it."

"The men he buys from have his money for their work, and a good many of the men he sells to probably make money from what they buy from him. The money doesn't all go one way."

"The thing is, *he* doesn't have to do any heavy work, doesn't have to put his back into anything," Piers said.

"He has to put his brain into it," Joliffe pointed out.

"I can do that," Piers said, plainly quite taken with the possibility of using just his brain and not his back to make a living. "Where we're going is where he keeps cattle and such until he can sell them to butchers and all, right?"

"You have it."

"But he doesn't own much land himself?"

"Maybe little more than what we'll see today." But the Fairfield properties might include lands, making them even more worth his while to keep.

"But he has the big house and all. I bet the people he buys from don't have as big a house."

"Some might. As well as from lesser folk, he likely buys from lords' stewards making money for their lords by selling surplus stock."

Piers was silent a while, swishing a stick through the branches of the hedge as they walked along, before he said, "I wonder if I could marry that Kathryn instead of Lewis?"

"Where did you hear of that?" Joliffe asked.

"Lewis told me. He likes that he's going to marry her. He says wives have to do what husbands tell them, so she won't be able to give him orders any more."

Joliffe did not point out the fallacy of that, only suggested dryly, "Wait to marry her yourself until she's his widow. She'll be richer then."

Piers brightened. "That's a *good* thought. I'll be older then, too." He frowned up at Joliffe. "You aren't going to try for her yourself, are you? I thought of her first."

"No. I promise I'll leave her to you," Joliffe said, not a difficult promise since they both had as much chance of hitting the sun with a snowball as wedding a rich widow.

Head down, now swishing his stick through the grass beside the road, Piers was silent again before asking in a smaller voice, "*Is* Lewis likely to die soon?"

Surprised by both Piers's quietness and the question, Joliffe said too lightly, "We're all going to die."

Piers looked at him with the scorn that deserved, and Joliffe answered him more fairly, matching his quiet, "Yes, he very likely is. They don't usually last even as long as this, his sort."

Piers went back to whipping the grasses, considering that for a while before saying, "I just hope he doesn't while we're here. I like him."

"Or before he's married to Kathryn and can make her a rich widow?"

Piers brightened. "That, too."

They walked on, Piers asking more questions about other things, but while answering them, Joliffe wondered how they all, even Piers, could talk so easily of Lewis being dead. He was an idiot, surely, born that way and never going to better, but Joliffe had known full-witted people with less warmth for life than Lewis had, full-witted people who used too little of their wits where Lewis used all he had. Who was to say which was more worthy in God's sight—someone who wasted God's gifts or someone who used what he had to the fullest that he could?

When they came into the yard among the byres and barns, Master Glover was leaning on the gate to the horse pasture, watching the horses graze. He looked around when Joliffe and Piers joined him and gave them greeting but did not shift. Joliffe leaned his crossed arms on the top rail beside him and said. "A peaceful life."

"Just now it is," Master Glover answered. "There'll be something come up before I've turned around, likely. Especially now I've had to send one of my men to Master Penteney's place in town to help ready for his lordly guests and two that are wanting to be away to whatever is happening in town as often as not."

Piers had been peering through the rails of the gate but now asked if he could look around. Master Glover said he could, adding. "Just don't touch or shift things, mind you."

Piers went off. Tisbe was drifting and grazing among
the other horses as contentedly as any of them. Joliffe said
something about her looking fit and settled in.

"She's made no trouble," Master Glover said. "She's a
quiet one."

"She's that," Joliffe agreed.

"How are things going for you there at Master Penteney's?"

"Well enough. No trouble."

"You'll be moving on after Thursday, like?"

"That's what we plan. Will you be free from here to
come into town for the plays on Corpus Christi?"

"I don't much hold with plays," Master Glover said easily. "Or crowds. I like it here, where it's peaceful."

They made a little more talk, mostly about whether this
summer would end up as wet as the last had been, before
Joliffe looked around for Piers and didn't see him.

"Went off around the end of the barn," Master Glover
said, pointing. "Not a paternoster ago. Toward the goose
marsh, though I've no geese here until more nigh
Michaelmas."

"A marsh," Joliffe said, pushing off from the gate.
"He'll mire himself to his knees if I know him, and his
mother will kill us both."

"Your wife?" Master Glover asked.

"No," Joliffe said; but something in the way Master
Glover had asked it had made him watchful and he saw the
hardness of disapproval come into the man's face so that
he added with deliberate lightness, pretending he saw nothing, "Nor is Piers mine, thank all the saints. I only work for
his grandfather."

He wished Master Glover well and left him with that,
unreasonably irked at him and irked at himself for being
irked. There were always people who looked for what they

saw as the worst in others. They couldn't be cured of it and so, like the plague, they were best avoided when might be and thought about as little as possible the rest of the time. Better to think about finding Piers, which he did by going around the barn and through a gate into a pasture that sloped down from behind the barn and Master Glover's house to obviously marshy ground along the stream that watered all the pastures.

Piers was already at the stream, poking with his stick at something in the water. Joliffe called him away, met him as he came, and steered him on across the pasture to a stile through the hedge and onto the road, thankful to see that he had had only time to muddy his shoes, not his hosen.

"If you're lucky," Joliffe told him, "the mud will dry and you can brush it off before your mother sees it."

"We're always getting muddy," Piers protested. "It's not trouble."

He was right about the muddy. They walked too many miles on dirt roads not to get muddy when it rained or snowed; it was simply part of their life; but Joliffe said, "We're trying to keep well-kept while we're with well-kept people."

"Why?" Piers demanded, offended.

"So they won't find out we're savages who eat small, wet-footed boys," Joliffe snapped.

Piers laughed.

Chapter 8

The Penteney yard was busy when Joliffe and Piers returned to it. Where it was cobbled, men were sweeping the cobbles clean and where it was paved outside the front door women were scrubbing the paving stones.

Piers looked at the busyness and with the sure instinct of someone who objected to being scrubbed himself asked, "What's all the cleaning for today? I thought it wasn't until tomorrow Lord Lovell comes."

"Better to start cleaning today. Less to do tomorrow," Joliffe said.

With probably fear it would all give his mother thoughts about him, Piers said, "I'm going to see if Lewis is in the garden," and sheered away in a dash toward the gap between the sheds. He paused to look back, to see if Joliffe was going to object, but Joliffe only shrugged at him and let him go on. It wouldn't save him, Joliffe knew. Sooner or later Rose would catch up to him and he would be washed but at least Joliffe wouldn't be the villain when it happened.

He went his own way, into the barn, to be greeted by Basset asking from where he sat on one of the cushions, "How goes it with Tisbe?" and Ellis saying as he picked up the water bucket, "Where's the whelp?"

"Tisbe is doing so well she may be too fat to fit her harness when we're ready to go," Joliffe answered. "And the whelp has run off to see if Lewis is in the garden."

Rose put her head out from the back of the cart. "Someone can fetch him, then. I want to clean him up for tonight. Joliffe, you had him last."

Basset started a slow climb to his feet, stiff with sitting. "I'll try to see Master Penteney now, before the afternoon's any later."

"What for?" Joliffe asked.

"About tonight. To be sure all's set for how and when. You know."

Rose put her head out of the cart again. "Best ask him about tomorrow, too, while you've the chance. Likely he'll be too busy for us then. Haven't you gone yet, Joliffe?"

"Just going."

"Ellis, have you done what I asked yet?"

"Just about to," Ellis protested. "Have a bit of mercy, woman." But he and Rose were smiling at each other as he said it.

Joliffe left them to their smiling and Basset to see Master Penteney, and before he reached the garden gate could tell by the noisy laughter that Piers had found Lewis. Stopping in the gateway to see what was worth so much noise, he saw an elderly maidservant seated on the bench among the trees with sewing on her lap and Lewis hopping up and down beside her, chortling, "Cold, cold, cold!" at Piers crawling around one of the trees on his hands and knees.

Not minded to stop their game in the middle of it, Joliffe went aside along the path to a wooden bench set against the housewall, warm in the afternoon sunlight. A gray-and-black cat already curled up there opened one green eye at him to see if he was going to spoil things, but Joliffe held up his hands to show he meant only peace and sat down at the bench's other end. The cat closed its eye and settled a little deeper into a comfort with which Joliffe silently agreed: there were few things better than sitting at ease in the soft summer sun of a quiet garden.

So long as there was not something better to be doing.

Joliffe smiled at the familiar restlessness of his own thought. Here and now was good but just a little farther down the road there might be something better. Or—at the least—something different. But for now he leaned back, head and shoulders against the house's stone wall, and closed his eyes. Across the garden Lewis declared, "Warm! Warm! Warm!"

As he sat down, Joliffe had vaguely noted the window near him, had vaguely supposed it was the one in Master Penteney's study from which he'd seen the garden when he and Basset first came here, and then forgotten it. Now a door closed sharply from inside, as if someone had contained an urge to slam it, and Master Penteney said with impatience and anger, "You've no business being here. That was agreed on from the first. From the very first. Why are you here?"

Joliffe half expected Basset to answer him but it was a voice he did not know that said back, "Agreements change." Joliffe hated when someone put that much sneer into their words. "So do circumstances. There's been trouble."

"That's not new. There's always trouble," Master Penteney snapped.

"He's been jailed. He needs money. Pay over and I'll get out."

"I don't 'pay over'. I give. There's a difference there you'd better remember, and the giving will stop if ever you show up here again for any reason. Nor do I want to know any more than what you've told me about what's happening. Just have him send word when all's well." There was a pause. Joliffe supposed something was being done, but he heard nothing that told him what it was, only soon Master Penteney said, biting the words short, "There. That's for love of my brother and no other reason. Remember that. How does he?"

"He lives. He does God's work. That's . . ."

A knock—at the door, Joliffe had to presume—was followed immediately by Richard Penteney saying, "Father, Basset wants . . ." before he broke off and started again, "I'm sorry. I thought you were alone. I'll . . ."

"No need. Master Leonard is leaving," Master Penteney said lightly, none of the anger of a few moments ago in his voice at all. He and Master Leonard made surprisingly polite farewells, with Master Leonard saying he would be in Oxford a while yet and Master Penteney saying perhaps they would meet again. It was all mellow, with not a snap or sneer between them, and then Master Leonard and Richard must have both gone out because at the soft sound of the door closing, Master Penteney said, "So, Tom, what do you think of that?"

Quietly but strained, Basset said, "Which is the saint against ill luck and bad mischance? Because that's what this just was, wasn't it?"

This was too easy, Joliffe thought, ready to go on listening; but the crunch of gravel told him someone was on the path and he opened his eyes, saw Kathryn coming toward him, and stood up to bow to her. She dimpled at him and motioned for him to sit, scooped up the cat and sat herself on the bench's other end, the cat in her lap where it circled, kneaded a little, and curled down, all comfortable again and never a baleful look at her at all, while she said, "You've come for your boy and I've come for mine, yes?"

Given she was some few years younger than Lewis, that came oddly but Joliffe understood the point and said, "Indeed, but thought to let them finish their game first."

"Then you won't go anywhere until dark. Lewis can play hot-cold for hours. He likes it because for a while he knows more than somebody else does."

"We'll give them a little while longer and pry them loose?" Thwarted of his eavesdropping now that their talking, if not Kathryn's footsteps, would have warned Basset and Master Penteney there were people near the window, Joliffe felt no need to thwart anyone else.

"Just a very little while," Kathryn said. "Mother expects me back."

She looked briefly back the way she had come, as if her mother might be coming after her already.

"Where's his Matthew?" Joliffe asked with a nod toward Lewis who had just rolled off the bench with laughing too hard at Piers now peering under the back of the maidservant's veil in search of whatever they were hot-colding over.

"Having a half day off. He's very faithful but needs to be away sometimes, too."

And you? Joliffe thought. When you're married to him, will you be given half-days off sometimes? Or will it be forenoons, afternoons, and night times, too?

Kathryn looked back toward the door again and by her open delight at the sight of Simon just coming out Joliffe realized it had not been for her mother she had been looking. Simon gave a quick look around the garden and seemed to hesitate when he saw Joliffe, but Kathryn waved for him to come on, and when he did, she slid over on the bench, closer to Joliffe, to make room for Simon to sit beside her, asking him, "Did you bring it?" in a conspirator's eager, uneasy voice.

Simon pushed his left hand, hidden until then, out the end of his doublet's sleeve. In it was a small, parchment covered book, perhaps four inches by six, that he handed to her with an air of triumph, saying, "Of course."

"Oh," she said with pleasure and satisfaction, taking it from him.

That she could read was no surprise. Any woman who kept a household had to read and reckon to keep her accounts or else be left to the mercy of servants and shopkeepers. Mistress Penteney would have been teaching her—or seeing to it she was taught—since she was small. The surprise for Joliffe, looking over her shoulder, was that the book was in Latin. "*De Caelo et Mundo*," he read. "*Of Heaven and Earth*, Albertus Magnus."

Simon and Kathryn both looked at him, surprised and showing it. "You read," said Simon.

"It helps if I'm to learn my part in plays," Joliffe said dryly.

"But Latin," Simon said. "Did you learn it in a grammar school?"

Not about to explain his Latin-learning, Joliffe was spared finding a side-ways answer by Kathryn saying, "Simon wants to have a grammar school. He wants to teach Latin."

"Kathryn," Simon said, warning her of something.

Kathryn leaned to the side, bumping her shoulder against his companionably while going on to Joliffe, "He's good at teaching. He's taught me Latin."

"*Kathryn*."

"Oh, he's not going to tell Mother or Father. Are you?" she said at Joliffe.

"I've no reason to if they don't ask me, and I doubt they're going to ask me," Joliffe answered. "But you should know your father is in the room behind us."

Kathryn and Simon looked over and up at the window with alarm, but Kathryn immediately eased and said, albeit in a lower voice, "He's talking with someone."

And I wanted to hear them, Joliffe thought, while saying, also quietly, "Your father and mother don't like you learning Latin?"

"They don't know about the Latin. What they don't like is Simon wanting to have a grammar school and teach."

"I'm supposed to become a victualler and travel and merchant for Master Penteney on Lewis's behalf," Simon said.

"You don't want to travel?"

"I want to travel. I just don't want to merchant or be a victualler." He said it lightly, but Joliffe thought there was unhappiness flickering behind the words. As well there might be if there were something else he truly wanted for his life.

Kathryn bumped against his shoulder again. "Once I'm married to Lewis, I'll get you the money for your school."

Simon smiled and bumped his shoulder to hers. "As if they'll let you."

Uncomfortable with the sudden feeling that the unhappiness behind Simon's smile and lightness was for something deeper than not wanting to be a merchant or a victualler, Joliffe asked, knowing he should let it lie, "When's this marriage to be?" Asking Kathryn but watching Simon.

Simon went on smiling but his eyes were suddenly sick, though Kathryn answered blithely enough, "Father thinks we should make our betrothal vows this Friday, with Lord and Lady Lovell here to hear them. Then the first banns can be read in church on Sunday."

"And they can be married before Lammas," said Simon. He stood up. "I'd best away." He pointed at the book. "Don't let your mother see it."

Kathryn made a face at him while tucking the book into the housewifely purse hung from her belt. "I won't. I never."

"You did once and she nearly threw it in the fire. My Latin grammer," he added to Joliffe.

"But she didn't throw it in the end," Kathryn said.

"No, but it took you a month to woo her into giving it back to me. She doesn't hold with the time I spend with books," he explained to Joliffe. "Kathryn had to swear she hadn't learned any Latin from me."

"Well, I hadn't yet," Kathryn said. "Nor did she make me promise I wouldn't. I told her I'd taken the book from him in sport, and that was true, too. Sport is done for pleasure, and learning is a pleasure."

If she was that well-witted at wriggling around things, it was a waste she couldn't be a lawyer, Joliffe thought. Or at least married to Simon. That she would be married off to Lewis seemed an even greater waste than it had at first.

Across the garden Piers yelled, laughing, at Lewis, "You didn't say it was the thimble on her finger! It's supposed to be something you hide!"

"Time we fetched our boys," said Kathryn.

The rest of the day and evening went all as planned and perfectly. Basset had settled with Master Penteney for the players and Lewis to have their supper before the household did, Matthew on duty again to help contain Lewis's excitment. Then, while the household dined, they readied for the play and at the meal's end came into the hall to do it while the household was still at table.

Joliffe, Ellis, and Basset somewhat raced through their

part of it, to bring Lewis and Piers on the sooner, and that was just as well since once Lewis and Piers were on it seemed they would never get off, chasing Ellis around and around while the household roared with laughter. When Ellis had had enough and made his escape, the two of them turned to pretending to attack people along the benches until Matthew collared Lewis and Joliffe collared Piers and made them take their bows to everyone's applause.

Ellis and Basset joined them, and when even Lewis had had enough, he was led off to bed and they returned thankfully to the barn.

"And the only time Lewis poked you was your own doing. You dodged the wrong way," Basset said to Ellis as they sorted themselves toward bed. "The boy is a wonder. And here." He tossed a coin toward Rose who was sitting on Pier's bed with her son's sleeping head in her lap. The coin in its momentary flight flickered gold in the lantern light. "Sign of Master Penteney's pleasure."

Rose caught it, held it into the light to see it better, and said, wonderingly, "A gold noble? He gave you a gold noble?"

"As you can see."

"Oh, Da," she said, smiling and sounding near to tears together. She closed her hand around the coin and pressed it to her heart. With that coin they were farther off from poverty than they had been for years.

Basset went to her, laid his hands gently on her shoulders, and kissed her forehead. "I know," he said, answering all the things she had not said but they all felt.

In that golden glow they went to bed. Joliffe slept deeply, and when he did awaken with the first graying of morning around the door, he made no move to rise, in no hurry to start a day he knew would be all work, readying the play for tonight.

So it was Ellis who arose first, yawning and scratching, and went with early morning bleariness out the door to see to his necessities . . . and a moment later stepped backward into the barn again, staring down at something on the ground outside.

And only after another long moment turned around to say slowly, stiff with disbelief, "There's a dead man out here."

Chapter 9

Except for Piers, still soundly sleeping, they all struggled up from their blankets to join Ellis at the door, Basset pulling it open wider so they could stare together at what was, beyond denying, a dead man lying on his back a very few yards away. A definitely dead man, because no one alive lay with such emptily staring eyes.

There was dawnlight enough by now to let them see that, and that meant there was light enough other people were surely up and around; and because it would be better if they weren't found standing there staring at a dead man, Basset said tersely, "Don't anyone touch him. Joliffe, go find someone. At the stables. That will be quickest. There'll be men sleeping there. Have someone from there go to tell Master Penteney."

As Joliffe went, Ellis was putting his arm around Rose, telling her, "Come back inside. You're shivering, love," while Basset muttered to himself, "There goes the day."

He made no mistake there. Joliffe gave word to a yawning stablehand just coming down the ladder from the loft, left him yelling to his fellows, and returned to join Basset and Ellis in guard over the body, that no one do anything with it until Master Penteney could take charge and give whatever orders would be necessary until the crowner came. As first-finders, reporting and keeping watch over the body was their duty, but more than duty, it was necessity and they knew it without need to say so to each other. Wandering, lordless players were always the first and easiest to accuse of anything that happened awry and a dead man was something very awry indeed, making it to their best interest to guard the body, that no evidence be spoiled before the crowner came, it being the crowner's duty to investigate, in the king's name, any unexpected deaths, to find out their cause and determine whether they were a matter for the sheriff.

Not that there would be much question of cause here, Joliffe thought, looking down at the dead man. In the rapidly growing morning light what had been a darkness all over the front of the man's doublet had taken on color, the dark red of dried—or drying—blood. Joliffe stooped and touched a finger to it. Dried. The man had been dead a while.

He wasn't anyone Joliffe remembered seeing here at the Penteneys'. His clothing was too good for him to be simply a servant anyway and, besides, he wore a rider's tall boots. Not of the best make, Joliffe noted, and well-worn with much use.

One of the man's arms was bent across his body. The other lay flung out to the side. Joliffe lifted the nearer hand a little from the ground. There was some stiffening in the arm, not much, but the night had been warm enough that stiffening would have been delayed. Or the man had been dead long enough the stiffening was wearing off rather than coming on.

"Joliffe," Basset said warningly.

Joliffe straightened.

"Here they come," said Ellis.

The man Joliffe had spoken to at the stable had already gone at a run to the house. Now his fellows from the stable, looking tumbled out of sleep, were coming from the stable.

"At least the fact he's stiffened and the blood is dried means Ellis didn't step out the door just now and stab him," Joliffe said before they were near.

"What?" Ellis said. Distracted between the coming men and Joliffe, he took a moment to catch up, then said angrily, "Of course I didn't stab him, you dolt. Tell him to shut up, Basset."

"Shut up, Joliffe," Basset said obligingly and Joliffe did, leaving it to Basset and Ellis to warn the men to stand back and, no, they didn't know how the man had come there but it looked like he'd been dead a while, stabbed, yes, by the look of it, no, best leave him for the crowner to see . . .

Master Penteney came striding across the yard, bedgown wrapped around him and shoes loose on his feet. The men already around the body stood aside for him. Others were following from the house, led by Master Richard somewhat more dressed than his father in hosen, shoes, and shirt, but before they overtook him Master Penteney had time to stand over the dead man, looking down at him in silence for a long moment. Then, just before the others caught up to him, he shifted his eyes without raising his head to look at Basset standing on the other side of the body from him.

Joliffe, drawn a little to one side, was able to see but not read the brief, deep look between them, something unsaid but understood passing between them before Master Penteney turned and began giving orders to the other men and the exclaiming maidservants flocking behind them from the house. Crisply, he named off two men who were more into their clothes than most were, ordering, "Jankin, go to Master Barentyne. He's crowner at present. You know where he's staying. Foulke, fetch the nearest of the constables. On your way, tell Father Francis what's here and that he's needed."

The men bowed and left at a run. Master Penteney sent others to take up guard at the two gateways into the yard. "To keep people out when word of this spreads," he said. "It's too late to hope to keep the murderer in. Whoever did this is long gone."

Or still here and set to dare it out, Joliffe thought but did not say.

Some of the maidservants cried out at mention of a murderer, ready to be fearful, but Master Penteney curtly shushed them and sent them and most of the men about their morning business, ordering, "We're all going to want our breakfasts and you all have your work that needs doing. Get on with it," so that at the end, only Master Penteney, Master Richard, Basset, Ellis, and Joliffe were left beside the body, with Piers craning his head around the barn door and Rose holding him there from behind with her hands on his shoulders.

"Not," Master Penteney said in a suddenly weary voice to Basset, "any of your doing, I presume."

It was not even a question and before Basset could say anything back, Master Richard interrupted, "It's the man who was here yesterday, isn't it? You talked with him yesterday afternoon."

"He was here and I talked to him, yes," Master Penteney said. "Hubert Leonard. Late of Abingdon."

And now, courtesy of a knife to his heart, of nowhere at all, Joliffe thought. So this had been the man with the sneer to his voice. He had no sneer now, only a slack-jawed blankness.

Mistress Penteney, dressed and her hair covered with a close-fitting cap, came from the house carrying something over her arm. Since Master Penteney's back was to her, Basset warned, "Mistress Penteney coming . . ."

"Stay here," Master Penteney said to his son and went to meet her, taking her by the arm and turning her away before she was near enough to see the dead man clearly. What passed between them was said so low it went unheard but to Joliffe it looked—to guess by her gestures—that Mistress Penteney's greater concern was not about the dead man but to have her husband into the house, out of the morning damp, and dressed. Master Penteney seemed to agree with her and called, "Come here for your doublet, Richard. Geva sent it. I'm going in to dress."

Master Richard went to his mother while Master Penteney started for the house, and as soon as they both were out of whisper-range, Ellis asked, "None of us know this dead man, do we?"

Joliffe readily shook his head that he did not but Basset said slowly, "When I went to see Master Penteney yesterday, this fellow was just leaving."

"Had they been quarreling?" Ellis asked.

"Not a word that I heard."

Joliffe kept silent but Ellis said, "That's all right then. We don't want anything should happen to Penteney. Not while he's doing us so much good."

"Ellis," Rose said, in the voice she used to remind Piers of his manners.

"Or any other time either," Ellis belatedly added.

Master Richard came back, fastening his doublet. "A bad business," he said.

"It is," agreed Basset.

A brief silence closed on them after that, before Rose said, "Come in and dress, you three," and withdrew into the barn, pulling Piers with her. With a murmured asking pardon of Master Richard by Basset, they followed her, dressed without saying much to each other, and suffered Rose to tidy them afterwards. As she pointed out while she did, "The more like honest folk we look the less trouble there'll be for us. Maybe."

Maybe. Besides that lordless players were always an easy mark when blame needed to be laid somewhere, it was not going to help that they were first-finders of the body. That much was such a given that Joliffe did not even dwell on it but was thinking over Basset's answer to Ellis. Basset had said he'd not heard Master Penteney quarreling with this Hubert Leonard and that was true enough. What Basset hadn't said was that he must know something about the man because why else would Master Penteney have asked him what he thought "of that." Which raised the question of what was "that" and why should Basset have any thought on it at all? And what was the "ill luck and bad mischance" in him being there at the same time as this Leonard? If that was what he had meant when he said it.

Rose brought out some of the hard-baked biscuits she kept for tight times, saying, "Eat. Food will help us keep our wits about us and there's no saying whether we'll have breakfast today or not. Piers, come away from the door," she added for something like the fifth time.

"I want to see . . ."

"You've seen dead men before now and you've seen this one enough. Just stay away from there. You and I will wait while the men handle this."

"Lewis . . ."

"Will be waiting, too, while the men handle it. You

couldn't be with him today anyway. We have two plays to rehearse."

And good luck to our getting to, Joliffe did not say, knowing the thought was in all their heads as he followed Basset and Ellis outside again. The sun was risen now, its light spread bright as daffodils across the yard, welcome for the promise it gave of another warm, clear day. Master Richard was still waiting beside the body, his back to it, but his waiting almost done if Joliffe rightly guessed that the two men coming through the streetward gateway were the priest and either the town crowner or else the constable.

Master Penteney's messengers had been quick but so had Master Penteney. He came out of his door to meet the men as they crossed the yard. He now wore a three-quarters-long dark blue houppelande belted low around his waist, the full sleeves hanging open from his shoulders to show the close-fitted sleeves of a dark blue doublet underneath. His hosen were black, but his low-cut leather shoes had been dyed to match his gown, and all in all Joliffe guessed that, like the players, he had dressed to show his respectability to the face of authority. A murdered man in your yard was a trouble no matter who you were. It was therefore best to make your importance plain from the very beginning if you could, and Master Penteney had far more with which to impress authority than the players had any hope of.

"The priest, I take it," Basset said to Master Richard. "The other man?"

"Master Crauford, the constable. But there's Master Barentyne come now, too," Master Richard added as a third man, accompanied by a clerk, came through the gate and joined the others now in talk with Master Penteney in the middle of the yard. "He's not properly crowner, is Barentyne. He's only helping out his cousin who badly broke a leg at Easter," Master Richard added, and Joliffe thought: not good, because it raised the chance of an inexperienced non-crowner who either knew he didn't know what he was doing, had been hoping nobody would die on him, and would make as short work of the business as he could rather than trying to do it right and well; or else he might be so overeager to prove he deserved his place that he would make more trouble about things than there had to be.

Master Penteney and the newcomers started down the yard toward the barn. He sent a look toward the men clustered by the stable door, silently reminding them they had work to do before breakfast; they disappeared into the stable. Someone else was probably doing much the same in the house; the faces that at been at all the upper windows were disappearing. Only Master Richard and the players stayed where they were, with Joliffe trying to guess something about the bailiff and Master Barentyne as they approached.

Master Crauford was the older, with the settled, irked look of someone who had dealt with students and their foolishnesses and the quarrels they made with Oxford townsfolk for more years than was good for him. The one necessary thing with him, Joliffe knew from experience with others of his kind, was never to let him think his authority was doubted or challenged. If once he took against someone on that account, neither rhyme nor reason would ever serve to put him on their side again.

Master Barentyne was younger and looked somewhat more eager to his work than the constable. If he were busy-brained to sniff out trouble, any trouble, whether it was there or not, he could well be more a problem than the constable, but if, on the other hand, he were set on finding out the truth rather than merely someone to blame, he could be the players' best hope of not being scapegoated. There was

nothing for it but to wait and see, and—waiting to see—
Joliffe put on his best "I'm here but I don't really matter"
manner. Ellis had once described it as, "As close to respectful as you ever bother to go," which Joliffe had
thought was somewhat unfair, albeit not entirely untrue.

The priest set to his prayers while Master Crauford,
Master Barentyne, and his clerk all took a long look at the
body and Master Penteney gave names all around. The
players bowed. Master Crauford returned them a beady-
eyed stare and a grunt but Master Barentyne looked at them
as if to be sure of knowing them one from the other later
on. That could be either a good thing or a bad, depending
on how this went, but it seemed a good start, anyway.

Even as a kind of under-crowner, Master Barentyne had
precedence over Master Crauford and asked him, although
with all courtesy, "Master Crauford, would you be so good
as to question the stablemen where each of them were last
night and when they came home to bed?"

Master Crauford accepted the charge with a grumping
nod and, "Aye." He bent and moved the dead man's head,
feeling for the stiffness, and added, "Dead since middle of
the night, maybe earlier. I'll ask if any of them heard anything in the night, too, and if they know the man or have
seen him besides dead here."

"He said his name was Hubert Leonard," offered Master Penteney.

Master Crauford gave him a sharp look but left it to
Master Barentyne to say, "You know him then?"

"He was here yesterday." A thing Master Penteney had
as well admit because enough people had seen the fellow
here that someone would say it sooner or later.

"'Said' his name was Hubert Leonard?" Master Barentyne asked.

"That's who he said he was," Master Penteney said carefully. "But he may have had other name or names. I think he may have been a Lollard."

Everyone, including Joliffe, startled and stared at him. Lollard might be a foolish-sounding name and Lollards were considered fools because of their heresies, but they had been very effectively plaguing both the Church and the law with their heretical arguments and disbelief and occasionally even armed revolts for sixty years and more. The more open of them were perforce pursued to the death for their heresies, but a great many more kept their beliefs secret, with even greater need to be secret of late, since one of their uprisings here around Oxford three years ago had been threat enough to need the king's uncle, the duke of Gloucester, with an army to put it down. There had been trials and hangings for treason afterward, but no one doubted there were still Lollards about. To admit to knowing one without having given him over to authorities was perilous. That gave Master Penteney reason to hedge what he said, but to accuse a man of maybe being a Lollard was an ill thing, too, and Master Barentyne demanded, "Why did you think that of him?"

"Because he wanted I should give him money for my brother."

"Your brother?" Master Crauford echoed with surprise and distaste. "St. Frideswide be with us. You mean your brother is still alive? I haven't thought or heard of him since I don't know when."

"Nor have I either," Master Penteney said, somewhere between anger and sorrow. "And wouldn't now if I could help it."

"Your brother?" Master Barentyne asked. "I've never heard you had a brother."

"To all intents I don't," Master Penteney said bitterly.

"He ran off years ago," Master Crauford said. "How long has it been? It was when that heretic Payne had to run for it."

"Payne?" Master Barentyne asked. "Peter Payne?"

"That's him," Master Crauford said. "You've heard of *him*, belike. He made trouble enough here in Oxford that he's still talked of sometimes. There's those of us here then that remember the man himself, damn his soul."

The priest stood up from kneeling beside Leonard's body, saying as he did, "No need for you to damn his soul, George Crauford." He nodded at Master Barentyne's clerk who promptly bent to start going over the body. "Payne has already done that for himself a hundred times over. I still pray for your brother, though," he added to Master Penteney.

"My thanks," Master Penteney answered.

"Payne was a scholar and master at the university here, yes?" Master Barentyne said as if digging remembrance out of far corners of his mind. "There was scandal about his teachings, wasn't there, and he left?"

"There was scandal and more," the priest answered. "His heresy became so open he was going to be arrested and tried for it, but he disappeared, fled abroad, and finally ended up on the other side of Europe, in that whole country of heretics, Bohemia. He's been writing his filth and making trouble from there ever since. Twenty years has it been?" he asked of Master Crauford and Master Penteney.

"At least," Master Crauford answered.

"What did your brother have to do with him?" Master Barentyne asked Master Penteney.

"He took up with Payne. Was taken in by him."

"He had to leave even before Payne did, didn't he?" Master Crauford said. "That business about the University's seal."

To Master Barentyne's questioning look, Master Penteney explained, "There was a flare of Lollardy about that time. The heretics here were in touch with others of their kind not only in England but across Europe. Somehow a letter went out to those in Bohemia, where they're the worst, that the University of Oxford supported them and their heresies. The University supported no such thing, but the University's seal was attached to the damnable letter. It was never proven who was responsible for it but . . ." he stopped, not happy with what he had to say but forcing himself to go on, ". . . my brother had something to do with it, that's sure. When he came under close suspicion, he fled. Our father disinherited him and that's the last we knew about him."

"I've never heard this," Master Richard said, sounding as if he only half-believed it now that he had.

"It was before I'd met and married your mother. Twenty-five years ago at least. Long enough that talk about it has long since died out. Until now." Master Penteney was openly bitter over that. "We've known where Payne has been all these years, but I didn't know whether my brother was alive or dead and I didn't care. Then this fellow shows up." He gave a hard glance at the dead man. "He says my brother has been with Payne all this time, has fallen into trouble and is in prison and needs my money. He asked for a note in hand to a French merchant I vaguely know, saying he could collect the money from him on his way back to my brother. I told him I kept my money for better things than traitors and heretics and sent him away."

"But you didn't report him?" Master Barentyne said.

"For what? He claimed that he'd never met my brother, was only a go-between for merchants, picking up this job on the side."

"But you thought he might be a Lollard himself?" Master Crauford asked.

"Afterwards, when he was gone, it crossed my mind. He never said anything to betray certainly he was but . . . there was something felt wrong about him."

Priest and bailiff nodded, understanding what he meant. Joliffe noted Master Barentyne gave no nod but instead asked, "Was he telling the truth, do you think? About your brother?"

"I don't know," Master Penteney said. "I didn't quite believe him but there was nothing I could point a sure finger at. He had a letter in what looked to be my brother's hand, but it's been twenty-five years since I saw his writing and I'd not swear to it. Whether this Leonard was telling the truth or not made no difference anyway. I wasn't going to give him anything except good-bye, and that's what I did."

"Did you keep the letter?" Master Crauford asked.

"He took it away with him."

Master Barentyne's clerk looked up from going through the dead man's clothing. "There's no letter on him now. Nor any money either. Or any weapon."

"He had a dagger and purse hung from his belt yesterday," Master Penteney said.

"Robbed," Master Crauford said. "Murdered and robbed and it probably had nothing to do with whether he was a Lollard or not. I'm off to question the stablemen."

He strode away.

"He's been stabbed once," the under-crowner's clerk said. He had opened the front of the man's doublet and shirt to see the wound. "Straight to the heart from the front."

"Was it a dagger?" Master Barentyne asked. "Not a sword?"

"Too narrow for a sword blade. A dagger, certes."

"Was he down or up when it was done?"

"We'll be better able to tell when we fully see the body but . . ." The clerk was fumbling under Leonard's back, feeling for the wound there. "But the wound is small back here. I'd say the dagger's point came out but barely. So either it was a short dagger or he was down and whatever he was lying on stopped the thrust."

"Sleeping, maybe."

"Maybe. Couldn't say. It's a very straight thrust, though. Not as if he were fighting it off."

Master Barentyne looked up from leaning over his clerk's shoulder and explained to Master Penteney, "Master Sampson has been the Oxford crowner's clerk since forever. Crowners come and crowners go and my cousin says that if they've any sense, they listen to what Sampson tells them."

"His knuckles on the right hand are scraped," Joliffe said. From the side of his eye he saw Ellis's arm twitch as if barely held back from elbowing him to keep quiet. "And there's a bruise on his chin."

Master Sampson looked at Leonard's chin and agreed, "There is."

"Like someone hit him," Joliffe suggested.

Master Sampson looked up from under his brows, maybe not liking help with his work, but instead of answering, he picked up the dead man's right hand for a better look and said, "They're scraped, right enough."

"Like he'd hit someone," Joliffe said. Ellis's elbow twitched again.

"Or something," the clerk said. "There's the possibility it was something he hit instead of someone." He felt along the sides of the dead man's head and under it. "There's a lump here, on the back. Someone hit him maybe."

He gave Joliffe a look but Joliffe left it to Master Barentyne to say, "Or he fell. He was fighting with someone, hit them, was then hit in the jaw himself and knocked down, maybe knocked out. Then someone stabbed him and robbed him. That would be possible."

"But why was he dumped here?" Master Penteney demanded. "Because you can see he wasn't killed here. There's not any blood except on him."

"He looks to have been dragged," Joliffe said. "There's mud on his heels."

Both Ellis and Master Sampson gave him hard looks, with Ellis's look, at least, suggesting the next murder might be of him; but Master Barentyne bent over to see Leonard's feet, touched the mud caked on the soft-leather heels of his thin-soled boots, and said, "It's dried but, yes, he must have been dragged through mud sometime, once he was down and probably dead." Master Barentyne straightened and looked around the yard. There were no muddy places. "Master Sampson, would you check the way outside the rear gate there, please you? See if there's any mud in sight."

Sampson immediately stood up and went. Joliffe held silent despite that he knew the lane's hard-trammeled earth had been dust-dry yesterday and there had been no rain to change it. Master Barentyne looked at the players. "None of you heard anything in the night?"

"Only the usual stableyard noises early on," Basset answered. "Then I slept and didn't wake until dawn."

Joliffe and Ellis said the same.

"None of you had to relieve yourselves in the night? That could give us some thought of when the body was left here."

Joliffe, Ellis, and Basset all shook their heads.

"There's just the three of you?" Master Barentyne asked.

"And my daughter and her son. He's nine years old," Basset said. "They've neither of them said they heard anything either."

"I'll ask them anyway. Not that there was likely much to hear." Because soft-soled shoes or boots made little sound even on cobbles, let alone the packed earth of this end of the yard. The laying down of a body need not be loud either, if care was taken. "Do you keep a guard here in the yard at night, Master Penteney?"

"Not this time of year. There's nothing in particular to steal and anything there may be is locked up. Master Barentyne. I have guests coming to stay. From sometime this afternoon until Sunday, Lord and Lady Lovell are to be here. Tonight I'm feasting them and Master Gascoigne and some of the others of the University. These men are to perform a play for us all." He indicated Basset, Ellis, and Joliffe. "Much though this man's death is to be regretted, it would be a great help if his body could be taken away and if your questions wait until later."

"There's no trouble about having the body away," Master Barentyne said easily. "If you could loan me two men to do it, I'll take it with me when I go."

"My thanks."

"The questions aren't so easily set aside, though. The sooner they're asked the better. I think I can have them soon done, though. Within the hour probably. Will that do well enough?"

Master Penteney said that it would. Joliffe was beginning to form a good opinion of Master Barentyne, with a growing suspicion that he was not actually of Oxford; he lacked the deference he likely would otherwise have had toward a man of Master Penteney's wealth and importance. He was respectful, yes, but out of courtesy rather than necessity, Joliffe thought. He was not someone who had to

worry over Master Penteney troubling his life once he was
out of office.

"I doubt we'll find this Leonard was murdered here,"
Master Barentyne was saying. "My questioning will
mostly be elsewhere, I think, and leave you untroubled.
Anything there, Master Sampson?" he asked of the returning clerk.

"No mud, sir, and the ground is too hard and dry for any
tracks that might mean anything."

"Worse luck. Rain all spring and dry weather just now.
Here's what we're going to do, because Master Penteney is
expecting Lord and Lady Lovell today and we want to be
out of the way before they come. When Master Crauford is
done with the stablemen, two of them can carry the body
away. By your leave?" he paused to ask Master Penteney,
who nodded ready agreement. Master Barentyne went on,
"While we're waiting for that, I'm asking you to stay with
the body while I go through the players' things to see if
there's any evidence there they had anything to do with
this. While I do that, Master Penteney is going to ready his
household for whatever questions Master Crauford and I
will then be asking them. If you please, sir?" he added to
Master Penteney, who again bent his head in agreement.

Since their agreement was not going to be asked, Joliffe
and Ellis simply stepped aside to let Basset lead Master
Barentyne into the barn ahead of them. Rose had surely
been listening. She was just inside the door, curtsying to
Master Barentyne as Joliffe and Ellis entered. Standing beside her, Piers was looking fierce and did not bow until his
mother, rising from her curtsy, slapped him on the back.

He bowed then, still scowling. Master Barentyne, pretending not to notice, said to her, "I beg your pardon, but I
have to look through your belongings. Will you help me,
that I do no harm to anything?"

Rose's stiffly courteous face eased a little. "Gladly, sir."

He turned to Basset, Ellis, and Joliffe. "First, though, may I see your daggers? And would you set the doors wider open, to give more light?" he asked of Piers.

With a slight shove from his mother, Piers went to do it while the three players unsheathed their daggers and held them out, hilts forward. Master Barentyne took them one by one and looked at each of them closely, especially near where the blade met the crossguard, the most likely place for blood to be left after a careless cleaning.

That done and nothing found, Master Barentyne went through their various hampers and the cart with Rose's help. He was quick at it but thorough and careful. He was on the last hamper, dragged from the far inside of the cart, packed with properties they did not need this week, when Joliffe gave way to his curiosity and asked, "So you think mayhap one of us—or several of us—was drunk enough to have killed this man and left his body lying outside our own door, but had wit enough to get rid of all the other evidence?"

Master Barentyne looked up from the folded clothing in the basket and smiled. "No, I don't think that. If you'd been drunk enough to leave the body lying there, I doubt you'd have had wit enough even to clean your daggers. Besides, none of you stink of drink this morning and you'd have to be stinking drunk to leave your victim's body at your own door. I'm only searching your goods so I can say afterwards that, no, there was no sign any of you had done it or even sign any of you had been drunk enough to do it."

"So you don't think it's one of us at all," said Piers indignantly.

"No."

Piers glared. "Then why bother us like this?"

"Because it's not enough that I think a thing. I have to show others, too, that it wasn't likely to have been any of you, no matter how much somebody might want it to be. Which very likely someone does, or the body wouldn't have been left here."

"Oh," said Piers a little blankly, seeing what he had not seen before.

"You believe the body was moved here, then. For certain," Basset said.

"For certain," Master Barentyne agreed. "Unless I can think of some other way mud got on his heels that way, and where the rest of the blood went."

Chapter 10

Finished with their belongings, Master Barentyne wandered through the rest of the barn, back and forth from one side to the other its whole length, presumably looking for mud, blood, or a discarded dagger but more for the form of the business than as if he expected to find anything. The players stayed where they were near the cart, watching him, saying nothing, waiting for him to finish and Joliffe thinking that despite how quickly, seemingly casually Master Barentyne went at his looking, he would have missed nothing if it had been there to find.

Thankfully, nothing was. Master Barentyne finished his search and came back to where they waited. "How long do you mean to be in Oxford?" he asked Basset.

"We perform at St. Michael Northgate on Corpus Christi and will likely stay at least a day longer before taking to the road again."

"Here?"

"By Master Penteney's leave, yes."

Master Barentyne turned to Rose. "My apologies to

you, mistress, for your trouble, and my thanks for your help."

"You've been all kindness, sir," Rose said back with a low curtsy.

Master Barentyne slightly bowed his head to her, then to Basset who in return bowed deeply but plainly, not spending a flourish he probably judged would be wasted on someone not likely to be impressed. Master Barentyne likewise nodded to Ellis and Joliffe, who likewise bowed. Then he left. Not needing to be told, Piers followed him to the doors, and when he had gone out, pulled one of them shut and the other almost shut, then waited, as they were all waiting, until they heard Master Barentyne begin to give orders for the body to be moved.

Assured by that that the man was indeed done with them, Basset heaved a great sigh. "That's it then. Unless something goes woeful wrong, we're off that hook. Thank St. Genesius for fair-minded men and may he send more of them our way. Right. To *The Pride of Life*."

No one protested being set to work. By not going into breakfast, they avoided the talk and questions there surely would have been, and work made a welcome refuge from thinking about anything else. They went at it with a will, keeping to it all the morning until by dinner's time even Basset was well-satisfied.

At the best, dinner would not have been much today, what with the whole household readying for tonight's feast. Even so, Joliffe guessed the thin-gravied, poorly seasoned stew ladled onto thick slabs of hard bread set at each place was mostly due to the morning's upset having reached the kitchen. Fairly enough, the Penteneys at the high table did not look to have much more, and oddly almost everyone seemed in good spirits. Leonard's death seemed to have darkened nobody's day, but that there was not even talk of it by anyone made Joliffe suppose that Master Penteney had warned his people off being distracted by it, must have even forbidden open talk of it, the business of readying for Lord and Lady Lovell being of more importance than an unknown dead man in their yard, by happenstance.

Only Lewis at the high table looked out of sorts, but that seemed to have nothing to do with the murder. He was restless, and over and over through the meal looked to be complaining at Simon and Kathryn beside him, pointing at Piers and making a show of not wanting his food. Once he started to slide down from his seat as if to make escape under the table but Simon and Kathyrn both caught him by the arms and Matthew stepped forward to help pull him, wiggling, back onto the bench. Mistress Penteney leaned forward then to say something at him and after that Lewis sat still, although his chin was sunk nearly to the tabletop and his lower lip thrust out, proclaiming his feelings no matter what he did not say or do.

At the end of eating, Master Penteney rose at his place to say he regretted the scant fare but trusted they all knew why. "I promise you," he said, "that there will be more than enough for all and everyone tonight."

That was greeted with raised cups and the laughter of a household well-pleased with their master and easily trusting his word. That he made no mention of the murder settled Joliffe's thought that he had forbidden talk of it for the time being. That left Joliffe, when grace was done and he and the others left the hall, to worry if Basset was going to keep them as hard at it this afternoon as he had through this morning; but when they were in the yard Basset said, "We did good work this morning. Unless we all lose our wits between now and tonight, the play ought to go well. What I think we must needs do now is see how things are at St. Michael's. Sire John promised their scaffold would be up

by now. We should see where we play tomorrow before
we're there to do it."

No one quarreled with that. Piers was sent to fetch the
men's hats from the barn and very shortly they were
headed down Magdalen Street and through the North Gate
into the town. Once through the gateway, the church's west
tower was close to the left around the corner, the church
stretching beyond it along the street there, with its churchyard at the far end for a fair distance farther, separated
from the street and its eastward neighbors by a tall wall,
with the town wall for its rear side.

As Basset had hoped, the scaffold was indeed standing
in the churchyard, set close to the town wall to leave room
in plenty between it and the street for an audience. It
looked encouragingly sturdy, made of heavy timbers and
thick floorboards, with the playing platform maybe six feet
above the ground and reached from behind by stairs almost
steep enough to be a ladder. It was a good-sized stage,
larger than their own, measuring maybe fifteen feet by fifteen feet, with the back third framed by wooden posts and
crosspieces from which curtains would hang to hide the
back of the stage from the audience. An elderly man, long
in his age-bent limbs and short of teeth, was seated on a
joint stool in the shade beneath it, leaning on a heavy-
headed wooden club. He narrowed his eyes as they came
toward him, hefted the club up to lie across his lap, and
crabbed at them as they came near, "The play is tomorrow
and ye've no business here before then."

Basset made him, of course, a flourishing bow. "Good
sir, here *is* our business. We're the players who will be using this scaffold tomorrow. We wanted to see it aforetime."

The old man went from crabbed to pleased. "The players, are you? Good! You'll find naught wrong with this
scaffold, I'll tell you. I made it myself, almost twenty years

ago, and it's done good service ever since with never a complaint from no one."

"I can see there wouldn't be," Basset said. While the old man talked, he was already looking to see how well the front posts joined to the stage, leaving Ellis and Joliffe to circle the scaffold, likewise looking at everything as the old man went on, "My sons put it together now I can't. They took over my carpenter's trade when I had to give it up, but I still keep my eye on their doings. There's no mistakes or I'd know the reason why."

There was indeed nothing to complain of. Scaffold and stage were well made and worth the old man's pride.

"And now you're guarding it?" Basset asked.

"Through the day. I've a grandson who'll do it tonight." The old man cracked a laugh. "And that won't cost the priest a penny. He set it to young Nick for penance, he did. Me, I get two pence for my sitting here, so I'm happy."

"You mean to fight troublemakers off with that club?" Ellis asked, jesting at him.

The old man cracked another laugh. "I'm smarter than that, you young louter." He reached behind him and lifted a long-handled fry-pan into sight from where it had been leaning against the stool. "I bang away on this and there'll be folk come do my fighting for me." He put the pan behind him again. "But there won't be trouble. There's nobody doesn't want to see the plays."

"Even Lollards?" Joliffe asked. "I hear Oxford has more than its share."

The old man spat into the grass beside him. "Lollards. They'd best know enough to keep their heads down and their mouths shut after the way Duke Humphrey finished with 'em, God bless and keep our good duke of Gloucester." He brightened. "Have ye heard there was a Lollard killed here last night? Not here but hereabouts? Stabbed

full of holes and thrown into somebody's stableyard with
his head beaten in and serve him right, God damn 'em all."

Rose who had been standing with her hand on Piers's
shoulder tightened her grip, warning Piers to hold his
tongue, while Joliffe and Ellis carefully showed nothing,
and Basset said smoothly, "We've heard that, yes. What a
pity to come to an end like that without chance to make his
peace with God."

The old man spat again. "If he'd not been a fool of a Lollard, he'd not have been in such need of making peace with
God. Probably wouldn't have come to such an end neither."

"May we go up, to have a feel for how much room we'll
have?" Basset asked.

"Surely, surely. Go on with you," the old man obliged
cheerfully. "You'll find no splinters or aught else to trouble you."

Nor did they. Ladder and stage were as smooth as hope
would have them. Likewise, a little subtle jouncing by Joliffe and Ellis made not even the slightest sway, and Basset
pushed and shoved at the frame that would hold the backcloth without wiggling it the least. Piers had scrambled up
the ladder after them but was content to stand at the forward edge, feet wide, hands on hips, gazing out on where
their audience would be.

Rose had stayed below, in talk with the old man, and had
him laughing when they descended the steps. Basset pointed
to the wooden pegs driven upward-slanting around three in-
sides of the scaffold's frame and asked, "For the hanging?"
that would close the understage and stairs from view.

"That's it, and a handsomer cloth you won't see at any
of the other churches, mark me. Here's Sire John. He'll
tell you."

A man in hale middle years, in a priest's plain black
gown and sober plain hat, had come into the churchyard

and was crossing toward them, smiling. As he came near, he exclaimed, "Master Basset!" and reached to grasp Basset's hand before Basset could bow, then turned his smile on the rest of the company. "And your fellow players." He rested a hand on Piers's curly head. "Our lamb of almost-sacrifice. Young Isaac, aren't you?"

Piers gave a bow worthy of his grandfather. "If it please you, sir, yes," he said in his brightest, I'm-a-good-boy voice.

"And Master Basset is God. That I know," Sire John said. He turned a questioning look on Joliffe and Ellis. "That leaves you two to be Abraham and the Angel."

They both bowed and Ellis said, "I'm Abraham, yes, and he'll be the Angel," with a nod at Joliffe.

"I heard you asking about the hanging," Sire John said to Basset. "You'll find no fault with it."

"I supposed not," Basset answered graciously.

"No, indeed. We've had it but four years. Some of our wealthiest parishioners paid for it and a mercer of the parish provided it. It will do you proud, I promise."

"We hope to do it proud, too," Basset said.

"There's provision made, too, for keeping folk from coming too far around the scaffold, just as you asked. Tomorrow there'll be some of our sturdiest young men to keep folk from seeing anything behind your curtains there." He nodded at the frame above the stage.

"You are a most excellent patron," Basset said. "I have to say we've never had better."

"My pleasure, I assure you. My pleasure indeed."

With mutual pleasures and their thanks to Sire John and the old man, they took their leave and were out of the churchyard and going back toward the North Gate before Ellis turned on Joliffe and demanded, "What is it with you and your mouth? What was that with bringing up Lollards for no good reason?"

"Ellis . . ." Basset started.

"Look!" Piers made to bound forward but Rose caught him by his doublet's collar and hauled him back.

"You stay with us," she said.

"But look! Something's going on!" Piers pointed more insistently and no one argued that he wasn't right. Ahead of them the flow of people had thickened and bunched and come to a stop with all their heads craned leftward, completely blocking any way onto Northgate Street and to the gateway. Across the street more crowd was gathered, looking the same way and now the players were close enough to catch the excited repeating of "Lord Lovell. It's Lord Lovell."

"That's what it is, then," Basset said. "Lord Lovell and his people are come and heading toward the Penteneys."

"I want to see!" Piers demanded. So did the rest of them, but there was small hope of pushing through the crowd. The best they could hope for was seeing past other people's heads, except Ellis swung Piers up to straddle his shoulders with the warning, "Don't kick me or you'll come down head-first, whelp."

Piers exclaimed, "Here they are!" as the first horsemen came into view. Their horses were mostly out of sight beyond the crowd but the riders were plain enough—men in matching livery of muted red, Lord Lovell's foreriders making sure the way was cleared for their lord and lady. Behind them came another rider bearing aloft the Lovell banner with its nebuly bars of gold and gules across it, and after him rode Lord Lovell and his lady themselves, both dressed in red that matched their banner but Lord Lovell with a green hat with a wide liripipe draped from one side of the padded roll and slung over his shoulders, while Lady Lovell had only the smallest of wimples circling her face under the slightest of padded circlets from which her white veil floated lightly back.

Lord Lovell looked a hale, long-faced man with a long-swooped nose; Lady Lovell showed as fine and fair a lady as comfortable living and good care could make her; and they both nodded and smiled friendliwise to the crowd on either side as they passed. It raised Joliffe's hope that they would be willing to be pleased by the play tonight. There were few things worse than playing to people determined not to be diverted.

They passed out of sight through the gateway. There was a glimpse of the top of the heads of two children riding behind them and then the rest of their household was passing pair by pair, men and women both—knights and ladies, squires and gentlemen, Joliffe supposed—maybe a dozen altogether and all in holiday finery of bright summer colors—greens and blues and flower-reds and sunshine yellow—and after them the necessary servants, easy to know in their Lovell livery. Not interested in servants, the crowd was breaking up, with grumbling from some that no coins by way of largess had been scattered to make it worthwhile to watch at all.

"Cheap, that's what he is," one man was saying as he and another elbowed between Joliffe and Basset. "Spend a fortune on himself and his, but never a half-penny for anyone else, I've heard."

Ellis, setting Piers down, muttered for only the other players to hear, "Why *should* he pay for them to gawk at him doing naught but ride by?"

"Because they want him to pay, that's why," said Joliffe. "What better reason than 'I want' do most men need?"

"Don't turn philosopher on me," Ellis snapped. "You'll philosophize to the devils dragging you down to Hell when the time comes."

"I'll not. I'll be too busy arguing mightily they've made a grave mistake and should be tossing me up the other way."

Piers bent over with a whoop of laughter. "Grave mistake. Because you'll be dead and buried in a grave. Grave mistake!"

The others looked at each other over his head, Rose fighting a smile before Ellis said grumpily, "Well, I'm not for going back to Penteneys yet, with that lot being sorted out all over the place. Who's for a drink to pass an hour until we can go back?"

Rose was readying a protest against that but Basset slapped him on the shoulder, said, "I'll stand you your drink, man," and sent Rose a glance that said he'd see to it being all right. "You, too, Joliffe?"

Knowing he would probably give way to the urge to aggravate Ellis and that this was not the time for that, Joliffe said, "No. I think I'll walk about a bit."

"Me, too," Piers declared. "I'll go with you."

"And so will I," Rose said, taking firm hold on Piers's hand.

"You're just afraid I'll lose him in the crowds," Joliffe said, unoffended because he supposed he probably would. Not that Piers was likely to come to harm and couldn't find his way back to the Penteneys easily enough if he wanted to.

"It's not your losing him I fear," said Rose. "It's what he'll get up to once he's lost *you* that I worry on."

Joliffe laughed, took Piers's other hand, and the three of them turned back past the church again, leaving Basset and Ellis to whatever tavern they chose.

If the crowding in the streets had not already shown the in-flow of folk for the Corpus Christi holidaying was well under way, the booths set and being set up along the street, ready to sell food and overpriced ale and wine, would have done it. So, too, would the gaudy-dressed jugglers, minstrels, and others with entertainments to offer spread through the crowd, hoping to catch people's eyes and farthings with their sports. Joliffe, all too certain that was what he and the others would have been doing except for Lewis and the Penteneys, turned a kindly eye their way but kept his farthings to himself.

Not so kindly, Piers said as they edged along the outside of a small gathering around a man juggling rainbow-dyed, leather-covered balls, "Ellis and I can do that better." Nor was he much more interested in a well-kept bear with shining black fur being led along on a chain, because neither the bear nor his bearward were doing anything, just going somewhere. The street widened where it passed another gateway through the town wall, giving space for a greater crowding of booths and people, but it was all much of the same with what they had already seen and Piers tugged at Joliffe and Rose's restraining hands, complaining, "I want to *do* something."

"Tomorrow there'll be things to do," Rose said.

"Tomorrow there's the play to do," Piers griped. "There's no sport in that."

"You didn't say you wanted sport," Joliffe pointed out. "You said you wanted to do something."

"You know what I meant!"

Rose, living not only with Piers but with three men who could turn cheerful talk into cheerful quarrelling as fast as she could turn a flat-cake on a griddle, was good at sudden distractions. They were just turning a corner in the street and she asked, "What's that place?" with a nod ahead of them toward yet another stone-towered gateway, this one with its thick oaken gates standing open to a wide, stone-paved yard surrounded by tall buildings.

Joliffe knew distraction when it was offered and answered readily, "That's New College. Not that it's all that new. Some bishop of Winchester founded it about fifty years ago. But it's the newest in Oxford, I think, unless there's been one made since . . ."

He broke off from what he had nearly said.

"Since when?" Piers promptly prodded.

"Since last I took any notice of colleges in Oxford," Joliffe said easily back.

"When did you ever take notice of colleges?" Piers
jeered.

"When it was either think about them or else about rude
little boys with no manners," Joliffe jeered back.

"Leave off," Rose said.

Beyond the gateway there was a sudden flurry of boys and
young men crossing the college's yard from one place to
someplace else, dark scholars' gowns flapping about them
and their voices raised in loud, confused talk with each other.

"Idiots," said Piers. "Shutting themselves up for years
with nothing better to do than read books and talk at each
other."

"May be," said Rose, "but those who see it through
come out fit for making a good living at more ease than
we're ever likely to know."

"You won't find me shut up like that for any reason,"
Piers retorted.

"That's sure," Rose agreed tartly. "Because even if you
wanted it, we couldn't pay the cost."

And yet behind the tartness Joliffe heard, even if Piers did
not, her half-wish—faint with knowing it was useless even as
she wished it—that there was hope of some other way for
Piers than this way they lived, uncertain of everything from
day to day and week to week, none of them even daring to
think about year to year; and because a little hope was better
than none, Joliffe said lightly, seemingly to Piers but meant
for her, "Well, if ever you change your mind, boy, there are
some get their learning here as someone else's servant. They
wait on a paying scholar and learn along with him."

Piers made a rude noise. "Shut up behind walls, stuck

with books, *and* having to wait on someone. Not for me, thanks."

"For which any number of scholars may thank their lucky stars," Joliffe said cheerfully.

The narrowing street took another turn and yet another, then straightened out toward Oxford's High Street, past the church of St. Peter in the East, St. Edmund Hall, and Queen's College. There were far less people here. The bustle and color were all ahead in the High Street except in Queen's College gateway where perhaps a dozen dark-robed scholars were gathered laughing around something or someone in their midst.

"Go see what's happening there," Joliffe told Piers.

"It'll just be another juggler or something," Piers scoffed but ran ahead anyway and began to burrow under elbows as a series of shrill yips that brought more laughter suggested that whatever was happening involved a small dog.

Rose and Joliffe kept their easy pace and stopped the other side of the street from the small crowd. Because there was not likely to be better chance than this, Joliffe asked, "About the dead man this morning. About him maybe being a Lollard."

"Oh, Joliffe," Rose sighed. "I only want to forget about him."

"There's nothing we have to worry about, is there?" Joliffe persisted. "None of us have had anything to do with Lollardy, have we? That you know of?"

"Not unless you were one before you joined us," she said so simply that he believed her because she was never good at lying. She refused to be that complicated. For her it was straight truth or nothing, and if she said none of them had ever had anything to do with Lollardy, then so far as she knew, none of them had.

To make a jest of his asking, he said, "No secret Bible

tucked away among the properties? No bundles of Lollard pamphlets in the hidden bottom in a basket that you go out secretly distributing when I'm safely asleep at night?"

"That Master Barentyne would have found them if I did, the way he went at everything. Why this sudden taking up of Lollards? Why look for trouble?"

"I suppose because I'd rather be looking for trouble than have it sneak up on me from behind. Master Penteney said the dead man was maybe a Lollard. That crowner and bailiff will both be taking hard looks at that."

"Um," Rose said, which might have meant anything.

They stood silent a few moments, watching the group across the street. Then Joliffe said lightly, "So Ellis has had nothing to do with Lollardy ever?"

With both disbelief and scorn, Rose said, "Can you honestly imagine Ellis talking on about the will of God and holy writ?"

In all honesty Joliffe could not. "What about Basset then?"

"I can see him talking about it. He'll talk about anything. But take it as darkly serious as Lollards do? Never."

"I've never heard him talk about religion at all."

"Then you can see how little he cares about it, if he doesn't even talk about it," Rose returned briskly. "Here, Piers."

The small crowd was breaking up around a short, bow-legged man and his rough little terrier dog. The man was bowing and turning in a circle, thanking all and sundry for the tossed coins ringing into the round-brimmed hat he was holding out while the dog balanced and bounced on its hind legs in front of him. Piers ran happily to his mother, a hand held out for a coin. Joliffe was quicker than she was, had a farthing out of his belt pouch before she had unfastened hers, and handed it to Piers who took it and spun to run back, nearly into collision with a skinny scholar who said, scowling, as Piers dodged clear of him, "*Puer inurbanus!*"

Without thinking Joliffe called after him, "*Stultus eruditus!*" The scholar stopped short and sharply turned around, his mouth open to answer that, then thought better of his dignity than to trade Latin insults in the street with someone so obviously beneath him, and went on into St. Edmund Hall.

Having tossed the coin into the man's hat. Piers came running back, exclaiming, "Joliffe, you know Latin! How do you know Latin?"

"What's the dog's name?" Joliffe immediately asked instead of answering.

"Riddelme," Piers said. "Did you see him? He can do backflips and everything. Mam, could I have a dog like him? I could train him and he'd show off and people would pay me . . ."

He was still trying to convince Rose he would *too* take care of a dog *and* train it and, *no*, he wouldn't lose interest in a week, when they came out into the broad High Street and turned right, heading back toward Northgate Street.

Oxford's High Street stretched east to west the whole length of the town, and since it was the main marketplace, the crowding of people and booths was greater here than everywhere else. In the crowding it was easier to let Rose and Piers, hand in hand again, go ahead, leaving it to Rose to sort out for Piers why he was not going to have a dog, while Joliffe trailed behind, keeping close but taking this first chance he had had today to think about this morning.

He had watched Basset as much as he watched the others. When Master Penteney began his lying to Master Barentyne and Master Crauford about Hubert Leonard, Basset had been almost not breathing, he was listening so intently. Only when the questions went beyond the dead man's pos-

sible Lollardy had Basset eased. Why? What about that
part of the questioning had mattered so much? There had
never been any sign of heresy about Basset in all the years
Joliffe had known him—and they all lived too much together for anything like that to have gone unseen. But this
morning Basset had been . . . afraid. Straight-forwardly
worried about the trouble that could have come to them because of the dead man would have been right enough, but
Joliffe would nearly swear he had been outright afraid of
something that could have been said. When whatever it
was had gone unsaid, he had eased.

Setting that against whatever he and Master Penteney
had secret between them and adding to it the fact that both
of them had known Leonard before yesterday—despite
what they had told and not told Master Barentyne—Joliffe
found himself having to think, to almost the point of certainty, that their shared secret might well have something
to do with this dead man. Because if it did, then the fact
that Master Penteney had so carefully lied about what had
actually passed between the man and him yesterday *and*
willingly brought up the Lollard could well mean their secret had to do with something even worse than heresy.
Worse enough that it was better to have people looking for
Lollards than some other way.

Joliffe began to be more than curious about Basset's secret with Master Penteney. He began to consider, following
Basset's lead, being afraid.

Chapter 11

By the time Joliffe, with Piers and Rose, had made their way back to the barn, Bassett and Ellis were already there, with Ellis beginning to be impatient for them. Rose turned his worry aside with a kiss on his cheek before setting to the work of persuading Piers that he was indeed going to lie down for at least a while.

"It will be a long evening. You'll want to stay awake for it," she said, laying out his mattress and pillow for him. "Now lie down."

Piers started a grumble that Basset cut off with, "That's your mother talking but this is your playmaster saying likewise. Lie down until she says differently."

Piers glowered and gave up. He could argue as well with his grandfather as with his mother or Ellis or Joliffe, but when "grandfather" turned into "playmaster" there was no more arguing and Piers lay down, flat on his back, stiff as a board, arms rigidly folded across his chest. Everyone else went on about their other business, ignoring him, and as usual in very little time his arms fell loose, he rolled over, curled onto his side, and was well away into sleep.

"He's so sweet when he's like that," Ellis said, lifting one of the garb baskets out of the cart. "Couldn't we give him a sleeping draught every now and then?"

"Say with every meal?" Joliffe suggested.

The four of them went over their clothing for tonight's play to be certain nothing needed doing—no trim restitched or button tightened or hem secured—but Rose had spent what time she could these past few days seeing to their garb for tonight and tomorrow; nothing needed to be done on anything. Then they brought out the properties, saw to them, packed tomorrow's away in one hamper and tonight's garb and properties into two other hampers, except Ellis kept out the King of Life's brass crown and sat down to polish it to a better sheen while Basset stretched out on his bed, laced his hands comfortably together over his stomach, and was soon snoring gently.

Rose smiled on him much as she had on the sleeping Piers, sat down on her cushion and took up a plain white shirt she was sewing for his everyday wear. When she had taken money to buy the cloth for it a few weeks ago, she had said, "Your old one is almost past scrubbable to whiteness anymore." And added as Ellis opened his mouth, "You'll have a new one next."

Rose would do as much for him, too, Joliffe knew, but he intended, maybe before they left Oxford, to buy a shirt for himself ready-made from a tailor and spare Rose at least that work. For the present, though, he occupied himself with sitting down, leaning back against the cart's near wheel, and running his lines for tonight through his head, shutting out the murmur of Ellis doing the same. It was Rose who kept an eye on the barn door's slant of shadow and in a while said, "It's probably time to go for our supper."

Joliffe stood up and stretched. "I'll go."

"Comb your hair first," Rose said without looking up and added to Ellis who had finished with the crown and was setting it atop the other properties in the hamper, careful his polished-smeared fingers did not touch it. "And you go wash your hands."

Joliffe and Ellis looked at each other and rolled their eyes.

Basset had settled earlier with Mistress Penteney that because they would be performing between two removes of the feast tonight, they would—like the servants who served the feast—eat before it started. Because it was always easier to be on their own rather than with others before performing, it had been likewise settled they would eat apart, in the barn. Joliffe only hoped someone in the kitchen had remembered that, because a cook interrupted in the throes of readying a meal always seemed to know where were the gristly bits of meat and the undercooked pastry and made sure of who got them.

Happily, having crossed the yard—presently clear of people and horses, the Lovells and their people long since settled in—and circled the house's far end to a small rear-yard and the kitchen door, he found that not only had the players been remembered but a skinny kitchen boy was loading their tray on a table just inside the door, almost out of the way of the bustling workers along both sides of the long worktable that stretched the kitchen's length well clear of the two fireplaces where pots bubbled and seethed and pans sizzled at one end while at the other something large had been roasting on a spit, to guess by the deep pan of dripping just being drawn off the fire for gravy-making. The smells were mingled and wonderful and Joliffe was instantly starving.

The kitchen boy, setting a covered platter on the tray beside a bowl of heavily buttered peascods, a dish of carrots roasted with herbs, and a large strawberry pudding, greeted him with a wide smile and, "I know you. You were the Devil when Master Fairfield was chasing that other man with a spear."

Joliffe rubbed himself behind as if remembering a wound and said ruefully, "You must not have seen when he missed the other man and got me."

That had not happened but the kitchen boy laughed as Joliffe had meant him to, while Joliffe lifted the cover from the platter and sniffed admiringly at the slices of roast goose in a spiced sauce. "Beautiful," he said. "If ever I give up playing, maybe I'll look for kitchen work."

"Do it in winter then," the boy said. "It's merciless hot this time of year." Like everyone Joliffe could see, he was red-faced and sweating. He looked the tray over and said, "One more thing. Wait here. I'll get it."

He dodged away through the flurry of elbows and aprons, and Joliffe could see why it might be better to be thin and quick here rather than fat or slow. Work might presently be past the slicing and chopping stage but the swing of a heavy ladle or collision with a heavy pan or bowl would probably do a person no good.

The boy had disappeared but a kitchen maid came toward Joliffe, wiping her floury hands on her apron. He gave her a deep bow and a deeper smile and she smiled up at him prettily as she asked, "You're one of the players, aren't you?"

Hand pressed to his heart, he declared, "I am whatever you want me to be."

"I saw you in the play the other night. All those words you have to remember. You're doing something different tonight at the feast, aren't you?"

"Tonight we do *The Pride of Life*. Will you be able to see it?"

"Master Penteney says we may watch from the screens passage if we keep quiet." She glanced around as if about to impart a dangerous secret. "Master Fairfield has to watch from up in the gallery. He's been carrying on all day because of that and because he hasn't been with you folk today. He's not happy about being left out tonight either."

"He's not going to be at the feast?"

"They won't let him sit eating among people who aren't used to his ways. You've seen him at table, haven't you? Well, they don't want such as Lord and Lady Lovell seeing it, that's sure. I don't know what Mistress Kathryn is thinking of, letting herself be married to him, I really don't. No, his man will see to feeding him in his own chamber. That's all settled. Then he'll be let watch the play from behind the minstrels in the gallery along with little Master Giles and the Lovell children and then be put back in his room again."

"Talking about that Lewis?" asked the boy, returning with a pottery pitcher covered with another towel.

"Master Fairfield," the maid said firmly. "You know that's what you're supposed to say."

"It won't make any difference," the boy said cheerfully. "He'll still be an idiot and he still won't be at any feast, even if he protests until he's gone blue—which he does do," he added to Joliffe. "They say his heart mis-beats and he goes all strange until it steadies again."

"As if you know everything," the maid scoffed.

Before that turned to an argument Joliffe asked with a jesting nod at the pitcher, "Wine?"

"A week past Hell freezing solid is when any of us will see wine come this way," the boy jested back. He set the pitcher carefully in the center of the tray for best balance. "You going to be all right with this?"

Joliffe slightly lifted the tray, judged the weight, and took it confidently. "Fine."

The maid gave him a flutter of floury eyelashes. "You're very strong."

"Have to be," Joliffe said, "to carry all those words in my head," and escaped out the door. Still, he wondered briefly what the odds were of keeping company with her a while before he left Oxford this time, but went on from there to thinking he might be no more wise than when he'd gone to the kitchen, but he knew far more about how things stood with Lewis. That there had been not one mention of the murder or the dead man suggested, too, how firm a hold Master Penteney had over his household.

At the barn Basset and Piers were awake, and as he set the tray down Joliffe voiced aloud his wondering about that lack of talk.

"Let go about the dead man," Ellis said. "If nobody is making trouble at us about it, why do you have to?"

"Somebody wanted to make trouble for us or they wouldn't have put the body where they did," Joliffe insisted.

"Or it was Penteney they wanted trouble for. We just happened to be here," Ellis said.

"Or maybe not. Basset, why do you think nobody asked me anything?"

"Likely because Master Penteney gave order that way," Basset answered before popping a peascod into his mouth, then saying around it, "Haven't you taken hold on the fact that for today at least, impressing Lord Lovell matters more than a happenstance dead body? If I was Master Penteney, I'd have given orders everyone was to tend to their work and save the talk for later. Come to that, I think I will give that order, because it's probably best we don't talk about it either."

"Piers," said Joliffe, "if you get your hand any closer to my food, you'll be playing your part in a sling tonight."

Piers took his hand back from the bit of goose for which

he had been hoping and the rest of the meal went peaceably. They had finished and Rose had the tray readied for return to the kitchen when a knock on the barn door was followed by one of the Penteneys' serving men coming in. Knowing he was a step or two better than players, he gave them no bow but said, friendly enough, "Master Penteney sent to tell you my lord and lady and their folk have gone up to ready for the feast. All's clear for coming in."

Basset thanked him with the grace of a lord bestowing a favor, which caught the fellow so unready that he bent his head in respectful acceptance of the thanks and left with the puzzled look of someone trying to reason out what had happened.

"There then," said Rose, taking up the tray. "You shift things while I see this to the kitchen and I'll join you in . . . the parlor, is it?"

"The parlor," Basset agreed. "We'll be there before you."

Rose made a sound that might have been doubt, but among them, Basset, Ellis, Joliffe, and Piers did have the hampers of garb and properties into the parlor before Rose rejoined them. Like Master Penteney's study, the parlor was beyond the dais at the high end of the hall. The problem of how the players would ready for the play and wait for the time to make their entrances to the hall without being seen beforehand or being in the servants' way—or the servants in theirs—was another thing Basset had settled with Mistress Penteney. By agreement players would come to the parlor before the hall had filled with people for the feast, to be out of everyone's way there and everyone out of theirs while they readied and waited for their time.

Reached by a doorway at the opposite end of the dais from the door to Master Penteney's study, the parlor was larger than the study, with equally much golden oak, including the well-polished floor, but where the study was meant for work, the parlor was plainly meant for pleasure and ease. The long, low-backed settle and all the curve-seated chairs around the room were softened with embroidered cushions in all colors. A long table to one side had a cloth woven in greens and blues laid across it, with silver candlesticks and beeswax candles waiting there for darkness. A blue-glazed bowl full of fresh-cut flowers was on the hearth in place of the unneeded fire and a yellow-glazed pot with a rosemary plant sat on the wide sill of the window that looked on out the yard. The walls were painted a creamy gold and on one of them there hung a tapestry showing the Holy Family's flight into Egypt, Joseph striding out happily along a road through green, very rolling hills while Mary and the Child rode a merry-eyed donkey.

Joliffe took in all of that with admiration while he and Piers set down their hamper beside the table. Not only were they going to have more than time enough to ready, they were going to do their waiting afterward in comfort.

He saw Rose give the room a long look when she came in, saw her face momentarily soften with pleasure and a longing that did not surprise him. But she put the longing aside almost before it was there and set to work, helping them all with what painting of their faces was needed, then sorting them into their garb and Joliffe into his wig as the King of Life's queen. By then the hired minstrels in the gallery above the screens passage at the hall's far end had begun to play and by the cheerful rise of voices it was easy to guess the guests were gathering to their places. The play was to come after the second remove, giving the feasters a long pause in which to digest before setting to the last remove. With plenty of time to spare, Joliffe moved in his trailing gown and long, false, fair hair—but without the queen's crown yet—to stand by himself at the window, looking out at the yard. Though the shadows out there were growing long from the westering sun, this near to midsummer there were hours of daylight left. It would hardly have thickened to dark even by the time the feast ended.

Whoever had murdered Hubert Leonard had not had very many hours of darkness in which to shift the body. The lightless back lane and need for quiet would have made slow going of the business, so besides wondering where Hubert had gone after leaving here, there was question of how far someone could have moved his dead body in the dead of night, given the few hours of darkness there presently were.

Of course the fellow might have been killed close by, in which case there was no bother over time. Any time in the night would have suited. But what if he hadn't been killed close by? Then someone had taken more than a little trouble to dump his body in the Penteney yard. Besides the why they had done it—to make trouble for Master Penteney, yes, but *why*—how had they moved it? Carried it over a shoulder, possibly, but that would likely mean the murderer getting blood on himself. By horse or mule then, or else a cart or wheelbarrow. Whatever it was, it should have made some noise. Hoofs plod, wheels creak, and there was always the chance that even in the middle of the night someone might be awake to hear them.

He was grateful at that point, knowing he was no further along than he had been and unlikely to get further, for Piers to bring a small gameboard and dice and challenge him to a game to pass the time. Since it was a game at which even Piers had trouble cheating, once Joliffe had made sure of the dice, they played peaceably through the feast's first remove. But during the interlude of singing by scholars from one of the colleges before the second remove, Piers, tired of the game because Joliffe was not los-

ing enough, suddenly left off playing and started across the
room toward his mother who was sitting quietly, leaned
back in a chair with her eyes closed and no work in hand.
Seeing no reason she shouldn't stay that way for a while,
Joliffe called Piers back with an offer to play coin-toss
with him. The promise of profit brought Piers immediately
back, and by the end of keeping score, when a servant
slipped in from the hall to say there was only one more
dish to be served in the remove, Joliffe owed him a penny
and they were both content to stop.

Basset sat up from his doze on the bench, stretched,
stood, and began to hum and mutter, loosening his voice.
Ellis stopped pacing, went to Rose to be tidied and straightened, and began working his own voice. Joliffe made sure
of Piers's hair and doublet, had him pull up and smooth his
hosen, then went to Rose for his own tidying. She made
sure of his wig and set the crown firm and straight on his
head, and then he and Piers set to trading odd noises,
readying their voices, too, until with a slight rap at the
door, the Penteney's chamberlain put in his head to say the
time was come.

Basset said, "Very well," and the man disappeared. Ellis
went to open the door all the way, letting them watch the
chamberlain proceed with great dignity past the end of the
high table, step down from the dais and go out into the
open center of the hall, cleared now of servants between
the two tables stretched the hall's length below the dais.
The several score of guests sat only along the tables' outer
sides, to make the servants' serving easier, meaning that
they were all facing inward to where the chamberlain now
rapped the end of his tall staff of office on the tile floor for
their attention. Talk dropped unevenly away to something
close to silence and in ringing tones worthy of a player the

man announced, "My lord and lady, my master and mistress, good sirs and gentlemen and ladies all, *The Pride of Life!*"

While he spoke, Ellis and Joliffe moved through the parlor doorway and stood ready. As he finished, there was a trumpet flourish from the minstrel gallery, Ellis held out his hand, Joliffe laid his free one upon it, holding his trailing skirts clear of his feet with his other, and in all the glory of royalty they swept forward together, past the end of the high table into the middle of the hall where they struck a regal pose. Behind them Basset came with stately stride. He was the Prologue and knew, to a fine-tuned instant, how long an audience would hold on their first sight of the players. He stopped on that instant, raised a hand, turned around, and began in a fulsome, rolling voice, "Peace and hearken, all you here! Rich and poor, young and old . . ."

Too used to great halls readied for feasts, Joliffe had given scant heed to this one as they had passed through on their way to the parlor but as he stood there now, his gaze set with serene adoration on Ellis's face (some parts were harder to play than others) he was aware of the rich play of candle- and lamplight on white-cloth covered tables; the glint of gold and silver tablewares finely crafted to catch the eye and light, the sheen of the guests' brocades and velvets and even silk. Was aware, too, of how the light must play like gold off his own and Ellis's brass crowns, giving them a spurious wealth to match that around them.

"Now disturb not this place, for this our play shall begin and end through Jesus Christ's sweet grace," Basset declared, ending the prologue as if bestowing a blessing on everyone here.

As he swept out the way he had come, hand still lifted in

that blessing, Ellis began, "King I am, with this wide world to rule as I will."

The play ran its course, although not quite the same course as the copy of it with which Joliffe had started. Theirs was too small a company for everything that script had called for, and he had trimmed, shifted, and tightened it until their few could play its many parts. Ellis remained the King throughout, but Basset, by way of dignified exits, changes of garb, and returns, went from the Prologue to a Bishop to finally God, while Joliffe held on as Queen until the King's death, then exited in tears to return as the Devil (yet again), his transformation covered, first, by the Bishop's somewhat prolonged prayer over the dead King and then, when the Bishop exited to become God, by Piers who by then had already been Page and Messenger and now was a Demon tormenting the King's soul until the Devil could come for it. The Devil and the King's Soul (still Ellis of course) then debated while the Demon left to return as a rather small Angel accompanying God for the final debate between God and Devil and the King's Soul over the King's final fate.

The trick of it—or of any play—was, when once started, never to pause but to go at it as if there were no chance of failure and that the end would crown all, as Basset was fond of saying. Fortunately, *Pride of Life* was something they had done often enough that, with the work they had put in on it these past few days, they had it firm and ran it straight without fumble or lost lines. At the end they took their bows to fine applause and glad faces all around, and escaped into the parlor to the flourishes of a trumpet and drum from the minstrels' gallery announcing the first dish of the final remove.

With the parlor door shut behind them, they laughed and quietly cheered each other and Ellis collapsed into a chair with a huge breath of relief. Rose promptly prodded him up again, to get his garment off him, while Joliffe saw to Piers's angel wings, telling him, "They don't suit you," and Basset stood waiting to have God's fulsome robe lifted off of him. Of heavy linen painted with gold, God's robe was one of their best garments and at the same time the most troublesome, made of so many yards of cloth it took up almost half a hamper by itself and always needing careful handling and the greatest care, both because of the paint and because they had no hope of affording another one anything like as good.

The angel wings safely given to Rose to put away, Ellis and Joliffe lifted God's robe off Basset and, with Rose's help, smoothed and folded it, ready for tomorrow. By the time a servant tapped at the door to be let in, their faces were cleaned and they were all into their usual clothing, with their hampers packed and closed and the servant eagerly welcomed because he carried a tray with sweet cakes, dried fruit, a pitcher, and goblets.

Crossing the room to set it on the table, he said, "Mistress Penteney thought you'd probably welcome this."

"We do indeed," Basset said. "Pray, give her our great thanks."

"She said to tell you that you well deserve it."

"Again, our thanks."

"But, also, Master Penteney asks you for the favor of waiting here past the feast's end. There's to be dancing afterward. While the tables are cleared away for it, he means to bring Lord and Lady Lovell and some other of his guests in here to be out of the way. He hopes you'll stay to meet them."

That Master Penteney requested rather than ordered was gracious of him, although it came to the same thing, and Basset said smoothly they'd very happily oblige, keep-

ing a straight face until the man was gone. Only when the
door was shut did he turn to the rest of the company as they
all of them broke into wide smiles and Piers did a quick-
footed little dance of delight. They had no need to say
among themselves their instant hope of what might come
if Lord Lovell was sufficiently impressed with them, but
when Ellis had poured the wine—"Wine, not ale," Rose
said wonderingly—they raised their goblets to one another
and Basset said for all of them, "To good fortune. May it
come and never leave."

Having drank to that, they put their hampers under the
table, out of the way and almost out of sight, then enjoyed
the food and the rest of the wine before, a while later, the
scraping back of benches across the hall's floor gave warning that the feast had ended. The players immediately drew
well away from the door, arraying themselves near the
window, Joliffe, Ellis, Basset and Piers side by side, Rose
standing behind Piers, her hands on his shoulders. Servants
came first, moving quickly, one clearing away the players'
tray, another setting a tray with silver pitcher and silver
goblets in its place, a third bringing a tall lampstand hung
with half a dozen lighted oil lamps that he set near the fireplace before lighting the candles on the table, needed now
that the last daylight was fading.

All that took them hardly more than a moment, and then
Master Penteney was outside the door, bowing low for
Lord and Lady Lovell to enter ahead of him. As one, the
players bowed, too, even lower, and Rose curtsied almost
to the floor. Only when they straightened up did Joliffe
have a first near, clear look at Lord and Lady Lovell.

He was a man of middle years and middle height and
wore his ankle-length dark burgundy houpelande with the
unconsidered awareness of his worth and dignity. Lady
Lovell was all graceful, wealthy womanhood in a gown of

heavy green velvet, one hand holding up the front of her trailing skirts to show the blue under-gown. Her headdress was far finer than what she had worn for riding, fashionably wide and draped with a pale veil that floated to the sides and behind her as she moved. Her dark eyes were lively, seeming ready to laughter, and her voice pleasantly matched them as she came forward from her husband's side toward the players, saying, "Good sirs, thank you for the pleasure your play gave us."

They all bowed again and Basset said, "The pleasure and honor were ours, my lady."

She smiled at Rose. "Much of the work to having them so lordly clothed was yours, I'll warrant."

"It was, my lady," Rose said with a curtsy.

Lady Lovell smiled down at Piers standing straight and bright-eyed, his curls particularly golden in the lamplight. "You, young man. However do you keep all those words in your head?"

Piers immediately hung his head and wiped at a feigned tear, murmuring, "They beat me, my lady."

She laughed at him. "They do not. You'd not have such a wicked glint in your eyes if they did."

Piers looked up at her, all smiles and charm again. "They maybe beat me just a little?"

"They well may for telling lies like that," she returned.

She smiled again at Rose, who said, smiling, too. "You must have children of your own, my lady."

"I do, and one of them reminds me very much of yours, for his mischief if nothing else."

Master Penteney had seen the last of the favored guests into the parlor and Lord Lovell was turned away to join them but Mistress Penteney—resplendently different from her everyday self in a bright blue gown with narrow bands of white fur at the throat and around the hanging sleeves

and a cauled headdress and veil—crossed the room with
another woman to join Lady Lovell. Joliffe silently wished
Rose and Piers well with them as Master Penteney beckoned for Basset, Ellis, and him. They of course obeyed, Joliffe falling behind Basset and Ellis with seeming respect
but in truth to give himself time to assess who else was
here.

One of the men with Master Penteney looked to be another prosperous townsman and it was likely his wife now
across the room, cooing something at Piers. Mistress Geva
was the only other woman present, still near the door with
Master Richard who was close in talk with Master Barentyne. As of this morning, the crowner had not been invited
to the feast, Joliffe knew from what Master Penteney had
said in the yard this morning, so it was clever on Master
Penteney's part to have him here now, welcoming him as a
guest instead of keeping him at wary arm's length. Or was
the cleverness equally on Master Barentyne's side? Joliffe
suddenly wondered. Had the crowner accepted the invita-
tion for the better chance it gave him to see things inside
the Penteney household?

If he had, it meant he had not yet let go the possibility
that someone here had indeed had something to do with the
murder. And that thought took away some of Joliffe's pleasure with the evening.

Chapter 12

Joliffe was turned from his worry by seeing, a few paces behind Master Penteney, John Thamys in intent, smiling talk with Simon Fairfield. He looked forward to hearing what Thamys would have to say about the play, but meanwhile had to join Basset and Ellis in bowing as Master Penteney presented them, first, to Lord Lovell, then to another man who, like Thamys, wore a scholar's dark gown. It was the gown of a far wealthier scholar than Thamys was—amply cut and of a worsted so fine it looked almost like silk, with the turned-out collar of deep velvet open at the throat to show a black doublet of worked damask underneath. Add to that the wide, jeweled rings enriching the hand fondling the gold chain spread across the man's chest and over his shoulder, and Joliffe altered his assessment from wealthy to *very* wealthy scholar.

"Doctor Thomas Gascoigne," Master Penteney said. "Chancellor of the University."

The players all bowed, and Doctor Gascoigne with

rather heavy graciousness said, "You gave an interesting display. I have seen worse in my time."

There was no telling whether he meant that for a back-handed compliment or simply failed to see the insult in it at all; but while Master Penteney's face went stiff and Lord Lovell frowned, none of the players was so unskilled as to show offense. Basset merely murmured faint thanks for the doctor's kindness and Ellis and Joliffe said nothing.

It was John Thamys who came to something like the rescue. Close enough that he and Simon must have heard what had passed, he said, just quickly enough that Joliffe knew he was trying to head off worse, "It must be difficult to find plays for so small a company, Master Basset."

"In truth, sir, it's nigh to impossible," Basset agreed. He was now playing the part of the bluff craftsman honored by his betters so graciously noticing him. "We'd be hard put but that we're fortunate in young Master Southwell here. He's reshaped a number of plays to our need. As he did the one we played tonight."

There were appreciative murmurs among the men, and Joliffe bowed his thanks.

"A literate young man," Doctor Gascoigne said, disdain tingeing his voice. He eyed Joliffe as if he were an interesting example of deformity. "What a pity to put such a skill with words to such illicit use."

"Sir?" Joliffe said politely, feigning ignorance of what the man could possibly mean but able to guess where he was bound and willing to help him along.

Not that Doctor Gascoigne needed help. Sounding much like a great lord being gracious to peasants, he explained grandly, "One must consider that your words are used by you and your fellows for the sake of dishonestly, shamefully displaying your bodies for the sake of profit.

Such display is a thing done only by players, whores, and others of such kind, and . . ."

"Do you mean 'shamefully' or 'shamelessly'?" Joliffe said.

Doctor Gascoigne drew himself up more straightly and stiffly, eyes widening, mouth tightening, plainly unused to being interrupted. "What?" he demanded harshly.

Very kind about it, Joliffe explained, "They're not the same, you know. Shamefully. Shamelessly. They mean different things."

"I know that," Doctor Gascoigne snapped. "But shame is at the root of both and both well apply to your so-called work. Only players and those benighted souls possessed by devils gesture thus." He made a cramped movement with one hand, meant to demonstrate mad flailing, Joliffe supposed. "So crudely. So . . ." He had to seek for another sufficient word. ". . . visibly."

"There being little use in gesturing *in*visibly," Joliffe suggested mildly.

Master Penteney, Simon, and the merchant looked uncertain they had heard him a-right, but Lord Lovell pressed a hand over his mouth, covering what might have been merely a cough, and John Thamys turned his head away, taking a smile with it. For his own part, Joliffe beamed with sublime innocence at Doctor Gascoigne who by now understood he was being sported with and thrust a finger at him, declaring, "In your profane plays you and all your kind blasphemously mock God's most precious creation—Man himself. You . . ."

"What exactly did we mock tonight?" Joliffe asked, all innocence. "We showed worldly pride in all its foolishness and doom. We showed the Devil's wiles and God's mercy. Where was the mockery in any of that?"

"The mere doing of it was the mockery! This play, any

play, and the japing and prattling of you and your kind are
a mockery of God's work. Your base display makes sport
of Man's struggle for salvation. You trifle with the awful
reality of Man and God and the Devil, too, and thereby im-
peril men's souls." His voice had begun to roll out in a
thunder of self-satisfaction. "With your follies, you stir
men's irrational fears and lusts rather than seeking to rouse
their minds to the pure contemplation of God and of salvation!"

Joliffe, doubting Gascoigne had ever contemplated anything more pure than his own exalted self, took advantage
of the man's pause for breath to look away from him to
John Thamys and ask in a sweetly reasonable voice,
"Would you say, sir, that the fears raised by tonight's debate between God and Devil for Man's soul were irrational? Or that we roused any lust except for salvation?"

Seriously and with apparently due consideration,
Thamys said, "I would say that the fears you raised are
fears we all must have. Of falling from grace to damnation
and the possible losing of our soul to the devil. As for lust,
I saw and heard nothing in the play that roused *me* to any
other lust than for salvation. I cannot speak, of course, for
Doctor Gascoigne."

While Gascoigne choked in his haste to answer—and
probably to protest—the implication in that, Joliffe said,
still to Thamys, "Then you would say that if someone
chose to be damned rather than saved after hearing the arguments presented in the play tonight, he could not by any
means be judged a rational creature?"

As if still considering a point of deep reason, Thamys
granted, "Considering that the arguments on both sides
were clearly presented and the choice obvious, I would
have to say that anyone who, after hearing them, chose
damnation over salvation could, as you say, by no means

be considered a rational creature. I might even say . . ."
There was a sudden gleam in Thamys' eyes despite he went
on judiciously enough. "No, I correct myself. I *would* say
that anyone who mistook the arguments of the play tonight
as raising unreasonable fears or as incitations to lust must
be someone already so far gone in irrationality as to be un-
reachable by reason."

"And therefore," Joliffe said quickly, cutting off Gascoigne yet again, "what we did was not, in itself, an incita-
tion to irrationality and base passions, as Doctor Gascoigne
has claimed, but in fact the play's point could only have
been taken wrongly by an already irrational and perhaps
even willfully sinning man?"

"I think that can be granted, yes," Thamys said. "It . . ."

Gascoigne burst in furiously, "But a rational man would
not need such a feigned demonstration! Being already con-
vinced that virtue is superior to sin, he needs no encour-
agement of his certainty. Therefore the whole business is
nothing but vanity and pointless display."

Joliffe drifted a long look down the rich length of Gascoigne's gown while saying, his voice only slightly edged,
"Yes. Vanity and pointless display are always things to be
avoided." He smiled into the man's face. "But from your
argument—that when a man is once certain that virtue is
preferable to sin, he needs no reinforcement of his certainty—it follows that all the preaching of sermons and
suchlike is a waste of time. A priest need only show once to
his people the folly of sin and damnation and then be done
with it, the matter being settled and certain in their minds."

Tight-faced with anger, Gascoigne snapped, "That's
fools' talk! I said rational men. Others must be taught and
taught again, must have the lessons against sin ever re-
newed because they are ever threatened by the Devil's
wiles and the World's lures."

"Then," Joliffe said with a slight bow, "might it not be well argued that such displays as ours serve the godly, goodly purpose of leading back to virtue those lesser minds? Those not so endowed with the powers of reason as yourself, shall we say?"

Red with irk, Gascoigne was certainly going to say something, but Mistress Penteney, crossing the room, trailing Lady Lovell and the merchant's wife behind her, sailed bright-voiced into the conversation with, "Good Master Basset and the rest of you, did you know my Lord and Lady Lovell's children watched your play from the gallery? And our grandson, too. They'll all be late to their beds but it would have been too unkind for them to miss it."

She did not mention Lewis, and for the first time Joliffe took note that, although he had glimpsed Kathryn at the high table during the play, she was not here. But Doctor Gascoigne, his mouth twisted with holding in whatever he had been about to say, pointedly turned away from Mistress Penteney's rush of words to engage Lord Lovell, Master Penteney, and the merchant in talk; and Joliffe, relieved to be done with him, joined Basset and Ellis in courteous heed to Mistress Penteney, not doubting for a moment that she had known his debate with Doctor Gasciogne had been on the verge of heating past courtesy into outright argument and that she had interrupted on purpose to stop it. He was grateful to her and smiled with unfeigned warmth when she said to him, "You played the Devil again tonight. That's twice I've seen you at that, Master Southwell."

Joliffe place a hand over his heart and slightly bowed to her. "But tomorrow you'll see me as the Angel at the right hand of God Omnipotent. I pray you, think of me that way, rather than this other."

"The question," John Thamys put in, having stayed

courteously attendant to his hostess, "is whether he's as convincing an angel as he is a devil."

That drew laughter from the women and mercifully no comment from Ellis.

Meanwhile Rose had followed Piers to the tray of cakes on the table, probably to forestall him slipping whatever he might into his belt pouch, and now Mistress Penteney urged the ladies and players and Master Thamys the same way. They mostly went, but Joliffe hung back and aside with Thamys who said for only him to hear, "St. Catherine bless the woman for breaking up you and Gascoigne. That was one of the most disordered attempts at logical talk I've ever encountered. Do you know how many holes there were in your argument?"

"Not as many as in Gascoigne's. Does he always go on like that?"

"Our grand Doctor Gascoigne loves nothing so well as the sound of his own voice demonstrating how uncommonly learned he is. Not that it helped that you goaded him. You didn't think he'd take well to being challenged by a player, did you?"

"I doubt he takes well to being challenged by anybody," Joliffe muttered. "And, yes, I know full well I should have let his windy opinions blow away on his own breath, but everything he had to say was old, dried, over-worked, and not even his own. I could name you the treatise they come from. It's fifty years old if it's a day, and there he was, pretending he was brilliant because he could trot out its arguments. He probably thinks that St. Jerome is still the greatest mind to touch theology in fifteen hundred years. He . . ."

"You," said Thamys, smiling, "are very angry."

Joliffe was and was not happy at himself for it, but he

smiled, too, and made Thamys a little bow, as if conceding a point to him, saying, "I'd hoped it didn't show."

"I only knew it by the way your eyes narrowed when you smiled at our Doctor Gascoigne. When you narrowed your eyes that way, it used to mean you were furious and about to do your best to make someone very unhappy."

"How do you know that?"

"Because I saw you the time Maydenlove said something with which you did not agree and you, smiling all the while, chewed his argument to pieces with fifty quotations from Augustine, Jerome, Aquinas, and I don't know whom else, then dumped a cup of wine over his head at the end of it."

"I doubt it was more than twenty quotations and I don't remember the wine."

"I'll warrant Maydenlove does. It was mulled and hot."

Somewhat raising his voice, Joliffe said, "Master Barentyne," both in greeting and for warning to Thamys as the crowner approached, having left Master Richard and Mistress Geva in talk with Lady Lovell.

"So you see," said Thamys, shifting into a pedagogue's clipped, condescending tone, "Doctor Thomas Gascoigne is hardly someone to offend as you were trying to do."

Joliffe lifted his eyebrows at "trying," being fairly certain he had succeeded, but Thamys turned from him to Master Barentyne, asking, "Isn't that correct, sir?"

"Happily, you know Doctor Gascoigne far better than I do, Master . . . Thamys, is it?"

"It is, and I thank your courtesy in remembering, Master Barentyne. But if you'll both pardon me, I should probably go be courteous to our chancellor. By your leave."

He bent his head to them, Master Barentyne bent his in return and Joliffe bowed. Thamys withdrew and Joliffe said, "Apparently Doctor Gascoigne wields much influence."

"He wields a strong tongue and a considerable amount of independent wealth. The wealth buys tolerance for the first," Master Barentyne answered.

"And the chancellorship of the University? Did it buy that, too?"

"I don't look at what the University is doing if I can help it. Come to that, I stay clear of the town's in-fighting, too, and as far from whatever town-and-gown quarrels the two get going between them. At any rate, you're safe from being asked to play at Oriel College anytime soon. That's where he resides."

"Is that who puts up with him? I shall avoid it like the stocks. Though I hope . . ." and this Joliffe meant unfeignedly, ". . . he doesn't take against Master Penteney on my account. I presume he was invited because of what influence he might have on provision purchases at his college and maybe elsewhere in the university?"

"Very probably, but Master Penteney should be safe. He is too good at what he does to be set aside on account of a player's ill manners."

Master Barentyne looked uncomfortable saying that, as if it were ill-mannered to remind Joliffe of what he was. Joliffe, knowing perfectly well what he was and what was thought of him by most people because of it, knew also what he thought of Doctor Gascoigne and his kind, and that rather evened the score. Therefore he only smiled and said, "But to shift to something other than Gascoigne, have you been able to learn anything more about the dead man?"

"Such as?" Master Barentyne asked in return.

Joliffe acknowledged the adroit trade of question for question with a wider smile and suggested, "Such as where he was staying in Oxford. Where else he'd been in Oxford besides here. Where was he seen after he left here yesterday afternoon."

"A very good set of questions," Master Barentyne said and gave way to a small smile of his own before admitting, "I've had men asking all of those things but so far to very little purpose. He doesn't seem to have stayed at any of the inns or other expected places. No one remembers him by name or description or is missing any guests. Nor does anyone remember if he was ever at any of the taverns around town where my men have asked. There are more taverns and alehouses to go to, though, so that run isn't done yet, but with the crowds here for the holiday I'm not leaning heavily on our chances of him being remembered. I've also sent someone to Abingdon to ask about him there."

"No one has been to the sheriff to say they're missing someone who was visiting them here?"

"No one, but maybe it's too soon for that. Or someone doesn't want to admit to knowing him. If he was indeed a Lollard or working for them, I assuredly wouldn't admit he was staying with me if I could help it."

"You've found nothing that shows whether he was a Lollard or not?"

"There was nothing on him, no. As Master Sampson said, there was nothing at all to tell who he was or what his business might be. If ever he had anything that way, it went with his belt pouch, dagger, and money."

Then maybe Master Penteney had made unnecessary trouble by identifying him at all. Except that he had had to admit knowing at least his name, since he was known to have talked with the man. And better to have brought out the suspicion of Lollardy and why the man was there, rather than make up a reason and risk having it found out. Always keep your lies as close to the truth as possible— that was a lesson Joliffe had *not* needed to be taught by Basset.

"Maybe he wasn't staying in Oxford," he offered. "Maybe yesterday he was just passing through. You've asked after his horse?"

"Supposing he had one and didn't walk or come some other way. I've asked, yes, but none of the livery stables say anyone of his look was at any of them."

"Maybe he didn't look like himself when he was there."

"Disguised?" Master Barentyne paused on that thought before asking, "But why then would he come undisguised to Master Penteney?"

"A well-taken point," Joliffe granted. "I'll try to think of a reason."

"Why should you bother?"

"Because someone tried to make us suspected of murder and might try to make trouble for us again."

"Why would someone want to do that?"

"I don't know, but besides worrying that they may try again at making trouble, Master Penteney has been generous to us. It would be shame if trouble came on him and his household because of us."

"Don't you suppose that my being here shows Master Penteney is unsuspected in the matter?"

"Does it?" Joliffe returned.

Master Barentyne laughed. "Now, before you ask me, I'll tell you I've had men questioning from house to house whether anyone heard anything along the back lane in the night. Voices. Quarreling. A cart. A horse or mule, for that matter, since the body could have been slung over a horse's back for carrying here."

"On Leonard's own horse maybe, and then the murderer rode off on it, and that's why there's no horse and no murderer to be found."

Master Barentyne made a wry face. "Very possibly. But since you're so eager with questions, here's something for you. When we stripped the body to see the wound better and find if there were any other marks on him . . ."

"Were there?"

"No. Just the stab wound, the bruised chin and knuckles, and the slight bump on his head. But his shirt was torn. The right sleeve. It looked to have caught on something and a small, ragged piece been ripped out of it. About this long and not so wide." He pointed at half his little finger's length. "It looked to be a fresh tear and the kind of thing easily done and overlooked in dark and haste to move and be rid of a body."

Bright and mocking, Joliffe said, "So all you need do is find a tiny torn bit of his shirt clinging to someone or a cart or a horse's saddle or whatever, and you'll have your murderer."

"Exactly," Master Barentyne said, bright and mocking back at him. "Keep an eye out for it, why don't you?"

They were interrupted by Master Penteney calling Master Barentyne to come tell Lord Lovell something, with a servant coming immediately thereafter to say the hall was cleared. While Master Penteney saw his guests back into the hall, the players took up their two hampers and were out the parlor door immediately behind the last guest, going down the hall along the wall to be noticed as little as possible, and out through the screens passage into the lantern-lighted yard.

They left the torchlight behind as they crossed the yard toward the barn, but the cool night darkness was clear and starlighted. Rose went ahead with the key, to unlock the barn doors and open them wide for the sake of thinning the darkness inside, rather than go to the trouble of lighting their lantern. Tired now the day was finished, they said little among themselves, doing by feel as much as by sight what little they had to do before lying down—Piers with a tired whimper, Basset with a weary groan that Joliffe could just about have matched as he dropped his own head onto his straw-stuffed pillow.

Unfortunately, along with his weariness, he took to bed with him remembrance that Master Barentyne had never answered whether his being here tonight meant he no long suspected Master Penteney of the murder. Joliffe had asked him—but Master Barentyne had never answered. Unless avoiding an answer was answer enough.

Chapter 13

Because Corpus Christi Day's business and pleasures so much depended on good weather, the morning might well have been expected to be, at the least, threatened with rain. Instead when Rose set one of the barn doors open to the day, the light of a shining dawn flooded in, promising a day as fair as hope.

"No corpse?" Ellis asked, still facedown in his pillow.

"No corpse," Rose confirmed. "You're safe to get up."

"I laugh," Ellis said, still into his pillow.

Piers rolled over, blinking his way to wakefulness, then cheered, "Play today!", bounded up and flung himself on Ellis. "Come on! We get to do *Isaac and Abraham* today!"

"*Abraham and Isaac*," Ellis growled and twisted onto his back to pull Piers down for a solid tickling. Laughing, Piers squirmed free, leaped up and ran out.

The rest of them went at the day more slowly. Basset, Ellis, Joliffe, and—under protest—Piers washed thoroughly with the clean water Rose had fetched in the bucket yesterday afternoon so it would not be cold from the well

this morning since they lacked a fire at which to heat it.
That meant the washing was not so bad; it was the shaving
afterwards that was unpleasant. Not until they were dressing did Joliffe bring himself to say, unsure why no one else
had spoken of it first, "About last night. I shouldn't have
started all that with Gascoigne. If trouble comes of it, I'll
take it on myself."

"You didn't start it," Ellis said, tying up his hosen. "He
did. The old bastard had been planning his little speeches
the whole time we were playing. You just gave him back
better than he was trying to give us."

"Still," Basset said, shrugging into his doublet, "you're
old enough to know better by now. Gascoigne's kind never
hear any argument but their own. Since they're always
right, why should they?"

"So don't do it again," Ellis grumbled, slipping his shirt
over his head.

It was a grumble more for form than actual irk, and to
cover how Ellis's unexpected support warmed him, Joliffe
muttered like Piers in a pout, "I'm never supposed to have
fun."

"You have too much fun," Ellis snapped, and they were
back to where they usually were with each other.

At breakfast in the hall, more than a few of the household met them with smiles and talk about last night's play,
but neither they nor anyone else was lingering over either
food or talk. Church bells were ringing from all of Oxford's churches, reminding people of the worship proper to
the day, but today was holiday as well as holy day, and
everyone who was going to be free of their duties today
was eager to be away to Mass and then into the streets for
everything that would be happening. Quickly though they
ate, the players were not among the first to leave and,
"Briskly," Basset said as they headed back across the yard.

"The men from St. Michael's will be here soon as Mass is done and I want to check the hamper again."

Living the life they did, they did not get to Mass so often as might have been right. Joliffe knew that bothered Rose, but today there was especially no help for it. Having made doubly sure they had everything they would need today, he and Rose were just strapping the second basket closed when four men appeared at the barn door. They looked somewhere between doubtful and eager, but once it was agreed that they were from Sire John at St. Michael's and that they had indeed found their players, it was smiles all around. They took up the two hampers, two men to each, and set out in a small procession across the yard and into the street, Piers leading, spinning and dancing while tootling merrily on a shrill pipe held in one hand, rattatapping with the other on a small drum slung at his hip by a strap over his shoulder. The men with the hampers followed close behind him, calling out "Make way! Make way!" while Basset, Ellis, and Joliffe came striding straight-backed, shoulder to shoulder, and heads up behind them as if daily used to having their way cleared through the streets. It was the best show they could make with so small a company and better than no show at all, but even so it was probably hardly noticed in the crowds of folk and the sellers of foods and drinks and this and that, everyone cheerful and loud and looking to have a good time by way of either fun or profit. Rose, having stayed to lock the barn, followed enough behind to make no show of herself at all.

Piers was just drumming and tooting their way into the churchyard when trumpets called out from the far end of town, announcing the beginning of the Corpus Christi procession outside the East Gate. The town fathers were moving things along at a goodly pace; some priests from farther churches must have had to bustle after their own

Masses to be there already, Joliffe supposed. He had seen enough Corpus Christi processions here and elsewhere to know how this one would go. Trumpeters, drummers, and staff-bearing officers of the town would come first, clearing the way. After them would walk the important laymen of the town—officers and officials of government and guilds; then the University's officers and heads of colleges and any others of the University with unavoidable claim to being worthy to be seen; then all the important churchmen of nearby abbeys, priories, friaries, and churches in a glory of ecclesiastical finery. There would be a high-colored glory of rich robes, furs, and gold-glinting chains of office; high-borne banners and holy images beautifully robed; burning torches and innumerable candles; a small army of shrill-singing choir-boys; and somewhere among all that, Lord and Lady Lovell riding as honored guests of the town. Here in Oxford the procession would make its way along the broad length of High Street, the crowd drawing back to either side as it passed, then closing in behind it, some simply to go on with what they had been doing before but a good many of them following the procession on its way out of the High Street past Carfax into Great Bailey and Castle Streets to its end on the green along the castle's moat, not far from the church of St. Peter-le-Bailey in whose churchyard the first of the day's plays—*The Creation and the Fall*—would be waiting to start.

Lord and Lady Lovell and others of sufficient worth would be escorted to the churchyard to watch from some favored place and then move on with the crowd to *Noah's Flood* at St. Martin's church. After that would come the turn of *Abraham and Isaac* at St. Michael Northgate, and that left time and enough to set up here and hopefully time to deal with any problems there might be.

Today, though, so far as problems went it seemed the company's luck was in. The scaffold was ready when they arrived, hung around the bottom under the stage with the curtains green and scarlet Sire John had promised, and the large chair for God's throne was already in place, raised on several shallow, broad boxes to make sure "God" was not blocked from view. Sire John was perforce not there, gone to be in the procession, but the men who had carried the hampers were ready for anything Basset asked them to do. Rose joined them while they were hanging the backcloth around the scaffold's upper frame and helped heave the large painted-gold cloth that would cover God's throne and the steps out of its hamper and onto the stage. Warned to be particularly careful of it, the St. Michael's men were but still made short work of unfolding and spreading it over the throne and steps. Then, while Basset was draping the throne cloth in ways that satisfied him, two of the men nearly elbowed each other off the scaffold's edge to be the one to take the ram-in-the-bush from Joliffe when he handed it up from the properties basket.

The ram-in-a-bush was not so large as a real ram but large enough, with polished, curving horns and a wooden face painted with a happier look than Joliffe had ever seen on a real sheep. Ellis and Piers had argued over that, Ellis insisting the ram should look woebegone, Piers insisting— more for perversity's sake than any actual conviction, Joliffe suspected—that the ram would undoubtedly be pleased to know it was going to die so worthily. Joliffe's suggestion that it was a sheep and not bright enough to know what was going to happen to it one way or the other had been ignored; and because Piers had done the painting, the ram looked positively smug. Besides that, it was covered with a real fleece and stood on a board with wheels that let it be rolled across the stage and served as a base for the flat, wooden, green-painted bush along the side toward the stage's edge.

The man who won the small tussle for the honor of lifting it lurched as he took it from Joliffe and exclaimed, "Saints! The thing's heavier than it looks."

Joliffe laughed and agreed it was.

"I thought it'd be no more than a straw-stuffed something," the man said, holding it out for the other man to feel the heft of it. "What have you? A real sheep in there?

"The body is a wicker frame stuffed with straw," Joliffe said, "but the legs are hollowed wood filled with rocks, to keep it from blowing away if we're using it on a windy day."

"That's right clever," the man said, as pleased to know it as if he'd thought of it himself. "No wind today, though. Couldn't be better weather for it."

Joliffe agreed wholeheartedly with that and left the two men telling each other about bad-weathered Corpus Christi days they had known.

Sounds from the procession, even muted by distance and buildings, had kept them aware of where it was, and now one of the men broke off, listened, and said, "They're to Carfax. I told my wife I'd meet her and the younglings for the play at St. Peter's."

Basset looked around at everything and said, "All we're still in need of are the hampers carried into the church. Then you're free to go."

"I'll stay," said the oldest of the men, the one who had been giving orders to his fellows all along. "I'm to watch the scaffold while you're away inside. Sire John said I should."

"Very good," Basset said. "If you'll just help the others carry the hampers in, while we finish here, we'll ask no

more of you. And the rest of you can go with our thanks.
Ellis, you'll go with them?"

Ellis did, not needing to be told he was to keep them
long enough so they would not see what else the players
would do. Not that what still needed doing took very long.
As soon was the men were gone inside, Piers and Joliffe
climbed the ladder to join Basset and Rose on the scaffold.
Working together with practiced skill, Joliffe and Basset
drove in the nail where it was needed on the right-hand upright post while Rose and Piers felt along the edge of the
throne-cloth for the loop that, hitched over the nail, served
to spread the cloth like a wide wing from that side of the
throne to the edge of the scaffold, hiding the hanging backcloth there to almost waist-high. With a bundle of thick
rods quietly taken from one of the hampers and laid at the
back of the scaffold for this chance, Basset and Joliffe
quickly put together a frame a little higher and wider than
the ram-in-a-bush and slipped it into place, the backcloth
draped over the top of it so it made a tunnel from backstage
to front, but out of sight behind the raised throne-cloth.

By then Rose and Piers had taken more of the carefully
made rods each with a metal loop at one end, and while
Piers fixed some to hidden ties on the side of the ram's
head and one jointed foreleg, Rose crouched to run others
under throne-cloth and backcloth and fix their looped ends
to the throne-cloth, so that when the time came and the audience was more set on watching Abraham and Isaac at the
fore of the stage than on anything else that was happening,
she could use the rods, while staying hidden herself, to lift
the throne-cloth, lay it across the low frame, and then push
the ram forward to just behind Joliffe who would be standing there beside the throne, his spreading angel robes and
long wings mostly hiding what she did. When he stepped

forward to command Abraham not to kill Isaac, Rose
would use the other rods to roll the ram forward, as close to
appearing miraculously as they could manage it.

Basset was fond of saying, "It's taking the lookers-on
by surprise when they think they know it all that helps
keeps them happy." That this was usually followed by, "I
have something I want to try," with some troublesome new
thing to be rehearsed made it no less true, and hence the
haste and secrecy now to set up the ram-in-a-bush without
any of their helpers seeing them because—sure as apples
in August—one or more of them wouldn't keep it a secret
if they saw it. Then, when the players most wanted people
to be heeding the play, someone in the audience would be
telling someone else just how that bit with the ram was
done, and that someone would tell someone else, and . . .

Their helpers came back and were seen away, save for
the man staying as guard. Rose and Piers went off to begin
laying out the garb but Basset, Ellis, and Joliffe lingered a
while with the man, making friendly talk because a
friendly guard was much to be preferred to an indifferent
one. Soon enough, though, Basset said, "Well, we'd best
get ourselves ready. You'll be all right on your own?"

"Not a trouble. There's some others will be here soon as
the procession is done. One of us on the ground at each
corner of the scaffold to keep people back. That's what
Sire John said. Nobody's to touch anything, he said, and
that's what we'll see to."

Basset gave him a bow and they went to join Rose and
Piers in the room off the church's chancel that Sire John
had had cleared for their use. Because Piers needed do the
least to ready himself—his face was hardly painted, his
garb simply a plain tunic of bright green with painted trim
around the neck and hem to look like rich embroidery—he
made himself useful, first to Rose, handing things to her

while she careful painted around Basset's eyes to make
them show the better from stage; then fitted and fastened
God's white wig and long beard on him. Time had been
when God was always played in a mask but that was done
less often of late and Basset preferred not to. That done,
Rose and Piers together lifted God's heavy robe over Basset's head, careful of wig and beard and eyes, and settled it
on his shoulders. As he was wont to grumble, "The weight
alone is enough to make me believe I'm truly God
Almighty bearing Creation's weight on me." But today he
did not. They were all of them working in almost complete
silence, too aware of how much depended on today's going
more than merely well. It was not only that they wanted to
honor Christ with their work on this day particularly dedi-
cated to him. There was the chance, too, that if they did
well enough, they would be hired for next year's Corpus
Christi here, and besides that, Lord Lovell would be watching, giving them another chance to impress him.

Even Joliffe forewent any jibes while painting around
Ellis's eyes and fixing on Abraham's dark wig and patriar-
chal beard, then sitting motionless while Ellis did his eyes
for him in turn. At least he was spared wig and beard, his
own fair hair and smooth face sufficient for an angel. On
the other hand, Ellis's robe was a straight-forward long tunic, easily put on and easily worn, while Joliffe now had to
endure Rose and Ellis strapping the tall angel-wings to his
back by a harness that went over his shoulders and circled
his chest and never rode comfortably no matter what he
did. Then came the floor-length white woolen gown—not
pleasant even to think about wearing on a warm day like
today—that trailed on the floor around his feet and had its
opening to the back, especially fitted to hide the harness
and make the wings seem actually to grow from his shoulders. Once burdened with the never-quite-steady wings

and the too-many yards of garment, Joliffe was perforce all slow-crafted movement and outward dignity. But then, as Basset had said to "comfort" his complaining the first few times he'd had to wear it, "After all, you're an angel living at the heart of all Creation, on the right hand of God who is the one immovable point in all the Universe. What else do you need to be but slow and dignified?"

"Able to breathe," Joliffe had snapped, pulling at the harness where it dug into his chest.

"You can still breathe?" Basset had said. "Best let me tighten that buckle for you. Angels don't need to breathe."

This angel needed to, Joliffe had said, and Basset had laughed.

Basset asked, "Everyone ready? Let's go then."

They returned to the churchyard where their guards were now at the four corners of the scaffold. Because the rough-and-ready entrances that were usually the best the players could have when performing in innyards or on village greens did not suit with the dignity of Corpus Christi day—or at least the dignity Sire John hoped for it—they were going to wait in the curtained back part of the scaffold from now until time to perform, rather than be seen taking their places by their audience when the time came. It couldn't be helped that a few people had already gathered—older folk who would rather avoid the jostle of the crowd as it moved from one church to the next and so had come early, bringing their joint stools and something to eat with them, to see at least this one play in comfort and probably because it was closest to their homes.

Piers easily scampered up the scaffold's ladder in his short tunic. Rose, too, made little of it, and together she and Piers held the curtains well aside so that the men, gowns gathered clear of their feet, could step from ladder to scaffold reasonably easily, Joliffe remembering to bend low enough to bring the wings in safely. That accomplished and the curtains settled into place, Rose checked to be sure all was well with the ram-in-the-bush and after that there was nothing to do but wait. Basset had had the foresight to ask for stools, so they did not have to stand. The waiting was made easier, too, when one of the men put his head between the curtains to tell them the first play had started.

"Sire John set up young Wat to run tell us when they start and end, the ones ahead of us here. So you'll know to be ready, like," the man said.

Young Wat did his work well. They knew when *The Creation and the Fall* ended and the while later when *Noah's Flood* began. By then Joliffe would have liked to walk a little but his wings kept him where he was: there was not room for them and pacing, too. Once Ellis stood abruptly up, as if he would have paced if he could, but sat down again, only to stand up again a few moments later. The space was growing warmer and Piers made to lie on his belly, probably to lift the edge of the curtain for a breath of air, but Rose caught him by the shoulder before he had more than reached his knees and stood him in front of her to fuss his tunic straight, then took a comb from her belt-pouch to tidy his curls. Only Basset sat composedly, upright and hands on knees, his quiet waiting betrayed only by the slight drumming of his fingers on his kneecaps.

Finally their man put in his head to say *Noah's Flood* was over. Soon after that there were the raised, excited voices of a great many people coming into the churchyard. Joliffe was past concern for anything by then but the play itself, his awareness of what was coming tightened in to only that, everything else forgotten.

Sire John put his head through the rear curtain, flushed with haste and eagerness. "All's ready?"

"All's ready," Basset said, already using his God-voice.

"I'll tell the trumpeter?"

"Yes."

Sire John's head disappeared, presumably gone with the rest of him to order the trumpeter assigned this duty today to give the flourished call that told the play was about to begin. Piers moved well aside, out of everyone's way. Rose went to the left side of the curtain that hid them from the fore-part of the scaffold and made ready to lift it aside. Basset, Joliffe, and Ellis lined up and stood with intense quiet of readiness, already more than half way to no longer being themselves. From somewhere overhead, probably at a window in the church's bell tower, the clear, bold notes of a long trumpet sang out, asserting the moment had come for all within its call to give heed. "Now," said Basset, and Rose, standing back so she would not be seen herself, lifted the heavy, painted cloth aside and up to clear the way for Basset, Joliffe, and Ellis to go out to the bright sunlight and hundreds of people watching them.

The trumpet cast a few last notes and ceased as Basset mounted the steps to his throne. He turned, seated himself with the immense dignity of Divine Majesty, fixed his gaze into a distance above and far beyond the audience's crowding heads, and went completely still.

Coming behind him, Joliffe, once the wings had safely cleared the curtain, moved with a dignity only slightly less exalted than God's own to in front of the throne, bowed to God the little the wings allowed him, was blessed by a godly hand raised toward him without any shift of godly gaze, and went stately on to take his place below the throne at God's right hand and—somewhat more importantly—in front of the hidden ram-in-the-bush, a single deliberate twitch of his gown spreading its skirts wide behind him as

he a quarter-turned toward God on his throne and raised
his eyes to gaze upon him with heavenly adoration.

That meant he was only slightly able to see Ellis as he
came on in his turn, going with no heed of God or Angel to
the front of the stage, where he knelt facing out to the audience, his head bowed over his clasped hands as if in deep
prayer. He held there while a waiting hush spread through
the crowd. When there was near-silence, only murmurs
left, he raised his head, lifted up his hands, and began
Abraham's prayer of thanks to God for his dear son Isaac.
In the hearing of God and his Angel, he swore, "I love no
thing so well as him, except yourself, dear Father of bliss."

After Abraham's stately prayer, Isaac's entrance was all
merriment. He skipped on, tossing and catching his
rainbow-colored hoop, his curls like burnished gold. When
he spoke to Abraham his voice was light and bright to
match, with hint of a childish lisp only lately outgrown.
Basset had worked him hard to get that, and as intended, a
cooing arose from a great many of the women watching.

Abraham and Isaac spoke lovingly together, lovingly
embraced each other—and stopped moving, holding where
they were while God, having listened to them with deep attention, told his Angel, "Fast go your way and say to Abraham that I command him take his young son Isaac that he
loves so well and blood sacrifice of him make. Thus will I
assay whether he loves better his child or me."

Abraham and Isaac parted, and while Isaac played alone
with his hoop at one side of the stage, the Angel gave the
message to Abraham who protested, accepted, and called
Isaac to him. The moment came that Isaac understood he
was to die. He first pleaded for his life, then accepted his
doom, saying with a little boy's innocent longing, "I wish
God had given me a better destiny." And when he asked,

trembling but with his chin up, "Father, hide my eyes. The
thrust of your sword I would not see," there were some
open, very satisfying sobs from the audience. It did not
matter that everyone knew the story and how it came out. It
was a tale that played to emotions that never staled. There
was probably no one watching who had not felt the pain of
losing a child, whether their own or someone's near to
them, and when the Angel stopped Abraham from the fatal
blow, declaring, "This day you shall not shed his blood,"
there were glad cries from women and even a few cheers
from men.

From there on to the end, it was pure glory. Saying,
"Make your sacrifice with this ram," the Angel stepped
aside, sweeping his gown's wide skirts clear of his feet
with one hand while with the other he pointed at the ram-
in-the-bush, apparently appearing from nowhere (except
for those people close enough on that side of the scaffold to
see it pushed out, and they should have been looking elsewhere, anyway). While it trundled forward on its wheels,
nodded its head, and pawed with its one jointed leg at the
ground, the Angel ordered, "Take up your son, alive and
free, while I to Heaven homeward go." The ram nodded as
if in agreement and pawed some more, and Abraham and
Isaac embraced in joy and relief at the front of the stage,
while behind them God rose from his throne and exited as
he had come, the curtain opening in front of him, his Angel
following after him. When they were safely away, Abraham and Isaac went, too, hand in hand, Isaac skipping
again. Rose let the curtain fall behind them and the ram-in-
the-bush stayed where it was, looking smug.

Applause burst up then, and Rose—smiling so widely
her face must hurt with it—pulled the curtain open again.
"God" did not do end-of-play bows but Piers skipped merrily out, followed by Ellis, followed by Joliffe still wary of

the wings. The more impatient of the lookers-on were already wiggling to get clear and on their way to the next play but most went on clapping long enough to see the players through three bows before Ellis clamped a hand on Piers's shoulder to draw him off and they all withdrew behind the curtain again, to find Basset grinning as widely as Rose, and Sire John scrambling onto the scaffold through the curtain at the back, as excited and pleased as any of them.

Their helpers were waiting for them on the ground, along with a few other men and some women who had not gone straight on to the church of St. Peter in the East for *Moses and the Israelites*. Joliffe left Basset, Ellis, and Piers to the congratulations and eager talk as soon as he could, wanting to rid himself of the wings. Rose had already gathered the rods and ram-in-the-bush and slipped away. No one had been interested in her because she had not been seen in the play, and she was waiting in the tower, still smiling, when he came wing-warily through the tower door. With no need to tell each other it had gone well, they merely embraced briefly before he turned his back to her, for her to unfasten and help him out of his angelic robe, then loosen and lift off the wings. He was both tired and gloriously borne up in the way that came only when a play had gone well for both the players and their audience.

By the time the others came in, laughing and talking together all at once, he had wiped down with a towel Rose had ready and was off to one side, dressing in his usual shirt and doublet, leaving room for first Basset and then Ellis to give Rose great hugs. She and Ellis kissed, too, both of them laughing, and Piers danced around and around, crowing his triumph until Rose pulled free of Ellis and caught him into her arms for an embrace he only pretended to resist.

Watching them while he fastened up his doublet, Joliffe

had the unwanted thought that *this*—*all* of this—was what
they were threatened with losing. Whether someone had
left the dead man outside their door deliberately to make
trouble for them or only by chance, they would have been
in deep, destroying trouble if Master Penteney and Master
Barentyne had been different men, willing to lay blame
quickly rather than bother to look further. Nor did their escape thus far mean trouble might not circle back and fall on
them after all. If no one else could be found to blame,
someone might well decide it was better to blame lordless
players than to blame no one at all.

And then there was Basset and whatever secret he and
Master Penteney dangerously shared between them. Joliffe
tried to stop the following thought: What if the dead man
and their secret were not two possible threats but parts of a
single, greater one, worse than either threat on its own?

He kept his outward smile but inwardly hurt with the
thought of losing all of this because of something not part
of it at all.

Chapter 14

With a strong inward effort, Joliffe shoved the dark thoughts and their fear-fed hurt away and finished fastening his doublet. There was nothing he could presently do about either of the troubles or any of his questions. Maybe nothing would need to be done. Maybe he and the others would leave Oxford in a day or so unscathed, problems and questions left behind. In the meanwhile, he wanted to enjoy the rest of today and, St. Genesius willing, he was going to.

Their helpers came in, bringing their curtain and throne-cloth from the scaffold, all as carefully folded as could be wanted. Sire John came with them, still full of praise but, better yet, ready to give over the well-earned coins to Basset, who bowed deeply and thanked him for the honor of performing at St. Michael Northgate. Everyone was pleased all around, and the Northgate men were willing to carry the hampers back to the Penteneys now if the players wanted it. That was to the good because it would save the trouble of retrieving the baskets later, but the play-

ers traded quick looks among themselves for who would
go to see the hampers safely locked into the barn. It would
mean losing some of the holiday, but Joliffe—to let Basset,
Ellis, Rose, and Piers spend the time together like the family they nearly were—said, "Give me the key, Rose. I'll see
to it and catch you up at one play or another."

But once the hampers were safely locked away and he
had given a half-penny to each of the men with his thanks,
he made no great haste to overtake the others. Instead, he
took his own time at making his way through the crowd,
enjoying the high good cheer all around him and everyone
dressed in their bright holiday best. Rich, varied smells
from food booths and tray-wielding vendors brought his
attention to his hungering stomach and he bought a fist-
sized pork pie to eat as he wended his way along. He joined
the play-following crowd at the churchyard of St. Peter in
the East just as Moses was smashing the Ten Command-
ments. Having no mind to edge and elbow his way into the
watching crowd, he hung at its rear edge. He knew the play
would have started with Moses seeing the Burning Bush
and gone on to his confrontation with Pharoah, followed
by the drowning of Pharoah's army. Now the Israelites
were being condemned to forty years wandering in the
wilderness for worshipping an idol. Joliffe didn't know
which company of players this was but they were good,
and he indulged in a strong tweak of envy at what a full
company—with undoubtedly a prosperous patron backing
them—could do in the way of a larger play. He wished he
had seen how Pharoah's army had been drowned.

Basset and the others were here somewhere, he supposed, but he did not try to find them. In fact, he tried not
to find them, losing himself in the crowd as it broke away
at the play's end. There would be a long pause now before

the next play, to give folk time for their dinners before the afternoon's plays began with Jack Melton's company doing *The Birth of Christ* at All Saints Church. Joliffe bought a beef pie and a bowl of ale at a tavern and sat on an outside bench in the sun to enjoy them.

He saw the Penteneys go by—Master and Mistress Penteney side by side, followed by Master Richard with Mistress Geva beside him and their small son on his shoulders. Then came Kathryn walking between Simon and Lewis, with Matthew close behind them. They would have been an ordinary family gathering, save for Lewis bobbing happily up and down, all but dancing with wide-smiled delight, refusing to hold Kathryn's hand, being kept from bumbling sideways into passersby only by Matthew taking hold on him and guiding him back to where he ought to be whenever he lurched too widely aside. Twice while Joliffe watched, Lewis lurched the other way, into Kathryn, and the second time she would have fallen if Simon had not caught her with an arm around her waist.

His arm was still around her waist when Joliffe lost sight of them in the crowd.

Only the rare pleasure of seeing a play instead of being in one brought Joliffe to his feet and on his way a little while later, when a town crier went past, crying the next play; but he only rejoined Basset and the others three plays later, at *The Harrowing of Hell* at St. Aldate's church. The company was good but Joliffe thought Basset would have better directed them in their business.

The day's last play, *The Resurrection* at St. Ebbe's Church, went the least well of any Joliffe had seen today. All too plainly some of the players had spent their waiting-while in drinking more than they should have. The apostles, running to the tomb to find Christ's body gone, stumbled into each other and had to hold each other up as they staggered their last few steps, giggling, bringing the audience to laughter with them and at them.

Unable to resist, Joliffe leaned to whisper in Basset's ear, "What would you do if any of us did something like that?"

Without taking his eyes from the stage, Basset leaned to whisper in return, "Give Tisbe a day off from pulling the cart and let you pull it instead, to sweat the stupidity out of you."

Joliffe laughed silently and did not doubt that Basset meant it. He had seen what Basset had done once to sober Ellis in time for a performance when Ellis had shown up waveringly drunk, and since then Ellis had never shown up drunk—waveringly or otherwise—for any play or practice.

As the crowd broke up to find what pastimes it would for the rest of the day now the plays were done, the players' way crossed with the Penteneys. Following Basset's lead, they would have done no more than bow respectfully and let the Penteneys pass, but Lewis broke away from Matthew, ran forward, and grabbed Piers's arm, exclaiming, "I saw you! I saw you!" He capered in a circle, awkward-legged as a colt, pulling Piers around with him, unheeding passers-by who had to swing wide to avoid them. Simon and Matthew moved as one to stop him, while Master Penteney said to Basset and the others, "On the chance you couldn't tell how many women were weeping while they watched your play, you were a success."

Solemnly Basset said, "We do indeed judge how well we've done with *Abraham, and Isaac* by the number of handkerchiefs we see among the ladies."

"We've been boasting to everyone that you're staying with us," Master Richard said. Even Mistress Geva was smiling on them all.

Matthew and Simon had subdued Lewis, but Lewis was still happily assuring Piers in an over-loud voice, "I didn't tell anybody about the sword not being sharp. Not anybody."

Joliffe saw Mistress Penteney send Matthew a look that said he should calm Lewis more, and her smile was somewhat forced as she said to Joliffe, "It was reassuring to see you as so noble an angel after your several devils."

Joliffe bowed to her. "My lady, you would be reason enough to turn any man into an angel."

Beside her, Master Penteney made a grumphing sound of doubt, teasing her. She lightly slapped his arm and said, "Behave!"

While they laughed together at each other, a well-bellied man dressed in the same richly sober manner as Master Penteney, with a face as round as Lewis's but without Lewis's bright-eyed warmth, paused in passing by to say, "Penteney, what about that dead man at your place? Found out anything about him?"

Master Penteney's smile lessened to nothing more than bare good manners, but his voice stayed friendly enough as he answered, "Nothing more than what we knew yesterday. If Master Barentyne has learned more, he hasn't told us, now that he's dismissed we had any part in it."

His voice also suggested that now was the time to drop the matter, but the man said, "I've heard the dead fellow was a Lollard, may his soul be damned. What about these players I've heard are staying with you? Think they did it? Or that maybe they're Lollards, too? You can't ever tell what that kind might be into and up to."

Master Penteney's good manners stiffened a little more openly. "I've seen nothing about them that worries me. You saw them yourself at St. Michael Northgate today and here they are for you to meet them yourself."

Rose, as usual, had managed to slip to one side and was

seeming not to be there, but at Master Penteney's gesture
toward them, the rest of them bowed. In return the man regarded them all with a cold eye and said, "These are the
ones that played at St. Michael's? They don't look the
same at all."

There was no way to answer than without pointing out
the man was stupid as well as rude, so no one did. Instead,
Basset said something polite to Master Penteney and they
removed themselves, leaving Lewis declaring loudly that
he wanted to go with them.

That hastened their disappearance into the crowd, and
as Rose appeared at Ellis's side again, Basset said fiercely
at all of them, "If any of you lets that fool spoil the day for
you, I'll rattle the teeth in your head. You understand?"

They chorused agreement and to prove he meant it Piers
tossed his hat in the air, caught it on a fingertip, and spun it
around. Ellis offered his arm to Rose, and Basset steered
them all to one of the food stalls and bought everyone
almond-topped cherry tarts that they ate while beginning a
slow drift back toward the Penteney barn. The long summer afternoon had hours yet to run and a long summer evening would follow, with the last reveling likely done by
torchlight, but they had worked as well as holidayed today
and the barn's quiet when they reached it was welcome.
Basset lay down immediately. So did Joliffe. Even Piers's
protest was brief and without heart when Rose told him he
should rest a while, and he and his grandfather were both
soon soundly sleeping.

Joliffe pretended to sleep, too, rolled onto his side with
his back to Rose and Ellis where they sat together beside
the cart, Ellis leaning back against the wheel and Rose
leaning against him, his arm around her and her head on
his shoulder. Their murmured talk was too low for Joliffe to
hear what they were saying nor did he want to hear. He

would willingly have been to sleep by the time they went past talking to something more, but since he was not, he deliberately set himself to thinking on how well, on the whole, the week had gone. They were well ahead on money and good will and with good fortune would leave Oxford tomorrow morning, ahead of the general out-flow of folk that would be bound homeward to villages and manors over the next few days. By leaving earlier, they would avoid an over-crowded road and hopefully make a bit of money playing to the stay-at-homes as they went.

With the thought that it would be good to be on the road again, he finally drowsed, to awaken when Basset and Piers did, with Piers immediately saying he wanted to go back into the streets to see whatever else there was to see.

Rose was spared answering that by a rap at the barn door and a Penteney servant coming in to ask if Master Basset would attend on Master Penteney presently. Taking it to mean Master Penteney wanted to see him now, Basset immediately smoothed down his hair, straightened his surcoat and left with the man.

Ellis, Joliffe, and Rose traded doubtful looks but said nothing aloud. Piers began to insist again that he wanted to go out, not spend a fine evening here in a barn. While Rose and Ellis debated with him, Joliffe briefly considered slipping away to listen outside Master Penteney's study window on the chance of overhearing something but decided that would be pressing his luck too far and lay back down on his bed, hands clasped behind his head, wishing he was better at waiting than he was.

Basset returned soon, though, and was smiling in a way that immediately eased everyone's worry, even before he said, "Master Penteney has asked one more favor of us and in return has promised we can stay here through Saturday night if we want."

Joliffe bit back his urge to say, "We don't want, do we?"
as Ellis asked, "What favor?"

"Lord and Lady Lovell dine at New College tonight. It's
a feast being given by the University in their honor and in
hope of their favor."

"Meaning far too many speeches in Latin," Joliffe said,
"but probably excellent wine."

"We may presume so," Basset agreed. "On the other
hand, the Lovell children are staying here for their supper,
nor are the Penteneys going out but are dining some of
their neighbors and others who are in Oxford for the holiday. Master Penteney has asked if we would perform."

"Another play?" Ellis said, ready to be displeased.

"Happily, no. Our street-business will be enough. You
can juggle. Rose do her tumbling, Piers sing."

That was none so bad. It was what they would have
spent much of the week doing in Oxford streets anyway if
Master Penteney hadn't taken them on; but Joliffe asked
warily, "And me?"

"Ah." Basset beamed at him. "There seems to be some
revolt in the nursery among the younger children at being
left out of things this evening. Or maybe it's the Penteneys'
nurse who's tired of being left out of things while having
extra children on her hands. I've promised you to them."

"To the children and their nurse?" Joliffe asked, his
voice going up into the range between surprise and protest.

"To tell stories or do whatever else comes to mind,"
Basset said cheerfully. "A little juggling. Whatever seems
to suit."

"Better settle for talking," Ellis said. "People get hurt
when you juggle."

"A mishap or two and no one ever forgets it," Joliffe
muttered.

"One of your mishaps came down on my head," Ellis jibed.

"Only the once and it was only a little leather ball that didn't have a chance of doing damage to your thick skull."

"The Lovell offspring might not be so lucky. Like I said, best hold to talking. Your tongue never fails you, that's sure."

Joliffe stuck it out at him for lack of any real defense of his juggling because Ellis was right—his juggling was not a thing to be beheld at close hand.

"So we're agreed we'll do it?" Basset asked.

"Certainly," Rose said. "I won't mind another two days before we move on."

"We can even work the streets a bit," Ellis said.

"But I wanted to see more of the fair," Piers protested.

"You'll see it if we're working the streets," Ellis pointed out.

"I want to see things like everybody else does—looking instead of being looked *at*."

"Why not go out now?" Basset suggested. "There's time. You and Rose and Ellis and Joliffe."

"Not me," said Joliffe.

"The rest of you then. Enjoy a little. Go on. But when the bells ring to Vespers, come directly back. Piers, you're in charge of seeing they don't dawdle. Right?"

Piers beamed. He loved being given charge of anything and would harry them back here with delight. "Right!" he agreed and put out a hand. "Money?"

Basset mock-glowered at him but dropped some far-things into his hand and did not even say it would come out of his share when they divided their earnings again, only, "Get on with you then."

Joliffe waited until they were well gone and Basset had

sat down on a cushion before he asked, "What else did Master Penteney tell you?"

Basset looked up a shade too quickly. "What else?"

"You were too eager to have them on their way. What is it you didn't want anyone to come around to wondering?" Joliffe sat down on his heels, eye to eye with Basset. "Barentyne?" he asked.

Basset grimaced. Answer enough.

Joliffe pulled a cushion to himself and sat down. "He's given Master Penteney the word we're not to go anywhere for a while yet? Is that it?"

"That's it." Basset was grave. "I saw no reason to spoil anybody else's day by saying so, though."

"We'll grant I've spoiled my own. You and Master Penteney worked up this business of our performing tonight and staying over as cover to Barentyne's suspicions and in hopes he'll soon be satisfied to let us go."

"You know, you might live happier if you weren't so sharp."

"You're not the first to say that. How much a part does the secret between you and Master Penteney play in this and how likely is it a danger to us?"

Basset froze, taken as much by surprise as Joliffe had meant him to be; but rather than being tricked into giving anything away, he narrowed his eyes and snapped, "What secret?"

"The one that has you and Master Penteney pretending you don't know each other. The one that had the two of you meeting in his garden in the dark the second night we were here. That one."

"You spied on me," Basset said, somewhere between indignant and incredulous.

"You gave me a feeble excuse for going out that night and made me curious. I followed you."

"What did you hear?"

Joliffe told him, ending with, "I don't need to know more than that, I suppose . . ."

"You suppose rightly."

". . . unless whatever it is has something to do with this fellow that was murdered."

Basset made an explosive, wordless sound and violently scratched at his right temple. "I don't know whether they're linked or not. Hopefully not."

"But this secret you have with Penteney has to do with Lollardy, doesn't it?"

Basset looked at him and said nothing.

"From how long ago?" Joliffe prompted. "Quite a while is my guess."

Basset still held off any answer.

Joliffe tried another way around, asking instead, "How did you even come to know Master Penteney?"

Tight-lipped, Basset seemed still ready to say nothing, then suddenly gave way and said, "I was apprenticed to his father."

"You were apprenticed to be a victualler?" Joliffe made no effort to hide his disbelief. "You?"

"Is that any harder to believe than that you were sometime an Oxford scholar?" Basset snapped.

"I wasn't," Joliffe denied quickly.

"Then you were something so close to it as makes no odds. But yes, I was supposed to be a victualler and, no, as you can see, I'm not."

"Because of this secret between you and Penteney."

"No. Because I didn't want to be a victualler. I wanted to be a player and keep company with people like you, all the saints have mercy on me." He glared at Joliffe, but there was more calculation than anger behind the glare and Joliffe waited, knowing Basset was making up his mind whether to tell him more or else nothing. Then finally Basset made an impatient sound and said, "Right then. It went this way. Back when the world was fresh and new, well before you were born, youngling, there was an Oxford master named Peter Payne who stood out for Lollard teachings more strongly than was liked by some. You've heard talk of him. There'd been none of the fool Lollard uprisings that finished the Church's and government's tolerance, but the tolerance was wearing thin even then. It was probably that made what Master Payne had to say all the more of interest to a good many people—most of us not old enough to know better. It was exciting talk and against so much of what we'd been taught to take unquestioningly, and yes, I was one of them, along with my master's sons. Hal, who's now Master Penteney, and his older brother Roger."

"His older brother," Joliffe said.

"Yes. The heir. Before their father disinherited him."

"For being a Lollard?"

"What do you think?" Basset said. "Now listen. Master Peter Payne finally had to give up his mastership of St. Edmund Hall . . ."

Joliffe tensed but kept quiet. St. Edmund Hall, where John Thamys was now.

". . . and go into hiding until finally he escaped overseas in 1413. Or maybe it was 1414. I don't remember. The point is that he'd talked too much and it was come down to escape or be tried for a heretic. He was a stubborn, bold man. If he were tried, he'd burn and he knew it. So he fled and ever since has worked with that great gathering of heretics in Bohemia, John Huss' madmen."

"The ones the Church has lately set crusades against every once in a while," Joliffe said.

"The same, with thus far the heretics generally having the better of it. For the better chastening of the Church's pride, I suppose. But to the point here. Master Payne almost came to grief a few years before he fled, in 1409—and that year I remember very well. A letter purporting to be from the University here was sent to these Hussites in Bohemia, saying they had the University's support of their heresy, and the letter was sealed with the University's own official seal."

"Falsely, I take it."

"Of course falsely. Someone had either forged the seal or made stolen use of it. That was never found out, but after the letter was learned of, Oxford was much like a henhouse with a fox in it. Uproar and flailing about and feathers flying everywhere. It was never proved who had done it, no matter how much they wanted to find Payne guilty, but they came near enough to the truth that Roger Penteney went into hiding and has not been seen in Oxford since then."

"He'd done it?"

"They were never certain. But they did find out he'd had too much to do with Master Peter Payne. There were a great many folk talking lollardy then, understand. It was only later it became far, far safer not to. Roger's trouble was that he went further than talk. By a long way."

"You and Master Penteney were never Lollards, were you?"

"No. Not seriously."

"Basset, even 'not seriously' is enough to get you eardeep in trouble these days."

"In those days, too, if you happened to catch a churchman's eye too boldly," Basset said grimly. "But all we did was listen to the talk that was going on. It would have been hard not to. Talk was everywhere and not just among addle-witted scholars. You couldn't avoid it. Roger and Hal and I even joined in now and again for the sport of it. It was never anything more with Hal and me, and before we were too deep in, Hal and I backed off, the way a lot of folk did as soon as the Church started to kick up worse about it all."

"But Penteney's brother didn't back off, I take it."

"He didn't," Basset agreed. "He went right on with it. Then the scandal over the University's seal broke out, and while Master Payne was talking his way around that trouble, suspicion started to come down on Roger. His father was furious at him, swore he had better clear himself or he'd find himself disinherited as well as damned. Roger's answer to that was to disappear. Old Master Penteney had to carry through on his threat then, partly to protect the rest of his family from suspicion, partly because he was indeed furious at Roger for being so stupid. There was nothing could stop the scandal, though. Search was made for Roger, of course, and questions asked of anyone who could be suspected with him. Hal and I were ordered in front of the archbishop and questioned because the three of us— Roger and Hal and I—had always been close. Hal's mother refused to see him until he was cleared and his father swore he'd disinherit him, too, if worse came to worse. Faced with disaster and an archbishop, you never heard two youngsters talk so hard and fast in all your life."

"You talked your way out of it."

"We did. We swore Roger had never told us anything about the University seal or that he planned to disappear. We swore that the last time we saw him, we argued with him against lollardy while he argued for it, and we swore he'd never said anything about running off. We swore it to anyone and everyone who asked until finally they believed us—both the archbishop and Hal's parents."

That answered much but not all, and carefully Joliffe asked, "Then why this unwillingness now to have anyone know you two know each other, if you were cleared so completely then?"

"Because we'd lied," Basset said flatly.

"Basset!"

"More than that, I think everyone fairly well knew we'd lied but they couldn't prove it."

"You mean you *did* know Roger was going to run."

"More importantly, we knew more than we wanted to know about that damned University seal. We knew Roger had helped Master Payne do it. We didn't want to know. The idiot told us. Worse than that, he told us how they had done it and what Payne was planning next. That was why Hal and I decided to lie and say we knew nothing about anything, because if once we admitted to knowing something, nobody would have left off until they had it all. If we were going to tell, we should have told it right off, at the first; but if we had, it might have meant Roger being found and caught. So we lied."

"And your lies succeeded and it's been, what, twenty-five years since then? You were cleared. The thing is over and done with and long since forgotten about."

"We were cleared, yes, but we weren't *in* the clear. The taint was there and it stayed. Roger was gone but we were still here—the boys who'd been questioned about heresy. Six months later there was still talk and people were still wary of us. Old Master Penteney had been trying to arrange marriages for his sons. Now Hal was sole heir to everything, but nobody was willing to marry a daughter into such a suspect family. His father finally had to deal through acquaintances all the way to Exeter to find someone who had a daughter they'd marry to Hal. About then was when I asked out of my apprenticeship. Old Master Penteney let me go so fast I was out the door and on my own within two days, with the understanding I'd take myself away from Oxford and stay away."

"You haven't, though."

"It was years before I dared come back. Not until I'd heard old Penteney was dead and I was changed enough no one would likely match me with the stripling boy I'd been. But I still kept away from Hal. You see, old Master Penteney had warned me that once I was gone, he'd let it be known I had been cause of all the trouble with his sons. That he'd finally found me out and thrown me out."

"You were the scapegoat. He put all the sins of the family on you to leave them clean."

"It was the price for being freed from my apprenticeship. I accepted it because it was worth it. I'd never have been able to buy my way out any other way. Even so it's always seemed best to stay away from Hal, for both our sakes. Us together would maybe remind people of what's better unremembered. We aren't so old that everyone has died off that ever knew about it. Like that fool in the street today. Fat-headed Adam we used to call him and he hasn't changed. I knew him, even if he didn't know me. If ever his memory was stirred awake, he's just one of the people who would make talk that would do neither Hal nor me any good."

"But you've stayed here at the Penteneys' despite that."

"Once we were here, it would have looked strange to back out, so Penteney and I have simply played it that we don't know each other and I don't doubt there would have been no trouble from it, except Hubert Leonard showed up and got himself murdered."

"And left outside our door."

"And that," Basset agreed. "Nobody would have looked twice at us and we would have been gone tomorrow and no one the wiser that Penteney and I ever knew each other. But now we have to worry someone is going to look too closely at things we'd rather not have looked at and start thinking things we'd rather they didn't think."

"Except you didn't kill Leonard, and I doubt Penteney did."

"Neither of us did, no."

"What Master Penteney has done is send his heretic brother money."

Basset looked surprised. A little too surprised. "Send his brother money? For all these years? Don't be daft."

"I didn't say anything about years," Joliffe said dryly. "Why couldn't it have been only once or twice? Except you know better."

Basset mouthed a silent curse.

Joliffe persisted, "What I've guessed is that this Leonard didn't come here out of nowhere, demanding money by pure happenstance. He knew something about Master Penteney and his brother and money. Now you've told me I was right and we can go on from there. Where is this Roger? Where's he been all this time?"

"Joliffe, this is no business of yours."

"It's my business if you're in danger because of it. Because you in danger puts all of us in danger."

Basset held silent, considering the ground beside them rather than answering.

"Basset," Joliffe said.

Without looking up, Basset said, "Roger is in Bohemia. With the heretic Master Payne. He goes by the name John Penning."

"So all these years, Roger has been in Bohemia, keeping company with heretical Master Payne and demanding money from his brother."

Basset looked up sharply. "No. Roger has never demanded or asked anything from Hal. After their father died, he let Hal know he was still alive. Penteney chose to send him money and has gone on sending it. In return he gets his brother's messages of thanks and word that he's still alive. That's all."

"How does he send it?" Since it was hardly something that could be done openly.

"By Lollards. From what Penteney told me—and he didn't tell me much, I'm guessing some of this—there's a net of heretics across Europe, working with each other, helping and hiding each other when there's need, passing along information when they can."

"Information and money."

"And money."

"But Master Penteney isn't a Lollard himself? His only interest is in helping his brother?"

"Yes. But that's meant he's had to deal secretly with Lollards all these years. If ever that's found out, he's ruined."

"So Leonard was here to pick up the present payment to Penteney's brother and . . ."

"No." Basset said. "Penteney isn't fool enough to have any of this come close to here. He does it all when he's away to other places about his usual business. He's even dealt through Leonard before now, because Leonard was exactly what Penteney said he was—a Lollard agent. The thing is that Leonard knew better than to be here at all. Whatever he said, I'll warrant he wasn't here for Roger, he was here to force money for himself."

And his being here had opened Penteney up to a danger he had been keeping distant all these years. That could have been reason enough for killing the man. But it was not a reason for bringing the body from wherever Leonard had been killed and leaving it lying in his own yard. That was someone else's doing. Someone who knew about Penteney and his brother and wanted to make trouble. It was probably that someone who had killed Leonard, too. But *why* this someone had killed Leonard and *why* they wanted to make trouble for Master Penteney, Joliffe had not even a guess as yet.

What immediately mattered—and it was danger enough—was that someone very probably knew about Penteney's present dealings with heretics.

"Maybe," Joliffe said with a thought so sudden he said it aloud, "he was killed simply for being here."

"Penteney didn't kill him." Basset said hotly.

"No, I know that. I mean, he was here trying to get the money from Penteney at an unsafe time and place. He can't be the only Lollard in Oxford. Maybe one of them found out what he was up to, decided he'd put them all in danger by it, and killed him for his recklessness."

"Or more than one," Basset said. "We don't know there was only one person in at his death. But, yes, whoever it was knew he had something to do with Penteney or the body wouldn't have been dumped here, and if they knew that, they knew about the lollardy side of it all."

"But if his coming to Penteney was the trouble he was killed for, why make the link with Penteney obvious by bringing the body here?"

"Good point and good question," Basset said. "Any good answer?"

"No."

"Then let's leave it where it is. It won't take Master Barentyne long to decide that either there's nothing against us or that he can't find it if there is, and then he'll give us leave to go. For now, if you don't mind, I think I'll have another nap." Basset shifted around and lay down. Only as he tucked his head comfortably onto the crook of his arm did he add, "And why don't you be a good lad and forget the whole thing, now that I've answered your curiosity and there's nothing more you can do?"

Chapter 15

Rose, Ellis, and Piers returned in good time, and while Joliffe fetched everyone's supper from the kitchen again, the others changed into their street-playing garb. Rose's rose-colored gown that she wore for her tumbling had the skirts gored with bright blue cloth so that the color flashed out as she somersaulted and spun. The same blue cloth—they had been paid with a length of it when they performed at a cloth merchant's wedding a few years ago—made Piers's tabard, setting off his blue eyes and golden curls. "And what we're to do when he outgrows it altogether, I don't know," Rose had lamented a year ago when adding a width of green cloth around the hem to lengthen it. "At least he's growing up instead of out."

He was doing both now and the tabard would soon fit him in no direction at all, but it served for the present, and the rest of the blue cloth had been used for half of Ellis's doublet and one of his hosen, parti-colored on the other half and other leg with onion-yellow cloth that Rose had bought cheaply and dyed herself. They made a bright

threesome, readily eye-catching and therefore more likely
to be coin-catching, too. As Basset said, "There's no point
performing if no one's looking and likely to pay you for it."

Basset, on the contrary, was soberly dressed in his
everyday brown surcoat and black hosen. When they
played in the street, his part was to be an ordinary passer-
by caught in the middle of the other's sporting, at first be-
wildered by Rose and Piers spinning and tumbling around
him, then indignant and offended as Ellis juggled balls
over and around his head. The sight of his blustering always brought the lookers-on to high merriment, and then
just when it seemed he would explode with indignation, he
would snatch the balls out of the air and be juggling them
himself and Piers would go skipping about with his cap,
collecting coins from the laughing crowd. If they were fortunate enough to have a crowd.

Tonight, in the hall, they would play it differently, the
others performing until interrupted by Basset coming in as
if to make a formal speech to the high table. Offended at
being interrupted, they would start performing around him
and things would go as usual from there. Then Rose would
tumble, and Basset and Ellis and Piers would juggle, and at
the end Piers would sing a merry song as the rest of them
left and then run out after them.

Joliffe, being a poor tumbler and a worse juggler, usually made do with wandering with his lute and singing. He
did not make as much as the others but "some is better than
naught" Basset said, and he balanced his lack in street-
playing by his skill at changing plays to their use. This evening his plan was to play music for the children to dance by
and set them to chasing games until they had worn themselves out, then tell them stories until he was rescued.

"You could juggle, too," Piers said as they left the barn.
"Then they could wear themselves out laughing."

"I'll wear you out with hickory stick one of these days," Joliffe said. At least he was comfortable in his everyday doublet, letting the bright ribbons hung from the neck of the lute be color enough.

Because he had been told when he went to the kitchen that the children were to have their supper and spend the warm evening with its long summer's twilight in the garden, he parted company from the others in the yard, leaving them to go on to the hall while he took the back way to the garden, shouts and laughter telling the children were already there. He stopped outside the garden's gate, unseen himself, to watch them a while and to judge into how much trouble he was bound. At least he wouldn't be facing them alone. A comfortably rounded woman in a plain gown, apron, wimple, and veil sat on one of the benches watching them swarm across the grass in some sort of tag-game. After counting several times, Joliffe decided there were eight of them and that none of them looked to be above ten years old, with Master Richard's little boy Giles the youngest. He did not know which were the Lovell children and which were some of this evening's guests' offspring but that did not matter. Of more interest was that there was no Lewis. That would make things easier and Joliffe did not mind things being easier, but why could Lewis be at tonight's meal but not last night's?

Confident that the nurse would have the answer and that he would have chance to ask her in good time, he shoved open the gate, announced his arrival with a loud strum of the lute, closed the gate behind him with his foot, and strode into the garden, starting to sing, "Upon a time a shepherd I was," a carol he expected the children would know.

They did. Or enough of them did. Already running toward him, they grabbed each other's hands and made a circle around him, dancing as they joined in the chorus, "With my fol de rol, a the riddle oddy O, With my fol de rol iday!"

He went through every verse he knew, the children dancing all the different ways the song called for—up on their toes through one verse, looking from side to side through another, then with backs to the circle's middle, and with baby steps, and giant steps, and with their eyes closed—until at the end they all collapsed with laughter and dizziness. He had them immediately on their feet again with another song that kept them dancing long enough that when he finished and said, "Whoever wants a story, sit down," everyone sat promptly down on the grass, willing to rest a while.

He sat down on the bench beside the nurse, they all scooted around to face him, and he told them, in varied voices and gestures, spinning it out, a tale about a Maiden, a Wizard, and a Ring. He had just finished when servants brought trays of food and drink, setting them on the grass for the children to help themselves while the maidservant who had talked with Joliffe in the kitchen yesterday set her tray on the bench between him and the nurse, ignoring the nurse but giving him a sidelong, eyelash-fluttered look. In answer he deliberately brushed his hand against hers where it lingered on the near edge of the tray as he reached for a piece of bread. She blushed very prettily, and he thought that having to stay a few days more at the Penteneys might have possibilities.

"How goes it in the hall?" The nurse asked her.

Without quite looking away from Joliffe, the girl said, "Oh, well enough. The second remove goes in soon."

"Master Fairfield? Is he behaving?"

The girl gave a shrug of her shoulders. "As much as always. Dav came back to the kitchen complaining he'd spilled the green mustard sauce all over the table but Master Simon and Kathryn are used to that, I suppose."

She was still looking more at Joliffe than the nurse as she answered and he was looking back. If he could find chance of time with her tonight . . .

Somewhat tartly the nurse said, "You'd best be back to the kitchen, girl. Everyone else is going."

The other servants were, and the girl did, with a little wave over her shoulder at Joliffe, who made a little wave back at her.

"She's betrothed," said the nurse, reaching for the pitcher.

Joliffe took it before she could, pouring a cup of ale while he twitched his mind clear of the girl, saying, "Poor man. He won't rest easy."

He handed the cup to the nurse. She took it with an appreciative crinkling around her eyes. "You see that, do you?" she said.

"And a good deal more. What I don't see is why Master Fairfield dines in the hall tonight when he didn't last night."

They were both setting to the food while they talked. The wine-cooked chicken looked particularly good but Joliffe took one of the mushroom pasties first.

"That's easy enough," Nurse said; but she had been watching the children while she talked and broke off to call, "Giles, no. Remember your manners." She waited a moment to be sure he did, and then went on, setting down her cup and reaching for a mushroom pasty for herself. "Last night was all business and folk to be impressed. Tonight it's folk who've known our Lewis all his life and will go on knowing him once he's married to our Kathryn." She briefly crossed herself. "The blessed St. Anne have mercy on our girl. So it's only right they're reminded now and again that he's family and to be treated as such. Besides, last night the silly thing fretted himself near into a fit, being left out of things. My little Kathryn had to leave all behind at the end of the feast and spend the rest of the evening with him in the nursery. Missed all the dancing she so dearly loves. Well, there's no help for that and she'll miss more than dancing ere long, since they're to be wed at Lammas, God willing."

"That soon," said Joliffe.

"Best to have it done and over with before she comes to understand all it's going to cost her, poor lamb."

"You don't favor the marriage?"

"Well, it's a shame she can't marry Simon instead, and everybody says so that says anything at all, but there it is. And once she's been betrothed to Lewis, even if he dies then, she'll never be able to marry Simon, Church law being what it is. Still," she said, looking to the better side of it, "some day she'll have her widowhood and a goodly dower to make merry on. She can find herself a better husband then. Though it would be good if she has an heir or two by Lewis first," she finished thoughtfully.

So the Penteneys could keep control of the Fairfield lands and all, Joliffe thought. Nurse was only being practical, but something under her voice made him ask again, "You don't favor the marriage, though?"

"It makes sense from all the ways it should make sense." She gave him a hard look and added, "To men anyway."

"But not," he said gently, meeting her look, "to any woman who can understand what the true cost is going to be to Kathryn."

The nurse regarded him with pursed lips, then gave a curt nod, approving of him as well as agreeing with what he had said. "The only present mercy is that I doubt she understands yet, and won't until it's too late for weeping over, poor lamb. Still, there's good chance the men-folk won't have it all their own way." She gave Joliffe a heavy wink. "My Kathryn knows her own mind about things, she does, and when the time comes they think to rule and run the Fairfield lands for her, she'll maybe surprise them with what she wants to do for herself. Giles! That's not what bread is for! Where did you learn that?"

She rose and bustled away to stop his happy throwing of wadded bread pellets at another child before anyone else took up the sport. Joliffe hastily finished his share of an herb custard, gulped the rest of his ale, stood up, and taking his lute, strolled around the children, singing a nonsense song that diverted them through the rest of their meal. Then he put his lute aside and set them to a run-and-chase game that tired them enough that they sat willingly down again for him to tell them another story.

He was to the point where the hero was about to face the dragon when a Penteney servingman came hurriedly out the rear door and along the path toward Nurse, again sitting on the bench. He might only have been coming for the trays, but something more than that was in his haste. Without faltering in the story, Joliffe kept half an eye on him and, indeed, the man ignored the trays and said something to Nurse that brought her to her feet. Joliffe looked openly toward her. "I have to go in," she called. "Can you see to them on your own?"

He nodded back that he could—it was a good thing she hadn't asked if he wanted to, because he didn't; he disliked being so badly outnumbered—and she hurried away with the servingman.

He spun the story out as long as he could, thinking she would soon be back. The hero took longer than usual to triumph over the dragon and was trying to decide if he would

take the rescued maiden home to her father the king and
marry her, or go on his adventuring way and leave her to
get home by herself, when one of the boys protested,
"That's not the way the story goes!" Joliffe deliberately set
up a merry quarrel with him over it, drew the other children into the argument, and soon had them all laughing.
But his sense was growing that something was wrong. The
garden was too far removed from the hall and yard for him
to hear anything for certain, but the nurse did not return,
nor anyone else come out of the house, and he only hoped
someone would remember him and come to his rescue, because even the long midsummer's twilight was not going to
last forever. What would he do if darkness came and he
was still here with the children?

He started a circle game with much chasing of the children by each other. His thought was that if he was going to
be worn out soon, best they be, too, and they were hard at it
and he was standing aside, cheering them on, when Piers
came into the garden. He did not look nearly so jaunty as
when Joliffe had last seen him. His face was strained and
white, and Joliffe took a few backward steps, putting more
distance between himself and the children so that when
Piers came to his side, he could demand, low-voiced
enough to be unheard by anyone else. "Piers, what is it?
What's wrong?"

Keeping his own voice low but his fear showing, Piers
said, "They're sick. Everyone in the hall. Horribly sick and
throwing up."

"Everyone?" Joliffe demanded, not letting his face do
anything but smile. The children had to be kept playing and
unfrightened, no matter what fear was gibbering up inside
himself: "Bassett and the rest and servants and all?"

"N . . . no." Piers was more shaken than Joliffe had ever
seen him. "No, not them. They're helping. But everyone

who was feasting. Almost everyone. They're all cramped over in pain and throwing up. Joliffe, if it's plague . . ."

"I've never heard of a plague that started with throwing up," Joliffe said strongly. Which did not mean there was not one. Or a new one. But plague did not bear thinking about and he said, "It sounds like the food has done it, that's all."

But that wasn't all. In the hot weather food could go off easily enough and sicken anyone who ate it, even kill them, God forbid; but two days ago someone had left a dead body in the Penteney's yard. That had been a deliberate making of trouble for the Penteneys. What if this were a deliberate poisoning, to make more trouble?

But if Basset, Rose, and Ellis were all right then it wasn't so bad as it might be, and he said to Piers, "There's no one dead?"

"No. But they're all throwing up. There's mess everywhere and . . ."

"Yes, fine." Joliffe did not particularly want to hear more than that about it. "Can you stay here? I'm going to need help with this lot."

Fresh air and being away from the hall were rapidly returning Piers to himself and color to his face. "I'm not going back in there, sure," he said, and together they were able to keep the children busy until, when the first stars were pricking out, Nurse came into the garden again. Seeing her, Joliffe went to meet her, leaving Piers showing how to do a cartwheel. Her white wimple, veil, and apron were moth-pale in the gathering dark and so was her face when he was near enough to see it.

"How goes it?" he asked quietly, quickly. "I've heard what's happening."

"It's bettering." Her voice shook a little. "The worst seems passed but, dear St. Frideswide, it was terrible for a time." She shuddered. "Twenty people all sick as sick could be, all at the same time. None of us could move fast enough to keep up. The hall . . . it's not good . . . everyone . . ."

She needed a strong drink of something to steady her, but Joliffe had nothing to offer but distraction and said, "I've kept the children as best I could, but it's getting late for them. They're tiring." Not to mention that so was he.

"The children. Yes. I've come for Giles and the Lovell children. The others . . . we've sent for everyone's servants to come help them home. They'll take the children, too. Could you take them to the foreyard to wait there? Not inside. It's . . . not good there. Do you know the way around without going inside? Yes, of course you do. You came that way . . ."

Her upset was overflowing into too many words. Joliffe gently told her to wait where she was, then brought Giles and the Lovell children to her and led the other five away to the back garden gate and out and around to the foreyard, Piers bringing up the rear, helping to keep it seeming like a game. In the foreyard lanterns glowed yellow beside the front door and at the gateway to the street, holding back the blue dusk for the bustle of people coming in and going out. Some of those coming out were not bustling, though, but leaning on servants' arms or walking with the carefulness of invalids unsure of their strength.

One of the little girls with Joliffe and Piers saw her mother and ran forward, calling gladly, and was taken into the circle of servants helping their master and mistress homeward. The other children were shortly sorted away to their families, too, and the last of the guests were going out the gate and Joliffe was wondering how long he and Piers would have to wait before Basset came out with the key to the barn, when Lord and Lady Lovell rode in with a haste

that showed they had heard at least something of what had
happened here, but not enough to relieve their alarm for
their children.

Mistress Penteney must have been just inside the house,
seeing her guests away, because she came out to meet them
as they dismounted, saying as she came—for them and,
probably purposefully, for anyone else to hear—"Everything's well, my lord, my lady. Something in the food, no
more. Your children had no part in it. They're completely
well and are being put to bed."

Joliffe heard Lady Lovell's gasp of relief from ten yards
away and saw the urgency go out of Lord Lovell, letting
him draw back into his dignity and ask, "But everyone
else? Your family?"

"It's passing off, whatever it was, God be thanked,"
Mistress Penteney said.

Lady Lovell laid a hand on her arm. "But you?" she
said. "You're not well either, are you?"

Mistress Penteney was surely not, Joliffe belatedly saw.
It was the lanterns' glow that gave her face any color besides the darkness shadowed all around her eyes, as if she
had missed days of sleep. Besides that, she had surely been
gowned for tonight's feast as richly as for last night's but
now her hair was barely covered with only a simple coif
and she must have taken off her many-yarded gown because she was in only a plain-fitting, tight-sleeved under-
gown, its cream-colored skirts spattered with dark stains.
But she said, "I'm not so bad as most. I'd eaten only a little
of what must have done it. It's my husband who . . ." She
broke on a small sob.

Lady Lovell made reassuring, questioning sounds and
Mistress Penteney said, unshed tears edging the words,
"He's past the worst, I'm certain. He'll be well. But it
was . . . very bad for a time. Very bad for everyone."

Lord Lovell began, "If it would be better we went elsewhere tonight . . ."

Mistress Penteney began a quick protest to that, but
Lady Lovell said even more quickly, "Of course not. We'll
stay right here as we meant to. We don't want to unbed the
children, for one thing, and for another our folk can help
with whatever needs doing. You'll let them, won't you,
Mistress Penteney." Stating, not asking.

Without sounding pathetically grateful, Mistress Penteney assured her that she would, and was still thanking
them as she led them inside.

"That's saved the Penteneys from some rumor-
mongering," Piers said at Joliffe's side.

"It did indeed," Joliffe agreed. As it was, the Penteneys
were going to be the center of unstoppable swirling rumors
and ill-reports, but if Lord and Lady Lovell had deserted
their house matters would have been even worse, which
Lady Lovell surely knew, so blessings on her good sense
and good heart. But where were Basset, Rose, and Ellis?
"Go in," he told Piers, "and find out what's keeping the
others."

"*You* go in," Piers said indignantly. "I've been in. You
take your turn."

"I'm not leaving you wandering loose out here." Nor
did he want in the least to go inside himself. "Go on."

Piers met that piece of cowardice with a glowering
stare. For not being Ellis's son, he could assuredly look
like him sometimes, Joliffe thought, clapped a hand on his
shoulder, said, "We'll go together then," and propelled him
toward the door.

No one hindered them. A last pair of guests were making their unsteady way to the door and servants were trudg-
ing into the great hall and out with basins and washbuckets
and mops. Joliffe and Piers had to stand aside for a maid

coming out with her arms wrapped around a bundle of white tablecloths before they could go in, finding a sorry change from last night's grace and show. Squalor and chaos were more the words tonight, and the smell did not bear breathing.

The Penteney servants were making what haste they could at clearing and cleaning. Whatever had happened, it had not happened to them and so this was not the hopeless mess it might have been. But where were Basset and the others?

Mistress Penteney, probably having seen the Lovells to their chamber, came from the screens passage and started across the length of the dais toward the door to the parlor. She was hurrying but the habit of a lifetime held even now and she swept the hall with a practical look as she crossed it, seeing what was being done. Among other things, she saw Joliffe and Piers and beckoned sharply for them to come to her. They readily did, but it was Piers whom Mistress Penteney wanted, saying, "Lewis needs you," as she took him by the arm and pulled him toward the parlor.

Joliffe, because nobody said not to, followed them and found this was where the Penteneys had retreated. They were all there, and Simon and Lewis, and also—less understandably but to Joliffe's relief—Basset, Rose, and Ellis. Like the hall, the room and everyone in it had lost all semblence to last night. Master Penteney was seated in a chair, bent over almost double, holding his head in his hands, his face hidden. Mistress Geva, with her headdress gone and her hair falling loose from its pins, was huddled in another chair, pale and clinging to Master Richard who, looking none so well himself, was leaning over her, an arm around her shoulders, his free hand stroking her hair while he murmured something to her.

Kathryn, white-faced and disheveled, was sitting near

one end of the long, backed bench, huddled against Simon who had an arm around her waist, his other hand holding one of hers in comfort and support despite he was huddle-shouldered and taut-faced himself, like someone who had lately seen too much awfulness. They were both looking at Lewis at the seat's other end, half-lying into the corner of it. He was mostly out of Joliffe's sight beyond Basset and Ellis standing close in front of him, but Matthew was there, hovered close behind him with hands wrung helplessly together.

Rose, just setting down a pitcher and turning away from the table with a goblet in her hand, sent a swift look at Joliffe and Piers that told she was relieved to see them, but it was to Geva she went, saying with all gentleness, "Drink some of this, my lady," holding the goblet to her lips. "Just a little. It will help."

By then Joliffe had sorted out that Basset and Ellis were, low-voiced, reciting from *Abraham and Isaac,* which startled him a little, until he realized it must be for Lewis'ss sake, to calm and quiet him. But Mistress Penteney interrupted them, pushing Piers forward, saying, "Here he is, Lewis. Here's your Piers."

As Basset and Ellis shifted aside, Joliffe had his first clear sight of Lewis. It was not a good one. His round face was clay-colored, under-shaded with gray, and he was drawing breath in labored, shallow, panting gasps. But he reached eager hands toward Piers who—after a frightened look at Ellis and Basset—went in reach, letting Lewis grab hold of his hand.

Feebly pulling him closer, Lewis gasped, "Piers. They're doing. The play. Do Isaac. For me."

Piers, wide-eyed with in-held fear, looked over his shoulder at Ellis.

Ellis stepped to his side and said firmly, "Rise up, my

child, and fast come hither—my gentle child that is so wise." He took hold of Piers's other hand. "For we, child, must go together, and to our Lord make sacrifice."

Piers gathered breath and answered, "I am full ready, my father, here. Whatsoe'er you bid me do, it shall be done with right good cheer."

Lewis, beginning to smile, let him go. Piers turned to face Ellis fully. Ellis, still holding his hand, went on, "Ah, Isaac my own son dear, God's blessing I give thee, and mine."

Master Penteney lifted his head from his hands. Mistress Penteney immediately went to him, looking as if she would have cradled him if she could have. "A priest?" he groaned softly. "The doctor?"

"Both sent for," Mistress Penteney assured him. "Meanwhile, I've fetched something." She dropped her voice to a whisper. "For Lewis."

"Good. It's taken him hard. Oh, God." Master Penteney cramped over his stomach and sank his head into his hands again.

Mistress Penteney looked to Rose just turning from Geva with the goblet, and said, "Pour it half-full." She slid the fingers of her right hand into the lower edge of her close-fitted left sleeve and fumbled out a small, parchment-wrapped packet. She undid the string holding the packet closed while Rose went to the table, set down the goblet, and poured wine from the pitcher there. Mistress Penteney took the goblet and dumped in a gray powder from the packet. "The doctor gave us this," she said low-voiced to Rose, swirling the goblet to mix the powder in. "For steadying his heart when he gets like this."

As she went toward Lewis, Ellis broke off at, "I am full sorry, son, your blood to spill . . ." and moved aside with Piers. Lewis, plainly familiar with taking medicine, held

out his hands for the goblet but she gently shook her head
and held it to his lips, her other hand behind his head to
steady him while he drank. When he had, she settled him
back into the corner and smoothed his damp hair back
from his forehead, looking long at his face. He feebly
smiled at her. His breath might even have been a little easier already, and she smiled back at him, said, "There's our
good boy," and took the goblet back to the table.

"Piers?" Lewis said. "More?"

Piers and Ellis took up where they had left off. At the
table Mistress Penteney paused at setting the goblet down,
gave a distracted shrug, and drank what was left in it, put
down the goblet, and went to her husband's side again. A
short while later a servant brought in a priest Joliffe did not
know. Master Penteney rallied enough to give the servant
thanks and bade the priest come to him. Joliffe, still standing just aside from the door where he had stopped when he
first came in, did not hear what was said between them but
by their gaze toward Lewis it had to do with him. Maybe
they were reassured by his steadied breathing. It was still
shallow but no longer ragged. He was not struggling for it
and his eyes were closed, his hands slack in his lap as if
maybe he was slipped into a doze, the worst of it over for
him. Ellis and Piers had lowered their voices almost to
whispers.

Mistress Geva whispered something to Master Richard
who said to his father and maybe his mother still standing
beside him, "We're going to bed now, please you. Unless
we're needed here?"

"Go on," Mistress Penteney said with a weary smile.
"There's nothing more to be done now. We'll all go to bed
shortly."

Master Richard was helping his wife to her feet when

Lewis's body spasmed. Once. Went still. Then spasmed again.

Everyone froze where they were, staring at him. His eyes were still closed but his hands flopped loosely and fell away to his sides as if no longer part of him. Again he convulsed. Then went still. Very still. Not noticeably breathing.

No one moved, not believing what was happening.

Then his chest heaved. He spasmed but less strongly and his eyes partly opened, a thin white band of gleaming eyeball showing. His mouth fell open and his wetly shining tongue moved up and down, thrust out, withdrew. His body slumped further down on the cushions, all of him twitched again, went still again. And did not move. At all. Anymore.

Chapter 16

There was a moment in which no one else moved either, staring. Then the priest came to himself, signed Christ's cross in the air and began to murmur something and move toward Lewis at almost the same instant that Matthew did, while Kathryn gave a small cry, drawing away from Lewis into the shelter of Simon's arms tightening around her, and Mistress Geva turned to hide her face against her husband. Master Penteney tried to rise from his chair, and Mistress Penteney caught him by the arm, steadying him. Ellis grabbed Piers and drew him backward, out of the way to the side of the room, Basset, Rose, and Joliffe joining them.

By then Mistress Geva had dissolved into wild tears, her face pressed against her husband. Master Penteney, on his feet now, leaning on his wife, said, "Take her out of here, Richard. She doesn't need to be here."

Master Richard gave his father a sharp nod, scooped his wife into his arms, and carried her from the room.

Master Penteney, with his wife's help, went toward

Lewis. Kathryn, after her cry, had gone silent, staring at Lewis and clinging to Simon, who still held her tightly, neither of them seeming to believe what they were seeing.

The priest, still praying, surely did. By their aghast faces, so did Master and Mistress Penteney. And so did Joliffe. Lewis was dead.

Master Penteney leaned forward anyway and pressed his fingers against the side of Lewis's throat, feeling for the heart-throb. When he drew back, he looked at Matthew standing behind Lewis, his hands resting on Lewis's shoulders, and shook his head. Matthew, silent tears running down his cheeks, put out a trembling hand and closed Lewis's eyes.

Basset began to herd Joliffe and Rose and Ellis, still holding on to Piers, toward the door. They were not needed here. They were better out of the way. But before they were clear Mistress Penteney suddenly broke into great, shattered, helpless sobbing. Her legs gave way and she would have collapsed to the floor except Master Penteney grabbed and held her; but he was hardly in better case and they might both have fallen except that Rose and Basset moved swiftly, Rose catching Mistress Penteney away from her husband, Basset taking steadying hold on Master Penteney.

Kathryn and Simon had come to their feet with Mistress Penteney's first cry. Now Simon came to help Basset guide Master Penteney back to his chair while Rose and Kathyrn gently sat Mistress Penteney into the other one. Her storm of sobbing was already done. Instead, in a stricken silence that was almost worse, she was starting to shake, and Kathryn had gone to the table and was pouring wine for her when a soberly gowned man and an equally soberly clad servant carrying a flat box appeared in the doorway.

They might as well have carried a sign announcing

themselves: a doctor and his man, even before the man exclaimed, "St. Luke's mercy, Penteney! What's been happening here?" He was already crossing toward Lewis. "Why didn't you send for me, man? I had to hear it from my neighbor when he came home and wanted my help."

"We did send for you," Master Penteney said. "You didn't come."

"I didn't come because nobody came for me."

"I sent . . ." Mistress Penteney started but stopped, shook her head. "I don't know. I told someone to go, one of the servants." Her voice was rising with distress. "But I don't remember who. It was all happening so fast. It was all so . . ."

Rose took the goblet of wine from Kathryn and pushed it into Mistress Penteney's hands, urging her to drink, while the doctor said, leaning over Lewis with his back to her, "Whoever it was, they didn't come." He had felt at Lewis's throat by then, was opening his eyes to peer at them, then looked into his mouth, laid a hand on his chest—a fairly useless set of gestures at this point but something to do to earn his fee, Joliffe supposed. The man shook his head and turned away. "He's dead, I fear. The strain was too great on his heart. I take it there wasn't time to give him the mixture?"

"Yes," Mistress Penteney said a little shrilly. "I gave it to him." She pulled the packet from her sleeve and held it out. "Just as you said. Here."

The doctor took and unfolded the paper, sniffed at presumably the remains of whatever powder it held, touched it with a moistened finger and tasted it.

"It's what you gave me!" Mistress Penteney said. "I didn't make a mistake!"

"No, no, no, of course not," the man quickly soothed. "I was only seeing if it had gone stale or some other thing but,

no, it's fine. The sickness was simply too much for his
heart to bear. It could have happened any time, for any reason. We all knew that. You must not distress yourself over
this, my lady. Give her more wine, Kathryn, while I see to
your father."

As the doctor turned around, Basset quietly asked Master Penteney, "May we leave?" Master Penteney nodded
that they might, and Rose instantly left Mistress Penteney
and moved toward the door, holding out her hand for Piers,
who still had his face turned away from Lewis and both
hands fisted into Ellis's doublet. He let go one hand to take
hold of his mother's and left the room clinging to both her
and Ellis. Basset followed, with Joliffe coming last, hearing Mistress Penteney behind him saying shrilly, "It's the
Lollards. They poisoned us. They did this. They meant to
kill us all!"

Servants were still cleaning in the great hall. All the
tableware and linens were gone now and some men were
taking the tables down, shifting the tops to lean against one
wall and the trestles to brace them there, while women
were starting to scrub the floor. Master Richard must have
passed through with Geva without saying anything, and
moving swiftly, the players almost escaped unquestioned,
too. Only one woman, as they reached the screens passage,
had chance to ask, "What's happening in there? How is it
with Master Penteney? He was bad taken. Worse than anyone, I think."

"Master Penteney is bettering. He's much better," Basset said and swung around her and away.

In the yard the tall gates to the street had been shut and
all of the lanterns but one were out and it was guttering,
throwing more shadows than light. There was enough
moonlight, though, by which to cross the yard and no one
around to stop them with more questions. Basset had to

fumble the key at the lock but soon enough they were inside the barn, the door left open and their eyes soon used to the dark as they felt their way to laying out their beds in the hurried silence of wanting to be done with the day.

It was Rose who spoke first with, for her, unusually open worry. "It was only the food, you think? Not plague of some kind? Or . . . poison?"

"Nobody would be getting over it so fast if it were some kind of plague," Basset answered. "No, it was the food."

"Lewis died," Piers said faintly.

"You've seen dead folk before now," Rose said, not unkindly.

"I haven't seen them die," Piers whispered.

"You saw that man hanged in Huntingdon last year," Ellis reminded.

As if he'd been accused of something, Piers protested, "He was a thief and he'd tried to set a barn on fire and . . ." His voice fumbled and went unsteady. "And we didn't know him."

Ellis reached out and put an arm around him, wordlessly holding him close for a moment, before Rose said, kneeling near them, "There. Your bed's ready, Piers. Come and lie down."

Piers went willingly, slipping under the blanket that the cooling night made welcome. Rose tucked it closer around him and settled to sit beside him a while. As she started to murmur some soft sleep-song, Ellis came to sit on the boy's other side and just barely in the shadows Joliffe could see him start to stroke Piers's hair.

Settling into his own mattress and blanket, Joliffe wished he had someone to stroke his hair and sing him to sleep, too.

* * *

he awoke in the morning to the same questions that had gone to bed with him. He would just as soon they went away but they stayed as he arose and dressed. The first and very obvious one was whether the sickness had been an accident or somehow by someone's doing, as Mistress Penteney had wildly accused. If by accident, then there was no particular need for much in the way of questions. Contrariwise, if someone had done it deliberately, there were too many questions, beginning with who and going on to why and how.

Mistress Penteney thought it had been done purposefully, had cried out against Lollards. Joliffe supposed they were as good as anyone else to accuse, especially with all the present fears against them. But why would they? A misguided revenge for Hubert Leonard's death maybe?

That was maybe a pointless question. Who could guess how a heretic's mind would work? If they could have a go at rising up against the king and all—and they'd already done that more than once—what else would they be fool enough to try?

But setting aside the question of who, if it was deliberant poisoning *how* had it been done? In the food or drink surely, but what would cause that much vomiting? The doctor or any apothecary could answer that and there was a start, and then questions could be asked about how much and where it could have been got in quantity. Always supposing something had been deliberately used.

But why was he even bothering to wonder? Thank St. Genesius, none of the players had been hurt by it.

Yet, his mind treacherously added.

Because, as with Leonard's death, they would be the first and easiest to blame if anyone decided blame had to be given.

So better he go looking for someone to blame before someone started blaming them.

Gone in his own thoughts, he had not been paying much heed to what was going on or being said around him. Piers was unusually quiet and the others talking in low voices, until Basset burst out, "Damnation! We may as well take up a house here. We're never going to get out of Oxford the way things are going!"

His vehemence startled the others to silence and Joliffe to attention, not knowing from what the outburst had come. Then Rose said hesitantly, "There won't be trouble over this. Some food went bad and people got sick. It happens."

"Someone died," Basset said curtly. "That brings the crowner into it. Again. Twice to the same house in under a week. That's not good. And here we are, ready to be blamed."

So his mind had been going the same way as Joliffe's, but Rose said, "You heard the doctor last night. Lewis's heart could have gone at any time. The sickness was an ill-chance and Lewis's dying not strange. There won't be trouble over it." She sounded as if she fully believed it, and Basset grumbled under his breath to silence. He raised a hand to comb his sleep-rumpled hair and winced.

"Here," Rose said, holding out her hand. "Let me if your arm is bothering you."

Grumbling more, Basset gave her his comb and sat down. He rarely admitted to his arthritics and, when forced to do so, was never gracious about it.

At the wash-bucket beside the cart, Ellis gave Piers's shoulder a shove. "What are you so quiet about? Picked up your grandfather's mopes, have you?"

"No," Piers snarled, rounding on him. His face was wet from washing but the red around his eyes suggested there had been tears not long ago. "I'm being sorry Lewis is dead. That's more than any of you are doing."

He grabbed up the towel and wiped his face ferociously dry while no one answered him until Rose said gently, "You shouldn't mind about Lewis. Not on his account, anyway. You'll miss him because he was a friend but he's gone to heaven, surely, and he's happy."

Piers stared at her stubbornly. "He was happy here, too. And is he still going to be stupid in heaven, or will God give him his wits back?"

"He was simple, not stupid, Piers," Basset said. "You've said it yourself. You knew him. He was simple but what wits he had, he used well. I've known people with more wits who used them worse. *That's* what stupid is."

"Will he have more wits in heaven and be like everyone else?" Piers demanded. "Will he even get to heaven? There wasn't time to shrive him full properly last night."

No one had quick answer to that, but finally Joliffe said, "We can't know, but for one thing, heaven isn't about wits. It's about how pure your soul is and I think that Lewis was far ahead of most folk with that, shriven or not."

Still fiercely, Piers said, "That's all right then," and disappeared behind the towel again.

Breakfast was scant in the great hall, and so was the welcome. Over the past few days the players had become familiar enough that people had begun to forget to stand off from them. Today people were standing off again and, "It's started," Ellis said into his ale cup.

They took as little time over their eating as they could and were going out when the household's chamberlain met them in the screens passage to tell them stiffly, "The crowner will be here before too long. You're not to go off anywhere. He'll want to talk to you."

They gave him a respectful bow of acceptance. Then they all had to move from the way of several servants going past, bearing trays well-laden with covered bowls and dishes. Breakfasts for the Penteneys and the Lovells in their own chambers, surely, which reminded Joliffe to ask before the chamberlain could go his own way, "Will my Lord and Lady Lovell be leaving or staying?"

The chamberlain fixed him with a hard look. "They were set to stay until Sunday and they will."

Joliffe thanked him and followed the others into the yard where Ellis turned on him with, "What was that for?"

"Just trying to judge how fast things might be going to the bad. If the Lovells moved out to less troubled lodgings, it would make worse talk against the Penteneys."

"And if they stay," Basset said, "it shows Lord Lovell thinks all that's happened is no more than bad chance and nothing of blame on Master Penteney."

"What about us?" Ellis said. "What are we to do?"

"What we were going to do anyway," Basset answered. "Wait until the crowner wants us. It would hardly be seemly for us to play the streets today."

So wait they did, though not so long as they feared. Piers hung about outside the barn and reported when the crowner and his people came. "Same fellow as before," he said, and that was good, Joliffe thought. Master Barentyne had not seemed given to judging players guilty simply because they were players.

"That doctor has come, and a couple of men with him," Piers soon added, and soon after that one of the crowner's men came to bid them to the house, too.

It seemed this was not yet a formal inquest. They were led to Master Penteney's study, where all was much as it had been the first time Joliffe was there. Lord and Lady Lovell were seated in the chairs; the doctor and his man were standing nearby; Master Barentyne was standing in front of the desk, leaving his clerk to sit behind it, waiting with pens and paper and ink to write down whatever was said. The Penteneys were at the window, Master and Mistress Penteney sitting on the seat there, Mistress Geva beside them, her hand held by Mistress Penteney while Master Richard stood at her other side, a steadying hand on her shoulder. Kathryn stood next to him with Simon beside her.

They looked what they were: a close-bound family no longer off-balanced by Lewis's strangeness.

And yet they likewise looked . . . Joliffe sought the word. They looked diminished, lessened without Lewis, who had brimmed with pleasures happily shared with anyone around him. Lewis's life and all his brimming happiness were gone and they were the less for it.

Whether they fully knew that yet or not, Matthew, standing a few paces beyond Simon, looked as if he did. He also looked as if he had spent the night in grief rather than sleep. Maybe he had kept watch beside Lewis's body, which made sense; he had been probably the one person best able to do it, since he'd not been sick with the others last night, Joliffe remembered. Attending on Lewis, he wouldn't have eaten any of the meal in the hall.

Thinking about who had been sick and who had not, Joliffe remembered neither Simon nor Katherine had seemed as badly off as the others. Nor had Master Richard, if he remembered rightly. They had all likely eaten less of whatever it had been, but happily this morning everyone was looking well or at least much better, only tired rather than unwell. Even Master Penteney was far better this morning, pale but upright and clear-eyed. Whatever had been the trouble, its after-effects seemed not to have lingered. Would that make it harder to determine what it had been?

Master Barentyne began with giving his sympathy to

the Penteneys and Simon on their loss. "I regret the need for troubling you more this morning but it's best to learn what can be learned as soon as possible, to be ready for the inquest when it comes."

"Will it be inquest into the sickness as well as Lewis's death?" Master Penteney asked.

"I'll be asking about both but they'll have separate inquests, if necessary," Master Barentyne said. "As I understand it, towards the end of the second remove at supper yesterday a general sickness spread among the guests. Most of them became sick-stomached and vomiting, quite obviously because of something they had eaten or had to drink here. I will ask more about that later, but at present I want to determine about the death of Lewis Fairfield. He was sick along with everyone else?"

Heads nodded in agreement to that.

"What happened then?"

Master Penteney's family looked at him, it being his place to speak for them all, and he said, "When the sickness started, Lewis's man Matthew . . ." at Master Penteney's gesture toward him, Matthew bowed to the crowner, ". . . took him into the parlor and saw to him while the rest of us were being ill in the hall and the servants were doing what they could for us. At the end of it all, when our guests had gone home and the servants were clearing the hall, we joined Lewis in the parlor."

"Who joined him, exactly?" Master Barentyne asked.

"Myself, my family, Simon Fairfield . . ."

"Lewis's brother and his heir?" Master Barentyne said.

"Yes. And those players." He pointed to Basset and Ellis, who bowed, and to Rose, who curtsyed. "Later the other man and the boy came in, too."

Joliffe and Piers bowed in their turn.

"Why?" Master Barentyne asked. "Why players at a time like that?"

"Because Lewis liked them so much," Master Penteney answered. "He'd even played for us with them a few evenings ago. Lewis never understood being ill. It always frightened him. I hoped seeing the players would cheer him."

"Did it?" Master Barentyne asked.

Master Penteney looked to Matthew, who said, "It did, sir. Even ill as he was, he asked them to say a play for him and they did."

"Was he more ill than anyone else?" Master Barentyne asked.

"More ill than some," Matthew answered. "Not so ill as others. I'd say, from what I saw, first and last, Master Penteney was worse off than Master Lewis by a long way."

"But Lewis died," Master Barentyne said.

"He did, sir, yes," Matthew said. The words broke a little with the grief in his voice.

Master Barentyne looked to the doctor. "You saw him die?"

"I came just afterwards. He was already dead when I arrived. There was nothing I could do except confirm it."

"What do you judge was the cause of his death?"

"I would say without doubt that his weak heart finally gave out. It was a long-standing condition. The strain put on it by the sickness last night proved too much for it. Even the medicine that had proved useful in strengthening his heart other times was insufficient to save him this time."

"You weren't here to give it to him."

"Mistress Penteney gave it. It's easily administered in wine. I provide it already measured, each dose of the powder separately paper-wrapped. She has given it before this and it's my understanding that she did so then. This time it did not avail."

Master Barentyne looked to Mistress Penteney. "You gave him this medicine?"

Sitting stiffly straight, braced for the question, she said, "Yes. As soon as I had chance among everything else that was happening, I fetched his medicine from my bedchamber where I keep all the household medicines. I should have given it to him sooner. I was too late with it." Tears rose in her eyes. "I'm . . . I'm sorry."

As her voice faltered, Master Penteney put an arm around her and Mistress Geva took her hand in both her own, holding it instead of having her own held, while the doctor said quickly, "No, madam. His heart was poorly. We all knew that. The sickness was too much for it, that's all. Nothing you did or didn't do made the difference, I'm sure."

Her head bowed, her face hidden, Mistress Penteney shook her head, refusing his comfort.

"You're willing, sir," Master Barentyne asked, "to swear to the natural failing of his heart as the cause of Lewis Fairfield's death?"

"I am, sir."

"Thank you."

Master Barentyne's clerk scratched mightily at his paper. Master Barentyne waited until the scratching stopped, then said to everyone, "That leaves the matter of how this sickness happened at all, and I must ask questions about that now."

"No one died of it," Master Penteney said quickly. "How does it become a matter for the crowner, then?"

"It can be argued that Lewis Fairfield died of it," Master Barentyne pointed out. "It can likewise be well argued that only by God's grace no one else did. This makes it a matter for the crowner. Nor does it help there's talk that Lollards are responsible for the sickness here last night. If I find that's possibly true, I have to give the matter over to the sheriff."

Mistress Penteney ducked her head and said on a soft sob, "That was foolish of me. I shouldn't have said anything about Lollards. I was upset by everything and by Lewis dying. You shouldn't take heed of what I said then."

"You're not the only one who's said it," said Master Barentyne, kindly. "Others are saying it elsewhere." He looked at everyone. "It would have crossed my mind anyway. You see what it means, though? That while I can rule that Lewis Fairfield died of his weak heart, I have to know more about the sickness here last night, so I can judge whether or not there's cause to set the sheriff on to find out more."

Slow nods of understanding and agreement passed around the room, and Master Barentyne addressed himself to the Lovells. "My lord and lady, do you wish to stay for this?"

"If we may," Lord Lovell said. He looked to his wife. "Yes?"

"Yes," she agreed with a kind smile at Mistress Penteney. "The more we know, the better we can tell people how things truly are and allay whatever fears and ill talk may be running."

Mistress Penteney smiled faintly back and said in a half-whisper of embarrassment and gratitude, "Thank you, my lady."

But even her faint smile faded as Master Barentyne said, not just to her but to all the Penteneys and Simon, "I'm sure you've begun to ask your own questions here in your household. Has any determination been made as to what was eaten or drunk that caused the sickness?"

Mistress Penteney started to speak but stopped and looked at her husband, leaving it to him to speak for all of them. He smiled at her a little and answered Master Barentyne steadily, "We've been thinking on the matter, yes, and have asked what questions there've been time for. The best we've been able to determine is that the sweetmeats served in the second remove were the cause. They were small date cakes soaked in wine. Partly we guess this because they're a particular favorite of mine, I ate more than my reasonable share, and I was among the sickest here."

"You said you partly guess," Master Barentyne said. "There's another part?"

"Except for the breads, the sweetmeats were the only food not prepared here. They were ordered from Master Wymund, the baker in the High Street."

"When?" Master Barentyne asked.

Master Penteney looked to his wife who said, "A week ago. Last week sometime."

"And were brought here when?" Master Barentyne asked her.

"The day before yesterday. In the afternoon."

"What was done with them then?"

"I took them into my own keeping." Which was good sense, given how costly such things were. "I had them put in my bedchamber until just before the feast began. Then I had my maid and one of the hall servants take them to the butlery." Where they would have been kept with the wine for the feast, under lock or else under the butler's guard and safe from idle greed.

And from anyone's meddling with them, Joliffe thought.

Master Barentyne returned his questioning to Master Penteney. "At the feast they were served to everyone?"

"Yes."

"And the sickness shortly followed?"

"Yes."

Master Barentyne turned to the doctor. "Do you have knowledge of anything that could have caused such a sickness, sir?"

"Groundsel and elder would both serve," the doctor promptly replied.

"And could that have been concealed in the sweet-meats?"

"Easily."

"Would it have to have been included when the sweet-meats were made? Or could it have been added later?"

The doctor considered, then answered, "To do it when they were made would have been easiest, but possibly they could have been soaked in a solution of either—or both—of those, sufficient to bring on the illness. Such sweetmeats are already dark and sticky. That would conceal much. They're likewise strongly enough seasoned to conceal what, if any, taste there might be from the herbs. But you do understand that the problem is most likely to have been no more than a spoiling due to the warm weather?"

"I do indeed," Master Barentyne assured him. "What I hope is to find that out in detail enough that people can be assured the sickness was no more than a matter of chance, not a deliberate poisoning by Lollards or anyone else. One thing, though. Are any of these sweetmeats left, that we could try on a dog, say, to see what happens?"

"No," Mistress Penteney said, with an unhappy, guilty glance at her husband, as if she had somehow failed him. "We weren't thinking about them last night. The few that were left were cleared away with everything else and . . . and thrown out." She began to speak more rapidly, to have her confession done. "With the sickness and then Lewis dying and because I didn't want to risk anyone else sickening—the servants or beggars if the food was given for alms, like I'd meant to—I had all the food taken—I'm sorry—and dumped into the river."

Master Barentyne was not happy at that but Mistress Penteney's distress and guilt were so severe that he took time to reassure her that it made little difference, before he asked that the butler be sent for. Matthew fetched him, a stout, stiff man who stated firmly that the sweetmeats had been given into his care late yesterday afternoon and had been under his eye or else the butlery been locked until such time as they were served at the feast. The maid and hall servant in their turn were summoned and confirmed the sweetmeats had been carried directly from Mistress Penteney's chamber to the butlery, with no chance for anyone to do anything with them. Then the two servants who had gone to the baker's and brought the boxed sweetmeats home were called in and to Master Barentyne's questions swore they had come directly back to the house, with no chance for anyone to have even seen the sweetmeats, let alone do anything to them. At the end of that, with no other questions to ask, Master Barentyne said that when he had talked with Master Wymund, the baker, he would almost surely be satisfied that last night's misfortune had happened by accident, not someone's ill-purpose, with no need to take the matter further. There might possibly be inquest held on Lewis's death, but with the doctor able to make clear that it was from natural heart failure, it would be a slight matter. For now, he was finished here.

Everyone eased at his words. He turned to say something to his clerk. Lord and Lady Lovell and the doctor went to speak with the Penteneys and Simon. The players quietly left the room, no word said among them until they were nearly to the barn, when Basset said, "That was none so bad," and Rose with her arm around Piers's shoulders gave him a little squeeze of relief and affection while Ellis with a friendly poke in Joliffe's ribs said, "For once you kept your mouth shut."

Joliffe, matching no one's relief and merriment, asked, "Last night, the empty medicine packet Mistress Penteney showed the doctor, do any of you remember which sleeve she took it from?"

Chapter 17

Basset, Rose, Ellis, and Piers turned outraged looks on him, but they were too in the open to give way to words and no one said anything until they had reached the barn and Basset had unlocked the door and let them in. Then, with the door safely shut, they rounded on him, Ellis's demand of, "What, in hell's teeth, do you mean by that?" cutting across Rose's, "Oh, Joliffe," and Basset's, "Don't be daft, boy," while Piers simply gave him a glare and stalked away to the cart, crawled up and into it, and disappeared.

"It was only a question!" Joliffe protested.

"It was more than only a question!" Ellis said back at him in a strangled shout. "It was halfway to some sort of idiot accusation. What's the matter with you?"

"All right," Joliffe granted sharply, starting to be angry back at him. "It was more than a question and I'm an idiot. Satisfied? But which sleeve did she take it from? Do you know?"

"No!" Ellis said.

Rose had Ellis by the arm and said, pulling him to come away, "We don't know, Joliffe. Why would anyone note anything like that? Ellis, come. Leave him to Basset."

Ellis went, fuming and trading low words with her as they went, leaving Joliffe and Basset still standing not far inside the door, with Basset's solemn regard on him making Joliffe wish he had never opened his mouth. But when Basset finally spoke to him, it was only to say quietly, "What made you ask that?"

Joliffe, looking at it straight on, had to answer, "I don't know."

"Something did. It didn't float into your mind like dandelion fluff on a gentle wind."

Joliffe grimaced at the slight edge of scorn in Basset's voice, went quickly through his thoughts, and said, "Kathryn and Lewis were to be betrothed today, and I'll warrant the first banns would have been read in their church this Sunday. Now, just before too late, Lewis is dead and she'll surely be married to Simon instead."

"A far better match for her," Basset said.

"Something any number of people could see. Kathryn herself, for one. Simon for another. They get on well together, and while they've both seemed ready to accept her marriage to Lewis, was one of them less ready than he seemed? Or she seemed? There was maybe more understanding on Simon's part than on Kathryn's of what she'd lose by marrying Lewis, but Kathryn's no fool. When it came to the point, she maybe decided she could not face it. Or Simon did."

"Or Mistress Penteney did. Joliffe, do you fully know what you're saying?"

"That Lewis's death was purposed. By Mistress Penteney or someone else. And that the tainted sweetmeats were no accident. That someone deliberately poisoned them."

"Why? To make all those people sick in the hope Lewis would die?"

"Maybe I'm wrong about Lewis's death being purposed. Maybe it was Lollards looking for revenge on Master Penteney for Hubert Leonard's death."

"Leonard's death wasn't Master Penteney's doing," Basset said.

"Lollards might think otherwise. Who knows? Whoever did it, maybe they didn't mean for anyone to die, just badly disgrace the Penteneys by ruining the dinner and make trouble for them."

"It has done that," Basset said. "*If* it was deliberate poisoning at all, which is unproven."

"But not impossible."

"No, not impossible. But impossible enough. You think someone at the baker's did it? Because there's no way it could have been done at the Penteneys'. The sweetmeats went directly to Mistress Penteney's keeping and from hers to the butler's . . ." Basset stopped, weighing what he had said and not liking it. He glared at Joliffe. "So, yes, she could have done something to them, but so could the butler. Why not suspect him?"

"I would if I knew he had any reason for it."

"What reason does Mistress Penteney have, you fool? Why would she want disaster at her feast and humiliation for her household?"

"So Lewis would die and Kathryn not have to marry him."

"St. Vitus give me patience. That marriage has been set and certain for years. Why would she balk at it now?"

"Because something that's bearable from a-far off is

sometimes too painful to face as it comes near. Or because there was always the hope that Lewis would die before it came to the marriage. And now he has."

"And you think she did it."

"I think she could have. I can see *why* she would."

"So she made everyone at the feast ill, in the hope Lewis would die," Basset said, unconvinced. "Not a very efficient way of murder. Wait. No. You think she made everyone ill so she could poison Lewis afterwards and it would seem nothing more than his weak heart failing under the strain. God's mercy, Joliffe, that's twisted. Let go of it. It's no concern of ours."

"It is," Joliffe said stubbornly, covering that he was somewhat desperate that Basset at least should understand. "Our concern, I mean. There have been two deaths here since we came to stay. One was undeniably murder, the other maybe. And there's been a poisoning that would have made talk even without Lewis's death, with talk of Lollards thrown in for worse measure. Master Barentyne may not be inclined to think us guilty of anything but that doesn't mean other people won't be. Talk against us will finish us as fast as anything. We won't be able to come back to Oxford for years. And what if it follows us? What if the taint 'Lollard' goes with us? We'll be finished within the year, one way or another."

Basset was scowling ferociously but more with thought than anger now. "Nor will it be good for Penteney to have Lollard talk around him again." His voice sharpened. "Nor good for him to have his wife found out for murder."

"Or himself considered a murderer. That's possible, too. It's his bedchamber as much as Mistress Penteney's, I assume. He would have had chance to taint the sweetmeats."

"And then eat enough to make himself very ill and somehow poison Lewis along the way? Joliffe!"

"It's possible," Joliffe said stubbornly.

"So's the chance that Judgment Day may come tomorrow but the likelihood is small to the point of invisibility. Suppose we come at it a different way. Suppose Mistress Penteney was right last night in her first suspicion—that it was Master Penteney who was supposed to die? It was probably no secret in the household that those sweetmeats are a favorite of his so he'd eat a great many. What better cover for murder than making a great many people ill and Master Penteney having the misfortune to die?"

"That's possible, too," Joliffe granted, "but as you said, not a very efficient way of murder. Seeing the sickness as cover for Lewis's death works better."

"Bringing us back to Mistress Penteney," Basset said with disgust. "Why couldn't whoever poisoned the sweetmeats have simply been hoping his weak heart would fail under the strain of the sickness and it did and there an end?"

"If that *was* going to be the end, maybe I could leave it lie as it is. But there's going to be talk and I'll lay you eggs to gold pieces that much of that talk is going to be against us."

Basset had not left off frowning since they had begun to talk, nor did he now as he asked, "So, supposing this poisoning was deliberate and done by someone, do you think you have any chance whatever of finding out who and proving it?"

"Probably not. But I've no chance at all if I don't try."

Piers had left the cart, unnoticed until now he sidled to Joliffe's side and said, very low, "Her right one."

"What?" Joliffe asked, stooping to hear him better.

"Her right sleeve," Piers all but whispered. "The packet Mistress Penteney showed the doctor last night. She took it from her right sleeve."

"You're certain?"

"After I thought about it, where she was standing and all, yes."

"Did you see where she put the packet she emptied into Lewis's wine?"

"No. But she took it out of her left sleeve and wouldn't she most likely put it back there? It was in her right hand the last time I remember it."

That was what Joliffe remembered, too; and Mistress Penteney was right-handed. How likely was she to have put the packet, left-handed, up her right sleeve? Not very, he thought.

"Piers, come away from him," Ellis snapped, so sharply that Piers actually took a step backward.

But before he altogether went he whispered to his grandfather and Joliffe, "I like Mistress Penteney."

"So do I," Joliffe whispered back.

Piers hesitated, then said, "But if she killed Lewis, she shouldn't have."

"No," Joliffe agreed. "She shouldn't have."

"Piers!" Ellis ordered and Piers went away to him, scuffling and ungracious.

Basset and Joliffe looked at each other—a long, assessing look, with neither of them very happy, until Basset finally said, tersely, "Why don't you go for a walk, Joliffe?"

It was an order more than a question and Joliffe took it, because Basset was right: they would all be easier if he was somewhere else just now.

Once outside the barn, though, he realized that where else he could go was a problem. Not into town. He was not in the humour for holiday crowds. Nor hanging about the yard. He would rather not have people here thinking about the players if it could be helped, or have to talk to anyone here. With little other choice, he went out the back gate to the lane. If nothing else, he could see how Tisbe did.

It was a solitary walk, which suited him well. Summer was coming into its greenest glory and he had the lane to himself, everyone probably gone to holiday in town. Almost he could lose himself in the pleasure of the sun warm on his back, the sky blue-shining overhead, the flirt of birdsong around him in the hedgerows . . .

Almost, but not enough.

Tisbe was doing well, though, he saw when he came to lean on the gate to the horse pasture. Even from a distance, grazing among the other horses, she looked sleek-sided, and when he whistled and she threw up her head and came to him, it was with a certain jauntiness, her days of rest and plentiful food having plainly been good for her. She even eyed him to see if he were carrying halter or rope before she quite came in his reach, and he chided her, "Grown fond of laziness, have you, girl? You've a few more days of it, by the look of things."

She put her forehead against his shoulder and shoved, telling him to make himself useful and scratch behind her ears. He obliged and they stood in silent, mutual satisfaction for a while, Joliffe letting himself ease into a quiet-mindedness that matched Tisbe's half-closed eyes and the drowse of flies around them, until the sound of a door across the yard behind him brought him to look over his shoulder and see Master Glover coming his way.

So not everyone was gone to holiday in town, Joliffe thought regretfully. He was more regretful when Master Glover joined him at the gate with a brief greeting and asked, "What's all this about trouble at Master Penteney's feast last night? Is it true the idiot is dead?"

"He's dead, yes," Joliffe said, succeeding at keeping his voice easy. He didn't know when he had stopped thinking of Lewis as anyone but Lewis, was surprised to find that he had, and more surprised by his flare of anger as Master

Glover went on lightly, "Well, that's God's mercy on everyone, including the idiot. What happened at the feast anyway? Poison, I've heard."

"You've heard as much as me," Joliffe said. He was giving more heed to scratching the long hollow under Tisbe's chin now than to Master Glover, hoping he would go away.

But Master Glover persisted, "I heard you players were there."

Word spreads fast, Joliffe thought while answering, "The others were. I was in the garden, keeping the children busy."

"Ah. I thought you looked over-well for someone who'd been poisoned. If you weren't, that explains it."

"I wasn't," Joliffe agreed. "Nobody was. Not of a purpose. It just seems to have been some food gone off."

"Is that what they're saying?"

"It's what the crowner is saying, anyway." Joliffe looked at him. "Why? What have you heard?"

Master Glover shrugged. "Lollards are what I've heard. Lollards taking revenge on Master Penteney for that Lollard found dead at his place the other day."

"How did you come to hear that?"

"You know how it is. People talk."

They surely did, but how had Master Glover heard so much, complete with flourishes and Lollards, all the way out here in the not over-long while since it all happened?

"You've been into town to the holidaying?" Joliffe asked.

"I've not, no. I don't hold with . . ." He seemed to think better of what he had been going to say and said instead, "I've let my men go in but stayed here myself. Everyone being gone is what thieves count on at holiday time. Mind you, Deykus is going to hear about only Dav making it back here last night, leaving all the morning work to the two of us."

"Dav is who told you about the trouble at the Penteneys."

"He did." Master Glover reached out and stroked Tisbe's neck. "He's courting one of the kitchenmaids, the poor fool. Was even helping at the feast, so knew about it all far better than he wanted to."

"How did he come to hear it was being said Lollards did the poisoning?" Joliffe asked.

"She has a carrying voice, does Mistress Penteney."

And of course there would have been servants listening as near the parlor's door as they could get. Joliffe realized he should have thought of that.

"But like I said to Dav this morning," Master Glover went on, "a man that has to do with Lollards, he should expect trouble from it, shouldn't he?"

"Master Penteney doesn't have to do with Lollards, does he?" Joliffe asked.

"He must. That Lollard was there to see him the other day and that wasn't by chance, I'll warrant you. His brother is a Lollard, you see. Master Penteney's brother. One of the worst, I've heard tell. He's off somewhere overseas with that arch-heretic Payne."

"I hadn't heard that," Joliffe said, lying with encouraging interest.

"Oh, yes. It's something everyone knows. They just don't talk about it to Master Penteney's face. Not that anyone thinks he's a Lollard, mind you, and good luck for him that he isn't, since everything his brother lost for being one Master Penteney gained, and every time Master Penteney gets richer, his brother is remembered."

There was an undercurrent to Master Glover's words, an edge that a satisfied man shouldn't have towards his master, but as if he had not heard it, Joliffe asked, "Do you think Master Penteney has dealings with Lollards? Besides with the dead man, I mean."

"Not likely, no. That fellow found dead at his place was probably just a useless troublemaker who ran into more trouble than he counted on in some back alley and only happened to be a Lollard."

"And only happened to be dumped in Master Penteney's yard?"

"Maybe. Or maybe somebody wanted to make trouble for Master Penteney." Glover left off stroking Tisbe's neck. "He didn't get rich as he is without making some people unhappy at him, whether they can do anything about it or not."

"So maybe one of them found a way to ruin his feast last night."

"Could be. Could be. Ended by doing him a favor though, didn't they? Killing off the idiot that way. I suppose they'll marry the girl to that Simon now."

"Very like," Joliffe said. He gave Tisbe a final scratch between the eyes, made his farewell to Glover, and left, making it seem he went in no great haste despite how much he wanted to be away from the man. It seemed that, like too many people, other people's trouble was meat and drink to Glover, and just now Joliffe was on a fast. Once away from the pasturage, though, he slowed his pace, matching it to the slow turn of his thoughts, and instead of returning to the barn, followed the lane past the Penteneys' back gate, took a side alley that let him wend back to outside the North Gate with his mind made up to something. Joining the happy crowds, he went through the gateway into the town and purposefully by the shortest way to Queen's Lane and St. Edmund Hall.

The porter, undoubtedly reconciled by the large pitcher

of ale and plate of cakes on a stool beside him to staying
where he was while others holidayed, grudgingly admitted
that Master Thamys was not gone out today, was probably
in his chamber if someone wanted to see him. After that, it
took two farthings to convince him to call out a servant—
who was grumpily less resigned to his day's duties—and
send him to see if Master Thamys would see . . . The
porter cocked a questioning eye at Joliffe, apparently not
impressed by what he saw.

"Master Joliffe of Gloucester Abbey," Joliffe said.

The porter looked as if he doubted that—rightly, as it
happened—but he sent the servant anyway, and the man
came back soon enough with word that Master Thamys
would see Master Joliffe if it pleased him to come up. Joliffe
granted that it pleased him well and followed the man into
the passageway beyond the door and into a long yard, went
slantwise across that to a door to a narrow stairway up to a
well-windowed room, not over-large and sparsely furnished
with several plain-backed chairs, two wall-shelves laden
with books, a small fireplace, and a large desk with a slanted
lectern for reading. Except for the books and fireplace, the
white-washed walls were plain, like the scrubbed-boarded
floor, but the desk from which John Thamys was rising was
laid out with carefully stacked papers, pens laid in a wooden
holder, and an ink bottle that Thamys was stoppering as he
said, "Master Joliffe, how good to see you. Thank you,
Henry. If you could bring some ale, please."

Henry took himself away and Joliffe said, looking
around the room, "Very good. And a separate bedroom,
too." He nodded toward the closed door at the room's other
end. "This isn't bad at all."

"And someone to light a fire for me on cold mornings
and a roof that keeps off the rain," Thamys said. "Not bad
at all, I find."

"And books." Joliffe had crossed to the shelves and was looking at what Thamys had there.

"You could have done as well, you know, 'Master' Joliffe."

"I couldn't have," Joliffe said, turning from the shelves to face him. They were both smiling. "My sense of jest would have come in the way." Over the years he had grown at ease with that certainty. Equally easily, he added, "But don't 'master' me in that tone of voice. I'm a master of my craft as surely as any smith or merchant."

"You assuredly are," Thamys agreed. "I neglected to tell you how much I admired *The Pride of Life*, and I've rarely been so moved as I was by your *Abraham and Isaac* yesterday. I could even forget it was you who were the Angel."

Joliffe bowed slightly. "Thank you."

"But 'of Gloucester Abbey'?"

"It seemed the easiest way to get in here."

Henry returned with a pitcher of ale, fetched two tankards from the other room, and poured while Joliffe and Thamys went to stand near the window overlooking the courtyard, making slight talk about the good weather and how Thamys was taking the chance of a quiet day to get on with his work instead of holidaying. Only when Henry had gone out and down the stairs did Thamys say, "I was sorry to hear about the trouble at the Penteneys and the boy's death. Were you sick along with the rest? You look well enough now."

Joliffe explained how he and the other players had stayed well and asked, "How do you come to know about it so quickly, shut up here with your work?"

"Henry and Cobbe at the gate are unceasing fountains of news of every kind. Word of Oxford's latest doings outside and inside scholarly walls comes along with every meal Henry brings me and sometimes between whiles if it's news enough to warrant it."

"Have you heard Lollards mentioned as part of last night's trouble?"

Thamys sobered. "I have and it doesn't make good hearing. Do you think it's likely?"

"No."

Joliffe's flat certainty of that surprised himself as well as Thamys, who asked, "You don't think at all it might have been Lollards taking some kind of revenge on Master Penteney?"

"For what?"

"For that man's death the other night?" Thamys said doubtfully. "Despite what the crowner seems to think?"

"That's a long stretch," Joliffe said. "Unless someone knows more than has been said about Master Penteney and Lollards. Or more than I've heard, anyway. Have you heard anything that way? Talk about Master Penteney and Lollards together? Before now, I mean."

"Until now, I've never heard aught but good about Master Penteney."

"Not even from nasty Gascoigne? If there's anything bad to say about someone, he surely would say it."

"You took a deep dislike to him, didn't you?" Thamys grinned.

"I did, and fairly enough, I think. He dislikes me and my kind for no good reason at all. Therefore, I feel free, for that very good reason, to dislike him in return."

"I suspect there's a severe flaw in that reasoning, on grounds of Christian charity if nothing else," Thamys said, "but I'm not minded to challenge you on it. What in particular are you wondering if I've heard?"

"About Master Penteney's Lollard brother."

"His Lollard brother? I've heard about him yes." Thamys seemed both surprised and puzzled. "But not until this week, as it happens."

"Not until after the dead Lollard was found?" Joliffe asked. "Nothing before then?"

"Before then, nothing."

"What exactly is being said? About him and against Master Penteney?"

Thamys paused, searching his mind before saying, "Nothing against Master Penteney, really. The talk that I've heard is merely that he had a brother who went to the bad, is long gone from Oxford and probably dead. All old news, but old news is still news when folk can't find anything else to say."

"But until now there's been no talk of him, this missing brother? Even by Gascoigne?"

"Even by Gascoigne," Thamys said soothingly. "I'd guess the matter was so forgotten it took a dead Lollard on Master Penteney's doorstep to drag it out of the depths of someone's memory and set the talk going. What are you up to, Joliffe?"

Realizing he was frowning with thought, Joliffe smoothed his face and asked blandly, "What about Master Wymond the baker? What's the talk about him?"

"You mean, is he a Lollard?" Thamys said dryly. "I haven't heard anything at all that way, and I'll thank you to start none. He makes the best apple tarts in Oxford."

"I mean is he well known for often being late with things ordered from him?"

"Master Wymond? Never at all. How long would he have anyone's business and a shop in the High Street if he couldn't be depended on? We use him ourselves here at St. Edmund. What are you about?"

Joliffe looked elaborately innocent. "About? I'm just asking questions is all."

"When a scholar asks a string of questions, it's because he's looking for an answer at the end of them."

"Ah, but I'm not a scholar, remember. Just a poor, wandering player without two wits to rub together," Joliffe said cheerfully.

Equally cheerfully, Thamys answered, "You're such a liar."

"I'm not!" Joliffe protested. "Some people make sport with quoits or balls of dice. You make sport with ideas. I make sport with questions. To each their own."

"I know you're not half the rascal you'd have me think," Thamys returned.

Joliffe laid a finger to his lips. "Let that be our secret." He moved away. "I'd best go now, but my thanks for the ale and talk."

"You're very welcome." Thamys followed him toward the door. "But only on condition you tell me later what you're at with all these questions."

"I will," Joliffe said, "if only to give you a goodly laugh at what a fool I'm being."

But if he was not being a fool, then something doubly dire was going on; and he left Thamys and went rapidly down the stairs because time might well be getting thin between now and worse.

Chapter 18

At the barn again, Joliffe found only Basset, sitting alone beside the cart, oiling a piece of Tisbe's harness. As Joliffe crossed toward him he looked up and said, "Rose and Ellis have taken Piers out and about. Better than moping here, they thought. Where did you go?"

"Out to see Tisbe." Joliffe sat down where he could reach oil and a rag and another piece of the harness. He had returned to the barn to try some of his thoughts against Basset's sharpness before he went further and was glad the others were gone. "I talked a while with Master Penteney's man there. Walter Glover. He . . ."

"Walter Glover?" Basset echoed, pausing at his work. "About my age? Thick sandy hair?"

"About your age, yes, and he has sandy hair, right enough," Joliffe said, surprised. "Not what I'd call thick, though. Especially on top."

"It could well be thin by now," Basset said complacently. He took open pleasure in his own barely withdrawn hairline.

"You know him."

"He sounds like the Walter Glover apprenticed to old Master Penteney when I was. What did you say he's doing?"

"He sees to Master Penteney's pasturing north of town."

"Huh," Basset said, taking up his work again. "Who would have thought it. I'd have supposed he'd be a victualler in his own right by now, if I'd thought about it at all. He was shaping toward it well enough when I left. Had a busy brain, he did."

Pretending more interest than he actually had in the rein he was oiling, Joliffe asked, "He was your friend, along with Master Penteney and his brother?"

"Walter? He was more just there than actually our friend. A few years younger and following along with what we did. You know how it goes."

"Taken up with lollardy like the rest of you were, was he?" Joliffe asked carefully.

Not carefully enough. Basset worked at the strap for a silent moment before, still working, he answered, "Pretty much."

"Or more taken up," Joliffe pressed. "The way Master Penteney's brother was?"

Basset gave up on the strap, gave Joliffe a long look, and said, "He shied off when the rest of us did. That's what I remember."

"Did he? Shy off, I mean."

For a long moment the twitter and flit of sparrows among the far rafters was the only sound in the barn, until Basset said, "You think maybe he didn't?"

"The way he talked just now, he sounded near to blaming Master Penteney for prospering at his brother's expense. As if Penteney were at fault for gaining everything that his brother lost."

"I suppose," Basset said slowly, "that if I had ever been asked, I would have said Walter followed closer on Roger's heels than on Hal's or mine in those days."

"Not so close as to follow him into exile, though."

"Not that close, no. But close enough that maybe, yes, he might resent Penteney had all the gain and his brother all the loss."

"And yet he works for Penteney to this day."

"Works for him," Basset said, "when he was apprenticed to be a victualler in his own right someday. Something went wrong somewhere, for him to be only a hired man instead of his own master."

"Master Penteney hasn't said anything about him when you've talked, though?"

"Not a word. Joliffe, what are you aiming at?"

"A target I'm just starting to guess," Joliffe said. He put aside the piece of harness and the rag and stood up, frowning not at Basset but at his own thoughts. "I have to go somewhere. I'll be back."

"I trust so," Basset said.

Master Barentyne was more easily found than Joliffe had feared he might be. The servant standing watch outside the Penteneys' streetward gate—whether to greet anyone coming to offer sympathy or on guard against the curious, Joliffe could not tell—was able to tell him Master Barentyne was staying at a cousin's house near the Guildhall, and as fortune would have it, Master Barentyne was in, rather than holidaying somewhere in the streets. The servant who met Joliffe at the door there was unwilling to admit that until Joliffe said he had come about "the Penteney trouble." That got him in but did not make him welcome;

he was left standing just inside the door while the servant went in search of Master Barentyne, who came himself, rather than having Joliffe brought to him, asking without other greeting, "Is there new trouble?"

"Just the old," Joliffe said. "It's about this Hubert Leonard and his lollardy and maybe Master Penteney's brother."

"Shall I guess here isn't the best place to talk about this?"

"A fair guess, yes," Joliffe granted, and Master Barentyne led him inside, into the house's hall. Like the house itself, it was an altogether more modest place than the Penteneys' but large enough that when Master Barentyne stopped in its middle and faced around to him, they were enough away from any doors to be safe from being overheard so long as they kept their voices down.

"What about Leonard?" Master Barentyne asked. "You're not thinking he was Penteney's brother, are you? Because he wasn't, worse luck. He's been named for certain by two men from Abingdon, come to Oxford with their families for Corpus Christi and to visit relatives."

"You've no reason to doubt them?"

"One is the abbot's bailiff there and the other a well-known merchant. They both say they've known this Leonard off and on since boyhood. He's been gone more than not these past years. 'In foreign parts,' one of them said. But they knew him well enough when they saw him. Neither of them seemed to mind much he was dead. I gather that had nothing to do with him being a Lollard, if that's what he was. They just didn't like him. So, no, he's not Penteney's brother."

"There was never much likelihood he was. What I really came to ask was how much you do truly know about Master Penteney's brother."

"What Master Penteney told us, and the talk that's come up about him since this started, the way talk does. That he was a Lollard and some way a troublemaker and he's long gone and probably dead. Why?"

"Had you heard about this brother before now? Not from Master Penteney, but from anyone?" Joliffe insisted.

"From what my cousin's wife says, the scandal is stale by twenty years and more. Even she couldn't squeeze much juice out of it. It's only the murder, with talk the dead man was a Lollard, has briefly freshened memory of it, that's all." Master Barentyne sharpened to a demand. "Why?"

Again, Joliffe slid away from answering directly, saying instead, "I went out today to check on our horse. She's being kept in Master Penteney's pasturage north from town. I fell into talk with Master Penteney's man there. Walter Glover."

"I don't know him."

"He was apprenticed to Master Penteney's father years and years ago, but never became his own master and works as a steward of sorts for Master Penteney now."

Master Barentyne was waiting for the point of this, but Joliffe made no haste about it, wanting to say the thing right, to see what Master Barentyne would make of it before he said his own full suspicion outright. "We didn't talk long, but Glover managed to mention Master Penteney and Lollards in the same breath a good many times. He made a point of linking last night's poisoning to Lollards, then said how Master Penteney should expect trouble if he has to do with Lollards, and that he must have to do with Lollards because why else had that man Leonard been to see him."

"The disloyal cur," Master Barentyne said. "He can make deep trouble for Penteney if he goes on like that."

"Then he saw fit to tell me about Master Penteney's brother. He said 'everyone knows' Penteney's brother is 'one of the worst' Lollards and lives 'off overseas' with the 'arch-heretic Payne'."

"That's more than my cousin's wife knows," Barentyne scoffed. "And she knows every morsel of talk to be had in Oxford. She . . ." He stopped, his brow creased with mingled frown and thought. He met Joliffe's waiting look and went on slowly. "She knows every morsel of talk and never stops repeating it. But she's never said anything about Penteney's brother being alive. The way she has heard and tells it, he's long gone and long dead."

"I've asked elsewhere," Joliffe said. "It seems to be what's generally said. Except by Glover."

They went on looking at each other a long moment more before Master Barentyne said, still slowly, "Since Master Glover seems to know more than anyone else does about this Lollard brother who may or may not have part in this Leonard's death, it's maybe time I talk a while with him."

"It isn't much," Joliffe said, willing to be cautious now that someone else besides himself had suspicion.

"A little is better than the nothing I presently have." Master Barentyne was giving way to open pleasure at thought of something to do, saying as he began to turn away, "I'll find some of my men to send out to bring him in."

Quickly Joliffe said, "I wanted to ask you about Lewis Fairfield's death, too."

Master Barentyne paused. "Are you going to say you think Glover had something to do with the poisoning?"

"I don't see how he could have. No. What I was wondering was if you knew any more about what was used to taint the sweetmeats. If it wasn't a chance spoilage."

"I've talked to the baker. He swears everything was fresh and that no one he doesn't know could have come at them while they were at his place. From what I know of Master Wymund, I lean toward believing him."

"But if wasn't chance spoilage, either at the baker's or the Penteneys', wouldn't it have taken a goodly amount of whatever was used—supposing something was used—to make that many people that sick? More of a poison than someone would likely have on hand?"

"It would. Yes." Master Barentyne was grimly certain about that. "That's why I have one of my men going around right now to every apothecary and herbwife in town to ask if anyone has lately bought much of any of the things the doctor mentioned. I'm hoping he finds out nothing. Then we can safely put all of it down to no more than ill-chance. Although," he added somewhat wishfully, "it would ease things if it turned out this Master Glover had been buying some such stuff of late."

Joliffe laughed. "It would, at that." He bowed respectfully. "I leave you to your business then."

Master Barentyne bent his head in return and again started to turn away. To his back Joliffe offered, "There's several sheds at the pasturage where carts are probably kept, and behind the house there's a muddy edge of marsh along one of the pastures. You'll maybe want your men to see if anything has been lying among the reeds there lately. And have a close look at any carts?"

Master Barentyne grinned over his shoulder at him. "A marsh and carts. Yes, those will bear looking at, thank you."

"And you might want to ask about the bay horse with the two white forefeet that wasn't in the pasture three days ago."

Master Barentyne's smile grew. He bent his head respectfully to Joliffe, then went on his way, leaving Joliffe to find his own way out, which Joliffe did, moving rather more quickly than was easy through the holidaying crowd. The afternoon was well along but there was no noticeable slackening of merriment. For most folks the roistering would likely go on until curfew and, for some, beyond curfew, but Joliffe's own sense of holiday was long gone. He was glad he did not happen on Rose and Piers and Ellis, but as he crossed the Penteneys' yard toward the barn he realized he did not much want to see Basset either. What he wanted now was chance to think and he didn't know how much time he had for it. Master Barentyne would learn whatever there was to learn about Glover. If it proved to amount to what Joliffe thought it might—if all the wrong notes Glover had hit in their talking together sang the song Joliffe thought they would—then Leonard's murder was taken care of. That left the poisoning and Lewis's death, and he had thoughts there that he wanted to lay out and look at, to see if they took the shape he feared they would.

But if they did, then his time was nearly gone, and with a quick glance to check that there seemed to be nobody to see him, he turned away from the barn, into the narrow alleyway to the garden gate. If someone were in the garden, he would simply stay out of sight in the alley, lean against the wall, and think there; but when he looked through the gap around the gate and saw Kathryn alone, sitting on the bench in the little group of birch trees across the garden otherwise empty in the afternoon sunlight, he only hesitated, then went through the gateway and across the grass toward her.

Head bowed, she did not notice him until he was almost to the trees. Even then she did not startle, merely raised her head and looked at him, her face a pale oval in the young birch leaves' dappling shadows. She was not crying but she had been; her eyes were a little red and there were tears under her voice as she said, "Master Joliffe."

Joliffe made her a bow and said, "Pardon me, my lady. Would you rather I left you alone?"

"Please," she said, lifting one hand toward him. "Please stay."

Joliffe stayed but came no nearer, warning gently, "It's hardly seemly for you to be here alone with me, my lady."

"Simon will be here soon. He said he'd come when they finished talking. They must be done by now. They're deciding about Lewis's burial and . . . afterward."

"Afterward," Joliffe repeated. "When you marry Simon."

He wanted to see how she would answer that, said out so plainly. She merely drew a long, trembling breath, let it out on a heavy sigh, and said unevenly, "Yes."

"You'll like that better than marrying Lewis, surely," he tried, still gently.

She fixed her eyes on him, wide and maybe a little frightened. "Much better, I think. How wrong is it of me to feel that way so soon after Lewis's death?"

That was very probably something she would have said to no one of her family. Only because he was almost a stranger, someone who merely happened to be there, was she that open, and he answered carefully, "It's not wrong at all. You're brave to face that truth so honestly. You don't mourn for Lewis any the less because of it, do you?"

"I've been crying for him," she said. "He was sweetness itself. But . . ." Tears welled up in her voice again. "I'm so glad I don't have to marry him!"

So when she had talked a few days ago about how she did not mind marrying him, she had been no more than putting a brave front on something expected of her, not her own choice.

"It will be much better to marry Simon," Joliffe agreed evenly. "Especially since you love Simon better."

Kathryn stared at him a silent while, her mouth twisted tightly against more tears, before she finally said faintly, maybe trying out the words aloud for the first time but certain of them, "Especially since I love Simon better."

She looked past Joliffe then, and by her gladdened face

he knew even before he turned to see for himself that Simon was coming.

Like Kathryn and everyone else in the family, Simon was garbed in black, but it was more than that made him look older than he had yesterday. Since yesterday he had seen death close up and had everything come into his hands that, all his life, had been just beyond his reach because he was the younger brother. Property and wealth and a firm place in the world—and Kathryn, who otherwise would have been lost to him forever.

She rose to meet him as he reached them, holding out her hands for his while asking, "It's settled?"

Taking her hands, Simon said, "Lewis will be buried tomorrow." He sounded tired as well as older. "Then, on Sunday before Lord and Lady Lovell leave, we're to be betrothed. You and I."

Kathryn sighed and closed her eyes. Simon took a step closer to her and leaned his forehead against hers. They both looked as if some great fear had gone out of them and left them too tired to feel, for now, anything but relief.

Regretting the need, Joliffe asked "Has anything more been heard from the crowner about the sweetmeats? Whether they were poisoned or not?"

Simon and Kathryn drew a little apart, each letting one hand go but keeping the other tightly held as Kathryn warned, "You're not to say 'poisoned'. Mother says it can't have been that. She's sorry she said 'poisoned' last night. They just spoiled, that's all. She says it's her fault for not keeping them well, and everyone is to know Master Wymond isn't to blame at all."

"So no one thinks it was Lollards anymore?" Joliffe prodded.

"No," Kathryn said firmly and with a little scorn.

But Simon, looking troubled, said, "Some people do. Father Francis was just here, telling Master Penteney that Master Wymond is going to be questioned by Master Gascoigne and some others of the university to see what he has to say."

"You mean to see if maybe he's a Lollard?" Kathryn asked, horrified. "He never would be!"

"His men are to be questioned, too," Simon said. "And all of our servants here."

"But why?" Kathryn cried in distress. "We're not any of us Lollards. Why would Lollards want to make trouble for Father anyway? He's never had aught to do with Lollards."

"It's because of the dead man the other morning," Simon said.

"That still doesn't have anything to do with Father!"

From the house door, Mistress Penteney called, "Kathryn, come in, please."

"Bother," Kathryn said but immediately let go of Simon and went. Simon made to go with her, but Joliffe said quickly, low enough for Kathryn not to hear, "Please ask Mistress and Master Penteney to see me here, now, if they will. Both of them. I've heard something about that dead man that they maybe should know and soon."

Simon paused, opened his mouth to ask something, decided against it, nodded, and followed Kathryn toward the house. Joliffe saw him stop in the doorway to say something to Mistress Penteney, who looked across the grass to Joliffe. He slightly bowed, then stood in a way that said he would wait. She gave him a brief nod and went indoors.

What, he asked himself, had he just done? Besides robbing himself of any time for thinking, he had just committed himself to something he very possibly should not be doing. But maybe Master and Mistress Penteney would not come out. Or not come out in time. If they didn't come soon, would he go in and demand to see them? Or would he just stay aside and let things fall out as they would?

He was spared finding that out by Master and Mistress Penteney coming together into the garden. As fitted their place in the world and his, they stopped on the path there, waiting for him to come to them and he did; but after his respectful bow, he stopped the beginning of a question from Master Penteney by making a small gesture that suggested they move farther away from the house, saying, "The better not to be overheard."

Master Penteney's questioning look deepened but he held out his hand for his wife, showing he was ready to follow Joliffe. Mistress Penteney had turned a little aside to pluck a stalk of lavender leaves from the tall plant beside the door. Twirling it in the fingers of one hand, she laid the other on her husband's and went with him as Joliffe led them back to the birches. There Master Penteney seated his wife on the bench and said to Joliffe, "Master Fairfield said you've heard something new about the dead man."

Master Fairfield was Simon now. Joliffe made that shift in his mind while saying, "I happened to meet Master Barentyne a little while ago. He was about to send some of his men to bring Walter Glover to him for questioning."

"Glover?" Master Penteney's surprise at that seemed complete. "What's Glover have to do with it?"

"It seems he's been heard saying things about you and Lollards."

Mistress Penteney had been smelling the lavender sprig. Now her hand with it dropped into her lap and she protested, surprised and angry together, "Master Glover? He'd never do any such thing!"

"Seemingly he has done," Joliffe said, watching Master Penteney rather than her. The man's face was suddenly stiff with wariness. As well it might be. Joliffe pushed on. "He's been talking about your brother, sir. How he's alive and that you've had dealings with him and Lollards all these years and that last night's poisoning was maybe by Lollards striking back at you for Leonard's death."

Stiffly, Master Penteney said, "I had nothing to do with Leonard's death."

"Besides," Mistress Penteney said, "your brother, God help him, has been dead for years. Everyone knows that who knows anything about it at all."

The silence in which Master Penteney did not answer that lasted too long, before Joliffe said, "I gather Master Barentyne thinks Master Glover was talking too much about the poisoning being Lollard vengence. He . . ."

"I wish I'd never said that!" Mistress Penteney exclaimed. "It's all foolishness!"

"Not that Master Barentyne sees any way Glover can be linked to the sweetmeats," Joliffe went on; but now he looked at her rather than her husband, laying his words out very deliberately. "The sweetmeats came straight from the baker's to here. Master Barentyne has begun to wonder, though, why you wanted them so much ahead of time." That was a lie, but if Master Barentyne had not wondered it, Joliffe had. "Master Wymond has never been known for being late with what's ordered from him. It would be more reasonable, in this warm weather, for you to want the sweetmeats to be made later rather than sooner wouldn't it?"

Mistress Penteney looked confusedly from him to her husband and back again. "It was . . . I don't know. It just seemed . . . I thought it would be better, that's all."

Knowing how much a fool and worse than fool he was going to look if he failed to bring this off, Joliffe pressed on, giving Mistress Penteney no time to regain her balance. "Of course, the whole thing is that everyone is thinking about the sweetmeats. Everyone has been wondering whether it was by chance or purpose they were tainted. If by chance, there's no problem. If by purpose, then whose purpose? Who would want to strike like that against Master Penteney?"

"No one," snapped Master Penteney. "What happened was simply mischance. I'm satisfied of that. If Master Barentyne isn't . . ."

"But suppose," Joliffe interrupted, still watching Mistress Penteney, "you weren't the reason for it at all, sir? What if the sweetmeats *were* tainted on purpose but it had nothing to do with Lollards or against you? What if, instead of all that, it's Lewis's death we should be looking at?"

"Lewis died of his weak heart," Master Penteney said at the same time Mistress Penteney demanded, her voice breaking with distress, "Make him stop talking about all this!"

Master Penteney put an arm around her shoulders and said at Joliffe, "She's right. This is pointless talk. Have done."

Knowing he had gone too far to have done, Joliffe said sharply, "Suppose the whole purpose was to make Lewis sick so that he could be given something not to *help* his heart but to stop it once and for all."

Master Penteney opened his mouth, closed it again, apparently unable to find words sufficient for the outrage suffusing his face, before he finally burst out, "Does Basset know you're a crazed young fool?"

But Mistress Penteney was staring, rigidly silent, at Joliffe and he turned on her, saying with seeming mercilessness, "I'm not the only one who saw you put the packet of whatever you gave Lewis up one sleeve and take the packet you showed the doctor out of your other."

It was a lie but she couldn't know that. Even so, a hard-ened woman would have faced him better on it, but Mistress Penteney shrank back, shaking her head with wordless horror.

Master Penteney took a furious, threatening step toward Joliffe, ordering, "Stop it!"

Joliffe took a step backward but said past him, still at Mistress Penteney, "Besides that, Master Barentyne has a man right now asking all over Oxford if anyone has lately bought quantities of any of those things the doctor said could have been used to taint the sweetmeats and bring on vomiting. Groundsel. A concoction from elder bark. Any-thing."

Mistress Penteney, dropping the lavender, pressed her hands to her mouth and went on—more desperately now—shaking her head. All color had drained from her face and her eyes were huge with fear.

Knowing he had to break her now or lose the game alto-gether, Joliffe said, demanding and begging together, "My lady, if he's going find out that it was you who bought any-thing like this, please, do you want to be here when he comes looking for you?"

The tear-wrought cry of protest and denial that broke from behind her hands turned Master Penteney from Jo-liffe to her. Too surprised to be alarmed yet, he said, "Anne? What is it? What . . ." He caught up to what Joliffe had been saying, matched it with the terror in her eyes, and said in a suddenly stricken whisper, "Blessed Saints. Anne, what have you done?"

Her hands slid down to clutch her throat as she turned her frighted stare on him. "What he said," she whispered hoarsely. "About buying the elder and groundsel. I couldn't let Kathryn marry Lewis. How did I ever think I could? I . . . I . . ." She lost breath and seemed unable to find more.

"But you never said anything," Master Penteney said, sounding still half-disbelieving what he was hearing. "You never said anything against it at all."

"I did!" Mistress Penteney cried out, anguished. "All this past half-year, when time started to run out, I tried. I'd start to say something about the marriage, but every time I did, you'd start in on what you could see coming from it! All your plans for Richard running the Fairfield properties and making a separate home for him and Geva. Everything. I couldn't make you hear me!"

"But all these years we've purposed it, Anne. There's been time and enough to say you didn't like the thought!"

"It didn't matter until now! We thought Lewis would die before now and we'd marry Kathryn to Simon. But Lewis didn't die and I couldn't bear it! I couldn't bear Lewis to be what Kathryn first knew of being married. Not with all the rest of her life to be lived through!"

Finally, fully, Master Penteney grasped what she was telling him, and like a man who had taken a blow under the ribs he took an unsteady backward step and gasped, short-breathed. "My God." Staring at her. "My God and all the saints."

Hands still clutched at her throat, Mistress Penteney stared back at him and saw in his horror that she had lost him. But in the instant that her face began to twist toward that knowledge and grief, he recovered with a gasp, took a long stride back to her and grabbed her into his arms, pulling her to him as if his life and hers depended on him holding her to him as tightly as he could.

"Sanctuary," he said fiercely. "Before Master Barentyne comes for you we'll get you into sanctuary. I won't let them have you. I swear it. We'll have you into sanctuary first."

Meaning into a church, any church. Once someone claimed sanctuary in a church, the law could not touch them for forty days, whatever crime they were accused of. And if, in that forty days, they confessed to the crime, they could not be tried or imprisoned, only sent into exile— given so many days to reach an appointed port and sail from England, forbidden ever to return.

In his arms, Mistress Penteney began to cry, but he looked past her to Joliffe and asked, "You say Barentyne is asking right now about anyone buying this . . . these things?"

"Yes."

Not loosing his hold on her, Master Penteney asked his wife, "Will he find out you did this?"

"Yes." She gulped on her freely flowing tears. "Yes. I bought groundsel at some places and elder at others all over Oxford this past week. They have good uses. That's why apothecaries have them. That's what I said I wanted them for. It's only if you mix the groundsel with . . ."

"Best we don't try for any of the near churches," Master Penteney said, planning aloud. "We might meet Master Barentyne on our way to them. St. Peter-le-Bailey would maybe be best, well away from any way he might take to come here. We can go by the back lane from here and around to come in by the West Gate. No. Not St. Peter. St. Ebbe's. That's straight in from West Gate, easier to come to."

He was already moving while he said it, pulling Mistress Penteney around and starting toward the back gate. She began what might have been a protest. "Hal . . ." But he said, "When you're safe, there'll be time for more. For now, sanctuary is what matters." He looked back at Joliffe, standing where they had left him. "If Barentyne shows here any time soon . . ."

"I'll delay him as best I can," Joliffe said. Was this how he had meant things to go? Too late to wonder, but, "One thing," he said. Master Penteney slowed, looked back, but did not stop. Joliffe raised his voice to reach him. "If ever Master Barentyne asks why you took her to sanctuary, could you just tell him she confessed to you and leave me out of it?"

Master Penteney gave a curt nod of silent agreement. Then he and Mistress Penteney were gone out of the garden and away.

Chapter 19

Joliffe followed them slowly enough that they were gone from the yard by the time he came from between the sheds. Since Master Barentyne had no reason to suppose Mistress Penteney would be warned and try to escape him, she would probably reach St. Ebbe's church safely enough. If they weren't followed too soon. And knowing he was being several ways a fool, he sauntered the length of the yard to the front gateway.

The gates were closed, only the small door through one of them standing open. He went out, giving a nod to the Penteney servant still on guard. The man nodded back with nothing to say, and Joliffe leaned back against the near side of the gateway, arms crossed, at seeming-ease as he took to watching the passing folk in the street. He had not watched long before Master Barentyne came striding along from the North Gate through the crowd with a grim look to him and four of his men following. That told Joliffe all he needed to know, and as the five men neared him, he straightened up with an easy movement that put him directly into their way to the gate-door and said with a bow and cheerful curiosity, "This is soon to see you again, Master Barentyne. You haven't found out anything from Glover already, have you?"

It was either stop or walk into Joliffe. Master Barentyne stopped and answered, "My men haven't brought him in yet. It will be a while longer."

Seeming not to see Master Barentyne's half-made gesture for him to stand aside, Joliffe said lightly, "What brings you here, then?"

"The other matter," Master Barentyne muttered, not wanting to be overheard, it seemed. Master Penteney's man was listening hard. The crowner's grim look did not ease. "Let us pass, man."

"Oh. Yes. Sorry." Joliffe confusedly started to go through the doorway ahead of him, thought better of it, started to step aside, thought better of that, made to go first through the doorway after all, and only finally settled on standing clear to let Master Barentyne go ahead of him.

Thrown off by the fluster of movements, Master Barentyne hesitated, waiting to be sure Joliffe was done before he went on. Joliffe bowed encouragingly, Master Barentyne finally went, and Joliffe followed him closely enough to cut ahead of his four men following him, fell into step beside him as he made toward the house, and asked, "The other matter? You mean the tainted food? You've found something out?"

They were to the porch. He stopped as he asked the last question, and Master Barentyne stopped, too, facing him to answer with taut impatience. "I've found out Mistress Penteney bought groundsel from at least three apothecaries and elder from an herbwife, all in this past week or so. I'm here to question her about it. Now if you'll pardon me." He did not wait for pardon but went on, his men behind him.

It had not been much of a delay. Joliffe could only hope

there would be a longer one once Master Barentyne was inside. Someone would be sent to bring Mistress Penteney to
him, would find she was not to be found. Then it would be
found that Master Penteney was missing, too. Only then
would the search for them spread out from the house, and
even when it was determined neither of them was there, no
one would know why or which way to send a search for
them, and by that time all that was straightened around,
Mistress Penteney would hopefully be into sanctuary.

And if she was not, there was nothing more Joliffe
could do for her anyway.

Tired all through and not certain what he was feeling, he
went to the barn, into its shadows and quiet, was glad to find
Basset still alone there, sitting on a cushion with the box
that kept their plays open beside him and papers in his
hands. He looked up as Joliffe came toward him and started
to ask, "Do you think maybe we should work over . . ."

Joliffe went past him, dropped wearily down beside the
cart, and leaned back against the wheel, his arms draped
over his updrawn knees, his head bowed, his eyes shut.

Basset changed his question to, "What's wrong?"

Without lifting his head, Joliffe said, "Master Barentyne
has found out it was Mistress Penteney poisoned the sweetmeats. He's here to question and probably arrest her."

Basset shot to his feet. "Blessed St. Genesius! Does
Penteney know?"

His eyes still shut, Joliffe answered, "Master Penteney
took her away to sanctuary in some church just before
Master Barentyne came for her. He knows she killed
Lewis, too. But Master Barentyne doesn't."

Basset sat heavily back down. "Joliffe." His voice was
flat. "What have you done?"

Briefly, Joliffe told him, first about setting Master Barentyne on to Walter Glover—"Though I don't know how

that will come out"—and then what Master Barentyne had
told him about the questioning being made of apothecaries
and herbwives. "Knowing that, I came back here, asked to
speak with Master and Mistress Penteney both, told her I
knew about the packets in her opposite sleeves and what
Master Barentyne was doing. She broke down." Just as he
had meant her to because all he had were suspicions, no
proof without she admitted to it.

"And Penteney?" Basset asked in a low voice.

Joliffe told him the rest of it, ending, "He took her out
the back way not much before Master Barentyne and his
men came in the front. They're at the house now."

But they were not. With a hard rap at the door and not
waiting to be asked, Master Barentyne stalked in, two of
his men with him. Basset stood up. Joliffe dragged himself
to his feet and stayed leaning against the wheel, his arms
crossed while Master Barentyne waved his men to search
the barn, then said at him, "I'm told you were with Master
and Mistress Penteney in the garden not long ago. Do you
know where they've gone?"

"The last I saw of them was in the garden."

"Why did you ask to talk with them there?"

"I thought they should know what Walter Glover had
been saying against Master Penteney and be told you were
going to question him."

"That was no business of yours," Master Barentyne
snapped.

"They've been our courteous patrons. I felt I owed them
that."

"After you told them that, then what?"

"I left the garden. I haven't seen them since." Which
was not a lie, merely the truth with bits left out and somewhat rearranged.

"You talked to them about Glover and then you left the

garden," Master Barentyne said. "You don't know anything more? Such as where they might have gone?"

"Back into the house?" Joliffe suggested.

"No one here has seen them since they went into the garden to see you. You don't know where they went?"

"No," Joliffe said, steadily meeting his gaze.

Master Barentyne turned on Basset. "Do you know anything?"

Basset spread out his hands, still holding papers in one of them. "I've been here all afternoon. No one has come in except Joliffe and now you, nor have I gone out. I haven't seen the Penteneys since this morning when you were here."

Since neither the barn nor the cart offered much in the way of hiding places, Master Barentyne's men had already finished their search. He swung his glare from Basset to them, then back to Joliffe and demanded, "You can't tell me more?"

"No."

Master Barentyne muttered an oath and swung away, leading his men out of the barn. For a long moment after they had gone, Basset and Joliffe stayed standing. Then Basset sat on the cushion again and Joliffe sank down where he was, this time holding his head in his hands.

"I hate it when I have to lie," he said.

"What you hate is when you have to *outright* lie," Basset returned. "What you prefer is to dance around the truth so fast no one can find it. Until Barentyne forced you into your 'lie outright,' you danced as pretty a dance around the truth as ever I've seen."

Joliffe lifted his head, smiling. "I did, didn't I?"

"You did. I've never seen it done better."

"Thank you."

"You're welcome. Now, as I was going to say, do you

think maybe we should work over the St. Nicholas play, since Piers is getting older and could take a part?"

They were still talking over how the play could be changed when one of the household servants put his head in at the door and said, "Hai, you fellows, Master Richard wants to talk with you."

Joliffe and Basset traded looks with each other and said nothing save Basset told the man "Certainly," and set to putting the papers and box away in the cart. The man waited, then led them to the house. In the usual way of things, the hall should have been busy with readying for supper. Instead, clumps of servants stood talking in fast, low voices, with wary looks at Joliffe and Basset as if worried that more trouble was somehow coming in with them. All the household's busy ease and friendliness were gone and Joliffe was glad to escape through the doorway into Master Penteney's study, where Master Richard turned from the window to say, "Thank you, Hew. Close the door as you go, please."

The man bowed and withdrew, closing the door while Basset and Joliffe both bowed to Master Richard, who beckoned them to come to him at the window. Outside, in the garden, Mistress Geva, Simon, and Kathryn were sitting in a circle on the grass, playing some sort of game with small Giles in their midst. Giles was laughing and, as Basset and Joliffe reached Master Richard, did something that made Mistress Geva laugh, too. Master Richard looked around and out at them, then back to Basset, and said, "You're my father's friend." And added, answering Basset's surprise, "He told me. After the dead man was found here, he told me about you and his brother and all. On the chance it would be necessary I know it." Until now, Joliffe had only seen Master Richard being his father's apparently willing follower. Now, with his father missing and the crowner come in search of his mother, he had justified his father's training and trust by having plainly taken authority into his own hands. He held it well, looking steadily at Basset as he asked, "Do you know anything about what's happening?"

"What I've been told," Basset said. "Nothing more. But Master Southwell does."

Joliffe found himself with both men looking at him.

"What do you know?" Master Richard demanded.

"Just tell him," Basset said as Joliffe hesitated. "Start with where Master and Mistress Penteney are."

Joliffe was spared that by a sudden silence from the hall. The talk from there had been a low, uneven background sound. Its stop made all three men look toward the door, just as Master Penteney entered.

"Father!" Master Richard said gladly, going to meet him. Only after he had grasped his father's out-held hand did he take in his father's disheveled hair and clothing and the strained unhappiness on his face, and say, far less gladly, "Father, what is it? Where's Mother?"

"She's safe," Master Penteney said. He had already taken in that Basset and Joliffe were there and seen beyond them to the garden. "Richard, fetch the others here, please. Geva, Simon, Kathryn. Don't send someone. No, don't call out the window. Bring them yourself. As quietly as may be."

"What do you mean by Mother is safe?" Master Richard asked.

"I mean she's in sanctuary at St. Ebbe's church. Please. Bring the others here."

Master Richard, his own face suddenly as strained as his father's, went out of the room. Master Penteney shut the door behind him and turned to Basset and Joliffe. "Master Southwell, I met Master Barentyne's guard at my front gate, so I know what happened here after we left, and Master Barentyne will surely be back here soon. He knows about my wife tainting the sweetmeats. Does he know about Lewis? That she killed him?"

"No," Joliffe said. "I've said nothing. He has no reason to suspect further than he does. That Lewis died of his weak heart."

Master Penteney heaved a great breath. "That's something, then. Will you keep it secret? The both of you?"

"We swear it," Basset said instantly, and Joliffe nodded to it, too, as Basset asked, "But what are you going to do about the other? About the poisoning. She'll have to give some reason for it."

"We've decided that already. She'll claim she doesn't know why she did it. That it was a kind of madness. If she doesn't admit to more, everyone will have to accept that."

"It was still a crime," Basset said. "She'll not be let lightly off for it."

"She won't be, no," Master Penteney agreed. "Aside from whatever punishment there would be if she wasn't in sanctuary, the disgrace of it will finish her here in Oxford. More than that, I'm afraid that if she's closely questioned, she'll break down and confess Lewis's murder and that would be the end of everything. No. She's claimed sanctuary, she'll admit the poisoning, and when she's exiled, I'll go with her. I have means enough overseas and know enough people there. We'll do well enough."

"You'll go with her," Basset said.

"I'll go with her. Part of the guilt is mine. I wanted the Fairfield properties badly enough I let it blind me to anything else. It was because I wouldn't see for myself or hear what she tried to tell that she did what she did. Besides that . . ." Master Penteney's voice softened and went low. ". . . how could I let her go alone? I love her."

It all came down, very simply, to that.

"What of everything here?" Basset asked. "You'll just leave it?"

"Richard is ready to take it over. More than ready. And Geva will be the happier, having a household for her own."

In the garden Master Richard was collecting the others, small Giles protesting the end of his game.

"It's Glover I'm wondering about now," Master Penteney said. "Have you heard anything?"

"Nothing yet," Basset said.

For the first time Master Penteney lost his certainty, shook his head with worry. "Damn. I hope he's done nothing stupid."

"You think he might have?" Basset asked.

"I've always suspected he never gave up lollardy so thoroughly as the rest of us but I've always been careful not to know for certain. What if that comes out in Master Barentyne's questioning? What if it comes out he knew this Hubert Leonard?"

"I think that's a matter about which you can do nothing," said Basset. "You've enough to see to here."

"And anything he accuses you of—about your brother or anything else," Joliffe said, "just deny it all and go on denying it."

Master Penteney looked at him, then back to Basset, and said quietly, "Just as we did all those years ago."

"Just as all those years ago," Basset agreed, quietly, too.

There was deep understanding in their looks at one another. Then Master Penteney held out his hand to Basset and said briskly, "Best you be out of it, then. If I've no chance of better farewell later, farewell now, with my wishes for good health and fortune on all your journeyings hereafter."

Basset took his hand in a hard grip. "My wish to you for

the same, and my thanks for all you've done for us. Good health and fortune to you and your lady."

He and Master Penteney looked long into each other's faces, then stepped apart, and Master Penteney held out his hand to Joliffe, saying, "Thank you for giving my wife this chance."

Joliffe took his hand in a brief clasp, with no answer to make to that. He did not want Mistress Penteney to face death for what she'd done, but he was still angry for Lewis's death, and so he settled for silence and a slight bow of his head before following Basset out of the room.

They passed Master Richard returning with Simon and Kathryn. Mistress Geva, carrying Giles on her hip, had stopped to direct a lingering group of servants toward setting up the tables for supper. Master Richard gave Basset a questioning look as they passed but asked nothing. Mistress Geva did not notice them at all, and when they were past her, Basset murmured to Joliffe, "I think we'll have our supper somewhere other than here tonight, all being as it is."

Joliffe was more than willing. The last place he wanted to be this evening was anywhere near the Penteneys and the wreck of what had been certainty and a family only a few days ago.

He and Basset came out of the house just as Rose and Ellis and Piers were coming in the gateway from the street. They met in the middle of the yard, Ellis asking, "What's this with the crowner's guard at the gate and asking do we know where Mistress Penteney is?"

Turning them around and toward the gate again, Basset linked one arm through Rose's and another through Ellis's, with Joliffe steering Piers with a hand on his shoulder after them, Basset saying as they went, "We're going out to supper tonight, in some inn the other side of town. Over a good cut of beef and other things I'll explain all. Or, better yet, Joliffe will."

"There's trouble, isn't there?" Ellis groaned. "And it's his doing, isn't it?"

Chapter 20

Despite of everything, the players went as usual to break their fast in the hall the next morning. They mingled unremarked among the household's ordinary folk and the Lovell servants, helping themselves to the bread, new cheese, and weak ale set out on the table. There was not much talk among the servants. Whatever the household had been told, they were subdued and no one lingered at their food but ate and went away to their duties. If this was sign that Mistress Geva had already taken the household in hand, it was a good one, but of the Penteneys and Simon and Lord and Lady Lovell there was no sign.

Like everyone else, the players did not linger but ate and left. Not that there was much to do but wait or anywhere to go but the barn. For them to take to the streets and make even seemingly merry at their work or anything else felt wrong. Like everyone else, they were set to wait for whatever word came next, and to pass the time Piers brought the wooden horse for Ellis to carve on and silently hung over his shoulder while he did. Rose took up the mending there always was and Basset and Joliffe tried to talk about what changes they could make in their plays to better use Piers.

Because they had set the barn doors wide open to the early morning light, a man's long shadow thrown ahead of him into the barn gave warning that someone was coming; they were all on their feet by the time Master Barentyne entered. He had no men with him, which probably meant he was not bringing trouble, but still there was a hint of wariness in Basset's greeting him with a bow and, "Good morrow, sir. How go things?"

"Well enough. Master Southwell, I've come to thank you for your help in the matter of Glover. He's refusing to admit to anything as yet but all the evidence lies against him."

"What did you find?" Joliffe asked.

"Most importantly, lollard pamphlets hidden under the floorboards of his bedroom. Not just single copies but many of each and paper for writing more. My guess is that Glover is not only a Lollard but a busy one. Living out there, well away from town, he could have people come and go without being much noted, bringing him news and whatever and taking news and pamphlets away with them."

"But he denies he's a Lollard?" Joliffe asked.

"He admits to that freely enough. He might as well. But he denies Hubert Leonard was there and that's a mistake. There's a place in the kitchen where what looks to have been blood has been lately scrubbed from the floor. Not that anyone with half his wits couldn't explain that away and Glover does, but it looks like far more blood than you'd expect to come from a killed chicken. And why was he killing a chicken in the house anyway? He doesn't know. Then there's the way the back of the house faces nowhere but a pasture closed in by hedges and runs down to a marsh, just as you said, and can't be seen from the road or anywhere else. Seems that when Master Penteney is

dealing in particularly fine horses, which he does sometimes, they're kept there, to be less obvious to thieves and
better under Glover's watch. The only gate into the pasture
is beside the house, but there's a narrow stile at the bottom
of it that makes an easy way in and out for a man on foot
and a private way for any Lollards who might want to come
and go secretly. In the mud of the marsh edge we found the
marks of what look like heels being dragged along. Besides that, there were two broken pottery mugs in the
kitchen midden."

"They quarreled over something," Joliffe guessed.
"They fought—there were Leonard's skinned knuckles and
the bruise on his chin—and when Leonard was down,
Glover did for him, likely in anger and not thinking ahead.
Otherwise he would have thought about the blood needing
to be cleaned up."

"That's how I see it," Master Barentyne said. "Unless
Glover talks, we'll never know for certain but it's close
enough."

And if Joliffe had his guess, the quarrel had been because Leonard had gone to Master Penteney for money
where and when he should not have. If Glover indeed kept
a way station for secret Lollard comings and goings, peril
to Master Penteney came too close to being peril for himself and everyone who dealt through him. That was surely
reason enough for him to be murderously angry at
Leonard.

Those thoughts he kept to himself, only saying aloud,
"Once he'd killed Leonard, he hid the body in the marsh
because if it was found there, at least he could deny any
knowledge of it."

"Then, after dark, with his men gone away to Oxford,
he dragged the body to the stile and over," Master Barentyne said. "Leonard being much about Glover's size, drag-

ging him would have been easier than carrying him. Likely if the ground wasn't so hard, we'd have found drag marks from the house to the marsh. Once over the stile, Glover had the cart waiting. That torn bit of Leonard's shirt? One of my men found it in one of the carts, just like we guessed, torn off on a rough splinter of wood. The first time anyone used the cart again, it would have been seen, but Glover did it all at night, by nothing but starlight, and it's been holiday since then, with the cart just sitting in the shed. Its wheels, by the way, had been lately and thoroughly greased."

"Could someone else have used the cart without Glover knowing? Can he claim one of his men there might have?" Joliffe suggested.

"Glover isn't a trusting man. There's a door on the cartshed with a padlock on it and he has the only key. No one else could have used it. No, he loaded Leonard's body onto the cart, brought him here, dumped him, and went home again."

"Why here?" Ellis asked, still aggrieved about that.

"There's a question," Master Barentyne said. "Since he won't say he did any of this, he hasn't answered it, but I've made guesses. From what you told me . . ." he nodded to Joliffe, ". . . about what Glover was saying against Master Penteney, my guess is that Glover hasn't forgiven Penteney for gaining everything his brother lost, nor maybe for being rich when Glover isn't. Glover and Penteney's brother have stayed true Lollards, but it's Master Penteney who's thrived in the world."

"I thought true Lollards are supposed to scorn worldly things," Basset said dryly.

"Apparently some don't scorn them enough," Master Barentyne said dryly back. "There Glover was with a dead body and a dislike of Master Penteney. Burying a body is a chancy business. People tend to note new-dug earth where there's no reason for it. In the general way of things, dead bodies don't stay hidden well, and just left lying about, they draw attention to themselves sooner or later, one way or another, and people ask questions. So he put the body where people wouldn't look at him about it and made trouble for Master Penteney at the same time. Whether he knew you players were in the barn . . ."

"I don't think I ever said so to him," Joliffe said. "But one of his men is courting a maid here and could have heard and talked about it."

"Lollards don't care much for plays and players," Basset said. "Seems Glover is a bitter sort of man. If he did know about us, I doubt he'd have minded making trouble for us as well as Master Penteney. More for the price of one, as it were. Will what you have against him be enough to satisfy a jury, do you think?"

"That's never easy to say ahead of the time, but even if we fail to get him for the murder, there's still the Lollardy. That will hold. More importantly for you, I'm satisfied he did it and you're all free to leave Oxford whenever you choose."

Relief bright as sunlight after a cloud moves past the sun showed on all their faces; but Rose asked, "What about Mistress Penteney? We've heard she's taken sanctuary and why—that she poisoned the sweetmeats—but why did she do that? Has she said?"

"That she has not. She only claims it was a kind of madness came over her. When she confessed her guilt to her husband, he saw her into sanctuary." Master Barentyne fixed Joliffe with a hard look. "Just before I came to accuse and arrest her. Almost as if she had had warning I'd come for her."

Joliffe tried for a look that said he did not understand

what Master Barentyne was saying. Master Barentyne answered that with a doubting sound in his throat and went on, "Master Penteney says he doesn't understand either why she did it, and it doesn't matter in the end, I suppose, since she's confessed to it and there's nothing more the law can do about it except see her into exile and be thankful that God was merciful and none but the idiot died."

Joliffe curbed the same spasm of anger he had had toward Glover's easy dismissing of Lewis's death. Whatever Lewis had lacked in the way of wits, he had been completely, honestly himself—a thing most people rarely were, even those *said* to be whole in their wits. More than that, Lewis had been full of eagerness toward his life and it had been roughly stolen from him. Whatever good came to Kathryn and Simon because of that did not in the least change the wrong that had been done to him.

Joliffe kept all that to himself, though, while Basset thanked Master Barentyne for their release and walked him to the barn doors, saw him away, and stayed there until he was well gone before turning around to say, "Let's load up. Joliffe, how long will it take to fetch Tisbe back?"

"If I go for her now, we can be on our way by dinnertime."

"After dinnertime," Ellis said. "Why travel with empty stomachs?"

"Why not?" said Joliffe, heading out the door. "You travel with an empty head."

"*Yours!*" Ellis shouted after him.

At the pasturage the fellow presently and somewhat bemusedly in Glover's place made no protest to Joliffe claiming Tisbe. "Given she's the scrawniest one in the pasture, you wouldn't be claiming her if she wasn't yours," the man said.

"What about that bay with the white forefeet?" Joliffe asked, pointing across the pasture.

"Odd. The crowner's man asked about that one, too."

"And?" Joliffe prompted when the fellow did not continue.

"I don't know nothing about it, is all. That's what I told the crowner's man and what I'm telling you. It was just here one day when I come back from Oxford. When I asked Master Glover about it, he said it belonged to a friend of Master Penteney's, that's all. Like your little mare here."

"What did the crowner's man say?"

"He didn't say nothing. Just nodded and walked away. That was just before he arrested Master Glover for that murder, like."

For some reason none of that seemed to stir the fellow's curiosity in the slightest.

Some people, Joliffe thought, have more luck with their curiosity than others did.

Tisbe butted her head at his shoulder half the way back to town, as if telling him she had had enough of those other horses and was glad to see him. At the barn the cart was waiting fully loaded, with nothing to do but put her in her harness, but neither Piers nor Basset was there, only Rose and Ellis, looking not so easy as they had when Joliffe had left, and he asked sharply, "What is it? Where are Basset and Piers?"

"Piers is gone to buy meat pies for us," Rose said. "After you'd gone, we decided not to wait but leave as soon as you came back and eat as we go."

"Basset . . ." Ellis started, but Piers appeared from behind Tisbe, his arms wrapped around the obviously very full canvas bag the players carried food in when they traveled.

"How much did you buy, in St. Lawrence's name?" exclaimed Ellis. "Where's my money? You were supposed to have some left over!"

"The pies looked so good, I bought some for supper, too, and there was someone selling spice cakes next to the pieman, so I bought those, too," Piers said cheerily. "I spent all the money."

"I'll bet if I check your purse I'll find a few coins," Ellis muttered threateningly.

"I'll bet their mine, if you do!" Piers answered, giving the bag over to his mother. He looked around. "Where's Grandfather?"

"Here," Basset said, coming into the barn.

With his back to the sunlight his face was too shadowed to read, nor was the feeling in his voice any clearer. Wherever he had been, something had happened and Joliffe braced himself as Basset came toward them, saying, "Joliffe. Piers. You're both back. Good." And to all of them, "It was Lord Lovell who wanted to see me. He and his lady are leaving today, too. He says the Penteneys have trouble enough now without guests on hand."

"Why did he want to see you?" Rose said, her worry plain.

"For this." Basset was to them now. He held out a several-times folded paper to her. Still watching her father's face, trying to read it, she took the paper. As she began to unfold it, Joliffe realized it was not paper but parchment. A document of some kind then, with the writing on it done in a fine hand, he could see when she had it open, and a seal attached to the bottom by a ribbon.

But Basset could not wait while she read it out to them or Ellis and Joliffe read it for themselves over her shoulders. Giving way to suddenly open pleasure, he exclaimed in triumph. "Lord Lovell wants us to be his players. He's offered to be our patron. He said Master Penteney had suggested it. This patent . . ." He slapped a triumphant hand on the parchment. ". . . makes it real. We're Lord Lovell's players! With forty shillings a year certain money from him, so long as we show up to perform at Christmastide and some other time of his choosing, wherever he happens to be. To start with, he'd like us with him at Michaelmas at Minster Lovell this year. We're made!" Basset cried, and grabbed Rose to him in a massive hug while Ellis caught Piers into wild, swinging dance and Joliffe laughed aloud.

Lord Lovell's players! No longer lordless. No longer unprotected against anyone who might take against them for whatever slight reason or no reason at all. Still on the road from year's end to year's end, surely, but . . . Lord Lovell's players!

They left soon thereafter, Joliffe leading Tisbe, Basset walking with Ellis in excited talk on the cart's far side, Rose following behind, hand-in-hand with Piers, out of the Penteney gateway, headed for the eastward road, for Aylesbury and places beyond, the world looking a far brighter place than it had looked for a while and a long while past.

Author's Note

Through Joliffe, this book links with the Dame Frevisse series of mysteries, taking place in the summer after *The Servant's Tale*.

Lollards were an ongoing trouble in England through the 1400s, though never so dangerous again as in their armed revolt of 1431, talked of in this story. The government and people of the time, lacking the comfort of hindsight, had very reasonable fears against what more trouble the rebellious heretics might cause. The heretics Peter Payne and John Penning existed and were in Bohemia at the time of this story, but the Penteney family is fictional.

As for the use of pamphlets for propaganda purposes before the beginning of printing, contemporary mention is specifically made of Lollard pamphlets circulating at the time of the revolt in 1431. In other words, pamphlets are period.

So are Dr. Thomas Gascoigne's arguments against players, though in this case they're drawn, ironically enough, from a Lollard treatise. Dr. Gascoigne is likewise real and quite possibly as unpleasant as he's shown here, judging by his extent work. John Thamys, too, existed, and St. Edmund Hall still does, now fully an Oxford college in its own right.

My particular thanks go to scholars Dr. Alexandra Johnston and Dr. Chester Scoville of the University of Toronto for their very necessary help with my questions about medieval theater in Oxford. One of the great helps to me in "seeing" medieval theater has been the volumes of the on-going *Records of Early English Drama—REED*—project at the University of Toronto.

My general thanks and very great appreciation go to all the people with whom I've worked, both onstage and off, over many years in many plays, indoors and out. I couldn't have put on a single play in this book without them.